A PROMISE TO KEEP

"Stay out of my things!"

Tricia took a breath. He was obviously still not himself. Holding her temper, she responded, "What is your name? If you'd tell me now, I could—"

"Just leave me alone."

The fellow's light eyes closed as he winced with pain. Regretting her brief annoyance, Tricia moved back to the bed and whispered, "I'm so sorry that you hurt yourself again. I should've prevented it but I—"

Startled when he grasped her arm unexpectedly and pulled her down so close to him that she could feel his sweet breath against her lips, Tricia was unable to protest. Her voice caught in her throat when he stared into her eyes and said with a heat totally unrelated to his fever, "You're available to anybody here who has the right price. That confused me at first, but it doesn't anymore. I may not be in a position to take advantage of what you have to offer right now—but I will be." Drawing her infinitesimally closer, he said in a voice that was more warning than promise, "You can depend on it—angel."

HAWK'S PRIZE

Elaine Barbieri

LEISURE BOOKS NEW YORK CITY

*To my dear friend, Constance O'Banyon,
it was great fun working with you, solving
the puzzles of our intricate plotline for the Hawk
series on an almost daily basis, and for sharing.
You're the greatest!*

A LEISURE BOOK®

November 2006

Published by

Dorchester Publishing Co., Inc.
200 Madison Avenue
New York, NY 10016

ISBN 0-8439-5638-0

Printed in the United States of America.

Visit us on the web at www.dorchesterpub.com.

HAWK'S PRIZE

Chapter One

Galveston, Texas—1866

The brilliant afternoon sun dropped slowly from its zenith as Tricia Lee Shepherd walked, silent and unseen, through the familiar wooded copse. Her suitcase in hand, she pushed back a strand of silky blond hair that had slipped onto her forehead from underneath the brim of her modest gray hat, then brushed away the perspiration that beaded her forehead and upper lip. Her suitcase seemed to grow heavier with each step.

She paused to catch her breath and her bearings, her green eyes narrowing with concern as she looked around her. Despite the foliage shielding her from the rays of the relentless sun, the moist air had heated to an uncomfortable degree. Perspiration trailed down between her breasts, staining her equally modest gray

1

traveling dress as she silently reasoned that it couldn't be much farther.

She had arrived at the Galveston train depot more than an hour earlier. She was aware that Galveston had been abandoned by the Confederacy, had been occupied by the Union Army, and had then been rescued by Confederate troops—only to have the Yankee forces blockade the port for the remainder of the war. Yet the changes that the resulting hard times had wrought had startled her as her carriage moved along the streets. The Yankee bombardment had left scars that were still visible on the city. Buildings and roads were pockmarked from the barrage; stately old homes were crumbling beyond repair; profuse foliage and lush gardens lay withered and dying underneath gnarled old trees that had been uprooted by the shelling and could never be replaced. Yet alongside the devastation were the sights and sounds of rebuilding and repair that seemed to be progressing almost routinely, while Yankees in uniform walked freely on streets where they had previously been scorned.

The past heavy on her mind, Tricia had instructed her driver to drop her off so she might walk the rest of the way. She had been startled when she turned a corner to see that other areas of the city seemed almost unaffected by the Yankee assault; they appeared to have suffered so little as to challenge comprehension.

She had entered the familiar wooded area at that point and had continued on unseen. She had forgotten how heavy the salt-laden ocean air could be, and how overgrown and difficult untended trails could become.

No, it could not be much farther.

A smile broke across Tricia's face when at last she came up behind the house she sought. Her smile faded into a frown of concentration as she assessed the rear staircase that led to the second floor. The alleyway was empty, but she wasn't surprised at that. The hidden walkway and high privacy wall that shielded it from prying eyes on the street discouraged entry by the average person.

But she was not the average person.

Tricia took a breath, scanned the yard to make sure it was deserted, and then moved toward the staircase. Her heart pounded as she pushed open the door to the second floor and glanced inside. Grateful that the hallway was empty, she ignored the sounds of laughter and lively conversation echoing up from the lower portion of the house.

Tricia was moving silently down the shadowed hallway when a plain young maid turned a corner. Obviously recognizing her, the young woman stopped in her tracks, and then scurried away without saying a word. Tricia mumbled angrily as she pushed open the door of the bedroom a few feet away. Once inside, she closed it quietly behind her. She had only to recall the look on the young maid's face to know what would soon follow.

Tricia raised her chin. It didn't matter. She was an adult. She had made a difficult decision, and had then followed through.

She had done the right thing.

So...why did that thought bring her so little consolation?

* * *

Drew Hawk stopped short in the doorway of Madame Chantalle Beauchamp's bordello, but not soon enough to avoid bumping into the back of his friend and fellow former Confederate soldier, Willie Childers. Drew's broad-brimmed trail hat pulled down on his brow, his casual cotton shirt and bandanna, and the gunbelt low on his hips would not have set him apart from other nameless wranglers walking Galveston's streets if not for the Confederate gray trousers and worn military boots that were all that remained of the uniform he had worn so proudly.

Drew stifled a pained groan as he shifted his weight to his stronger leg. He frowned as Willie continued gawking almost comically at the interior elegance of Galveston's most infamous brothel.

Drew silently acknowledged that he too had been impressed at first sight of the graceful, two-story brick mansion that sat back some fifty feet from the road. The path leading to the front door was lined with great live oaks and curtained with Spanish moss that fostered an aura of anonymity for any patrons who might desire it. The great pink oleander bushes dotting the manicured lawn lightly scented the air, adding to the building's understated gracefulness. He had been even more impressed, however, when Willie and he had dismounted and were greeted by servants who took their horses to the stable as if they were gentry, instead of down-and-out Confederates making their way home.

Drew revised that thought. Actually, it was Willie who was making his way home to the backcountry nearby; Drew had just come along for the ride. Galveston wasn't his home anymore. It hadn't been for a long time, and although the period he had spent there with his family had been one of the happiest of his life, it was also painful to recall.

So many years had passed, and so much had happened in the time between. The luxurious life he had lived in Galveston as a boy had come to an abrupt end when his father's gambling left the family destitute and his mother deserted them for another man.

Years in an El Paso orphanage followed while his older brother Whit and he held out hope that their father would return for their sisters and them. It didn't happen.

Whit left the orphanage as soon as he came of age, promising to return, but that didn't happen, either.

Determined to find his brother, Drew left the orphanage a year later, but his search proved futile. He returned to El Paso for his sisters shortly afterwards, only to discover that they had been killed in a fire that had destroyed the manor house and everything in it.

He still cursed the day he had left them behind.

Drew's expression grew taut. He had felt strongly about the Confederate cause when the war began and had joined the boys in gray. His fellow soldiers had been like family; but that had finished badly, too, with Yankee bullets ending many of their lives before the war and their cause was lost.

He supposed it was for that reason that he had accepted Willie's invitation to go home with him to meet his kin; but he was only too aware that he must maintain his anonymity in a city where Yankees kept a prominent force. Having led a secret Confederate raid on a Federal gold shipment forwarded by rail during the war, he had accomplished his mission, only to be wounded for the second time. He had delivered the gold to his superiors but was immediately hospitalized. He learned when the war ended shortly afterward that the Yankees never recovered the gold. He also learned that the Yankees were searching for him because of his role in the theft.

One of thousands of defeated Confederates ostensibly heading home, he had become a wanted man.

Drew's leg began throbbing painfully, and he tensed. He had not expected that the wound in his leg—which had never fully healed—would start acting up again. Nor had he expected that Willie would be determined to stop off in Galveston on the way so he might "visit a woman of quality," unlike the camp followers he had become accustomed to during the war.

Willie was still gawking, and Drew unconsciously shook his head. Willie was of medium height, slight, snub-nosed, blond, and freckled. He looked younger than his twenty-four years, an appearance that contrasted vividly with Drew's dark hair, strong features, penetrating hazel-eyed gaze, and the broad, muscular physique he had earned the hard way after leaving the orphanage eight years earlier. Drew knew the differences in their personalities were even greater than the physical contrasts. Willie was instinctively trusting and optimistic, almost naive despite his war experiences and the sober, intensely loyal part of his personality that most people did not have occasion to see. Drew was cautious and deliberate, a man who was realistic almost to a fault, impatient with deceit, and dangerous to cross. Yet despite the differences between them, the friendship struck between Willie and him had been spontaneous and true. Drew valued it.

Valuing their friendship, however, did not make Drew patient with the time Willie wasted gaping at the flamboyance of the mansion's interior. To his mind, the gilded mirrors and red velvet draperies and furniture bespoke the house's function clearly, as did the magnificent, prominently displayed stained-glass image of Aphrodite resplendent in a transparent toga. The great oak bar and unpretentious gaming parlor that he glimpsed through a doorway were unexpected, but the curved staircase rising from the parquet floor to the second story—where he assumed the true business of the establishment was conducted—was not.

He glanced at the relaxed, laughing patrons of the establishment, unconsciously noting that business appeared to be in full sway—a surprise since it was barely past noon. That thought coincided with another twinge in his leg, and Drew caught his breath. He and Willie had taken time after breakfast to stop off at the baths, to get their hair trimmed, and to change into clean shirts, but their attire still made them a little too obvious for his comfort in this setting.

Drew steeled himself as a middle-aged woman with outlandishly bright hair turned the corner into view and started toward the staircase. Her red hair was upswept in complicated swirls; her red velvet gown was obviously expensive and cut deeply enough in the bodice to reveal the curves of an ample, matronly figure; her makeup was artfully but heavily applied. She was a handsome woman who Drew reasoned had probably been a beauty in her earlier years. She stopped short when she saw them at the door. The look in her eyes made Drew suspect that their stay might be limited.

Smiling unexpectedly, the woman walked toward them and said, "Good afternoon, gentlemen. My name is Chantalle Beauchamp, and this is my establishment. You appear to have recently arrived in Galveston ... perhaps from the war." Her smile faltered as she added more softly, "If so, I'm glad you have returned safely. It pains me that so many young men did not. You are welcome in my house."

Her distraction obvious, Chantalle turned gratefully toward two young women approaching them. Without allowing Drew or Willie to respond, she said, "Let me introduce you to Angie and Mavis. I'm sure they will do their best to entertain you."

Chantalle started up the staircase without another word, and Willie winked in Drew's direction when the young blond woman named Mavis took his arm with a flirting glance and drew him toward the inner room. Drew did not smile when the dark-haired woman moved to his side and purred, "Like Chantalle said, my name's Angie." She swept him with a heated glance before pressing herself closer. "You sure are a handsome fella. It's going to be fun getting acquainted with you. But even before you tell me your name, I want you to know that I'm up to anything you have in mind, because just looking at you puts me in a real playful mood."

Drew stared down at the voluptuous whore. His leg was throbbing painfully, sobering memories were returning, and despite the young woman's obvious assets, he had not a speck of desire for her. He was beginning to regret coming to Galveston, and his visit to the brothel even more.

His primary concern at the moment was his increasing inability to stand steadily on his feet, and he responded flatly, "You're wasting your time, honey. I'm heading for the bar."

"What are you doing here?"

Tricia glanced up from the suitcase she was emptying onto the bed as the door of the room bounced open. At a loss for words, she stared at the woman who stood framed in the opening. Her red hair blazed in the sunlight, her red dress was provocatively cut, and her painted, mature face was tightly composed.

It was Chantalle, and she was angry.

Yes, what *was* she doing there?

Tricia shook her head.

"I asked you what you're doing here."

Aware that she could avoid a response no longer, Tricia replied, "I wanted to surprise you. I went to great trouble to make sure no one saw me approaching so you would be the first one to know I was here."

"But Polly saw you and recognized you from your photograph on my desk. And if she saw you, others did, too."

"I don't think so—but right now I don't really care. I had hoped you'd welcome me."

"You know you're not welcome here."

"This is my *home*, Chantalle."

"No, it isn't! You don't belong here and you know it. I made sure of that when you were still a child."

"Did you?" Tricia pushed a blond wisp back from her forehead with a shaky hand. "You may have tried, but despite all those years of private schools up North, when I kept hoping you would take me back home with you each time you came to visit, I knew where I belonged—and that's here, with you."

"I promised your mother—"

"I know what you promised my mother." Tricia took a stabilizing breath before continuing softly, "You've told me that story often enough. You promised my mother on her deathbed that you'd take care of me and raise me to be a woman she'd be proud of."

"That's a truth I've lived by."

"I know, but—"

"Your mother wouldn't want to see you in a bordello, much less have you *living* here."

"Living in a bordello ... you mean, like she did?"

Chantalle shook her head stiffly. "Your mother and I didn't live in a bordello when you were little, although I almost wish we had. We shared a miserable little room where we hid you from the 'friends' we brought home when we were driven to desperation because there was nothing for us to eat."

"But no matter how bad things were, you kept your promise after she died. You took care of me."

Her ample breasts heaving with suppressed emotion, Chantalle whispered shakily, "And it was hard, Tricia. I had made so many mistakes in my life. I had failed too many times to allow myself to fail again with such an important trust. In the end, I took the only way out. I was lucky enough to find a 'house' that allowed me to keep you with me. I was lucky enough to find a special 'patron,' too, an old man who I truly believe loved me in his way. When he died unexpectedly, he left me a sum that enabled me to leave the house where I was working and bring you here with me when I set up a house of my own. The day that I was able to send you up North to school—as far away from this place as I possibly could—was a triumph for me."

Chantalle brushed away a tear as she continued, "That day was a triumph for you, too, whether you want to believe it or not, and I will not allow you to sacrifice it all now."

"It's no sacrifice for me to come home, Chantalle. It's the realization of a dream."

"No! You're beautiful and educated. You're a *lady* … a woman who will make a wonderful wife for a man of substance."

"I can find a man of substance here in Galveston."

"Not if you're considered Chantalle Beauchamp's daughter. Not if you're living in a bordello!"

"I wanted to come home, Chantalle."

"That was a mistake. There's no place for you in this house."

"I didn't mean I expected to work as one of your girls."

"Whether you did or not doesn't matter, don't you understand? You'll be considered no better than one of the women here simply by association with me."

"I *am* no better than the women here. If not for you, I might be one of them."

"But you're not."

"I know what I am … and I don't care what people think of me."

"I do!"

"Chantalle ..." Tricia's throat tightened as she continued, "My mother wanted me to be happy, didn't she?"

"Of course, but—"

"I can't find happiness by forcing the past out of my life—a life I owe to you."

"You don't owe me anything. All I did was keep a promise that was worth keeping."

"You did so much more, Chantalle. You made me believe I was worthwhile. You gave me a sense of who I am, and who I can be ... and you gave me love."

Chantalle's shoulders stiffened as she pressed, "If you want to repay me for what I did, you can do it by leaving here and by becoming the woman your mother and I both dreamed you would be some day."

"I can become that woman here."

"No, you can't."

"You said it yourself, I'm educated. I can read, cipher, embroider, sing, play the piano. I can also do *useful* things, like I did when I volunteered in Union hospitals during the war."

"Useful things? You don't consider having a rich, full life useful?"

"I can't be happy without doing what I know is right ... without doing what my heart tells me to do."

"Tricia—"

"And my heart told me to come home."

"Tricia—"

Her throat thickening, her slender frame trembling, Tricia said softly, "I just need to hear you say you're glad to see me, Chantalle…that you're glad I'm here."

"I can't say that to you."

"You're … my mother, Chantalle."

"No, I'm not!"

"But you're the only mother I've ever known."

"Tricia—"

"Please."

Tricia's soft plea reverberated in the quiet room. She saw the impact of that single word on the woman she loved as a mother. She saw Chantalle's eyes fill as her bared shoulders began shaking.

Chantalle's trembling was echoed in Tricia. Truly uncertain which of them took the first step to close the distance between them, Tricia sobbed with happiness when Chantalle's arms finally closed around her.

"Look at him. He's so drunk he can hardly stand up!"

Jake looked at the big fellow standing at the far end of Chantalle's bar, then back at Angie's livid expression as he responded, "I've been bartending for more years than you've lived, Angie, and I've got to say I've never seen a man his size get so drunk so fast."

"What difference does that make?" Angie shrugged. "You should throw him out before he makes trouble."

"He's not bothering anybody."

"He's bothering me!"

Jake's white handlebar mustache quivered with suppressed amusement as he said, "That wouldn't be because he told you to find somebody else to entertain, would it?"

Angie responded haughtily, "Mavis has been upstairs for over an hour with that skinny blond fella who came in with him, while this big fella hasn't done anything but hang on the bar. It isn't normal."

"He looks pretty normal to me. Maybe you just don't appeal to him."

"I appeal to every man who deserves the name."

"Oh—insulted that he turned you down, are you?"

Ignoring Jake's amusement as well as his question, Angie pressed, "Look at him. Look at the way he's dressed, wearing those pants and those worn-out boots. The other fella is dressed the same way. They're saddle tramps. We don't cater to their kind. Chantalle never should have let them in here."

Stiffening, Jake said, "Those pants are part of a Confederate uniform, and if I don't miss my guess, those are military boots, too."

"So?"

"So if a man served his country—"

"He didn't serve *our* country. The Confederacy lost the war, remember? The soldiers wearing Union blue are the ones we should be catering to now."

"Not behind this bar they ain't."

Scoffing at Jake's irate reply, Angie turned toward the slight, blond fellow approaching. She smiled stiffly as she asked, "Where's Mavis? Are you done with her for the day ... finally?"

"Ma'am?" Uncertain how to respond, Willie said, "If you're asking whether Mavis did a good enough job to satisfy me, I can truly answer that I'll remember my hour with her for some time to come."

"Too bad your friend can't say the same."

A grunt from the bar turned Willie in its direction.

One look at Drew's red face and squinting expression and Willie blurted at his friend, "What have you been doing while I was gone, man?"

Willie's question reverberated shrilly in Drew's ears, and he winced. It was hot, and Willie was talking too loud. The sound started Drew's head pounding anew and upset his equilibrium. It further unsettled his queasy stomach, too; and the truth was, he couldn't take much more without losing control.

"You look terrible." Willie walked closer. "I thought you were going upstairs. Was you drinking all the while I was gone?"

Drew attempted to draw himself upright, but the effort to put weight on his throbbing leg was beyond him and he stumbled against the bar.

"Dammit, man, you're drunk!"

"Is that so?" Drew's response was slurred.

"You shouldn't have come here if you wasn't in the mood."

"My mood has nothing to do with it." Every word he spoke seemed to unsettle his stomach even more, and Drew silently cursed. No one had to tell him that the whiskey he'd drunk had nothing to do with the way he felt. The wound in his leg was acting up again. He had ignored the doctor who told him he was leaving the hospital too soon. The war was over, and the choice of whether to leave with a partially healed leg or remain in a filthy, infectious hospital until the Yankees found him had been a simple one.

Drew scrutinized his irate friend. Willie had settled his business and was now anxious to be on his way home. He was angry because he thought Drew would delay their departure. The problem was, if Willie knew his true condition, he wouldn't leave until Drew was able to travel with him—and there was no telling what the result would be.

Drew stared at his friend through his fevered haze. No, he couldn't let that happen. Willie had waited a long time to see his family. He couldn't put him at unnecessary risk while Willie waited in Galveston out of loyalty to him.

His decision made, Drew said gruffly, "You may be in a rush to leave now, but I'm not. This bar serves some of the best liquor I've had in a dog's age."

Willie's frown was disapproving as he retorted, "My family ain't going to be too happy if I bring home a drunk, even if he did fight beside me in the war."

"That's too bad, isn't it?" Drew forced a lopsided smile. "We all have our ways of enjoying ourselves, and I've found mine."

"That ain't true, and you know it." Willie shrugged as he approached him. "Come on, let's go."

Aware that he would not make it across the room without revealing his true problem, Drew ordered, "Stay where you are. I don't need your help and I'm not moving until I'm good and ready."

"Drew—"

"Go home. You know where to find me if you want me."

"This ain't like you, Drew."

"Maybe it is." Drew breathed deeply, disguising the escalating pain. "And just maybe it's better this way."

"Drew, you said—"

"I said I'd go home with you. Well, I changed my mind. Besides, I've got some unfinished business to take care of here." When Willie searched his face uncertainly, Drew added sharply, "How many ways do I have to say it? I'm going to stay here awhile. Go home, Willie!"

Willie did not respond.

His expression darkening, Drew repeated, "Go home!" He then turned back to the bar and downed his drink in one gulp.

He did not look back at the sound of Willie's departing footsteps.

"You never should have let the two of them in here."

Angie's nagging tone turned Chantalle toward her sharply. She had left Tricia upstairs minutes earlier so the dear girl could clean up after her long trip. Chantalle was still disturbed by Tricia's reference to the bordello as *home,* and despite their tearful, bittersweet reunion, she had not yet decided how she would handle Tricia's decision to remain. Uncertain, she had come back downstairs, aware that her guests expected her to welcome them at the door. What she had not expected was to be assailed by Angie the moment she stepped down onto the floor.

Annoyed, Chantalle replied, "What are you talking about? What two fellows shouldn't I have let in here?"

"Those two new fellas who came to the door an hour ago ... the ones Mavis and I took on." Angie's lips twitched with irritation. "You know, the ones who walked in here still wearing those Confederate trousers."

Chantalle felt heat rise to her cheeks as she replied softly, "I didn't hear you complain when Miles Whitestone came in here wearing his *Yankee* uniform."

"That's different."

"Is it?" Chantalle's voice dripped ice as she continued, "Those two fellas looked fine to me."

"The Confederacy lost the war!"

"Unfortunately."

"They're losers!"

"You didn't look at that big fella like he was a loser when you went sauntering up to meet him. What happened? Didn't he like you?"

"Any man who *is* a man likes me."

Chantalle raised her brows. "Except …?"

"Except for drunks that hang on the bar without taking the time for any woman in this place!"

"Is that why you're angry?"

"He's still hanging on the bar. And if you ask me, he's not going to leave it until he falls down."

Dragging Chantalle by the arm, Angie pulled her to a spot where she could see the tall man leaning against the bar more clearly. She said haughtily, "He doesn't belong in here."

"I'll be the judge of that."

"Look at him! He's drunk!"

Chantalle stared at the tall fellow's back, thinking that it was a waste of a lot of man if he was drunk. Yet the way he was standing off-kilter, the flush on his face, his squinting expression—she hated to admit that Angie was right this time, but obviously she was. The policy of the house was to tolerate a less than sober condition among regulars, but this fellow was a stranger. Since it was apparent that he wasn't interested in any of the women, and since it was impossible to gauge what to expect from him in his condition, she had no recourse but to ease him toward the door before any possible problems could start.

That thought in mind, Chantalle moved to his side. With an expertise developed over the years, she said gently, "It looks to me like it's time for you to go home, fella. You can rest up a bit before coming back here to finish your business, if that suits you."

Pinning her with his unsteady gaze, the big fellow responded, "Are you throwing me out of here?"

Startled by his intense reply, Chantalle was momentarily at a loss for a response. She said more softly, "You strike me as a sensible fella, and we both know you're not in any condition right now to go upstairs with one of my ladies. You're welcome to come back here anytime, but for now—"

"—for now I'm going to stay right where I am."

Chantalle said more forcefully, "There are other places in Galveston where you can indulge yourself at the bar, but not here. This bar is maintained for the convenience of my customers only."

The big man turned more fully toward her. He swayed as he said, "I'm not leaving yet."

"You're making a mistake." Chantalle felt the rise of anger as she continued, "My memory isn't so short that I enjoy asking a former Confederate soldier to leave; but I will not allow any man to become drunk and disorderly in this establishment."

The man did not reply.

"Please go."

The big fellow remained silent.

"If you don't go, I'll be forced to—"

Chantalle was unprepared when the man fell suddenly toward her.

Breaking his fall with a clutching grip, Chantalle gasped at the heat radiating from the man's body. The startled bartender rounded the bar and shifted the fellow's unconscious weight onto himself as Chantalle said breathlessly, "This fella's not drunk, Jake. He's sick ... fevered, if I don't miss my guess. Get him upstairs so I can call Dr. Wesley."

Speaking up from behind her, Angie said, "You'd do better to throw him out onto the street. He doesn't deserve anything else."

"Maybe he doesn't." Nodding thankfully at the helpful patron who stepped up to help shoulder the man's weight, Chantalle continued harshly, "But no man wearing Confederate gray in any form is going to be thrown unconscious onto the street from this house!"

When the two men carried the stranger toward the stairs, she instructed, "Put him in the spare bedroom at the end of the hallway so Dr. Wesley can see to him undisturbed."

Still breathless, Chantalle turned back to the occupants of the barroom. With a forced smile calculated to erase the tension of the moment, she ordered Angie behind the bar and announced, "Drinks are on the house, gentlemen."

Scraping footsteps in the hallway ... mumbled curses ...

Tricia raised her head from the washstand as the

sounds filtered into her bedroom in the private quarter of Chantalle's house. She had been attempting to refresh herself, but the all-too-familiar sounds echoing down the corridor raised harsh memories. She reached for her dressing gown to cover her seminakedness, flicked her unbound hair free of the garment, and walked to the doorway to peer out cautiously. She went still at the sight of two men carrying a third, unconscious fellow into a bedroom at the far end of the house. The hallway was not a hospital corridor filled with the mutterings of the wounded and dying, and the men transporting the fellow weren't wearing Yankee uniforms, but the scraping sound of a helpless man's dragging feet was the same.

It chilled her.

She turned abruptly toward the sound of Chantalle's voice as the older woman ordered, "Go back inside, Tricia."

"What happened? What's wrong with that man?"

"I said, go back inside." Chantalle shook her head. "I don't have time to talk right now."

"What happened to him?"

Chantalle gave her a despairing glance. "I don't know who that fellow is, I don't know where he came from, and I don't know what's wrong with him. I only know he passed out at the bar downstairs. He's sick ... burning up with fever. For all I know, he may be contagious, and I don't want you exposed to any disease he may be carrying."

"You've been exposed, and so has everyone downstairs."

"That's different."

"No, it isn't."

"Just do as I say."

Tricia felt a familiar shuddering begin inside her as dark memories of hours spent at the bedsides of suffering soldiers returned. She did not bother to reply but fell into step behind Chantalle as the older woman continued on down the hallway. She came to an abrupt halt at the bedroom doorway when she saw a muscular fellow with a white mustache struggling with the man on the bed, who had regained consciousness and was trying to stand.

"Lie still." Chantalle approached the sick man's bedside, partially blocking Tricia's view with her broad figure. "You passed out downstairs," she said tersely. "You're sick. I've called for a doctor."

Tricia heard the large man's grunt of pain when the mustached fellow attempted to restrain him by pushing down on his leg. "I'm all right now," the big man said with a shaky voice. "You wanted me to leave, so tell this fella to let me go."

"I'd let you leave if I thought you could make it out the door, but I don't think you can."

"I can make it."

"As far as the stairs, maybe." Chantalle continued more softly, "Just wait a few minutes. The doctor will give you something to take care of your fever, and then you can leave."

"I want to leave *now.*"

Tricia heard the determination in the man's tone. She had heard it many times before from men so badly wounded that they were not fated to survive. She remembered the many times she had heard that determination gradually weaken until it went still forever.

The sound haunted her.

It kept her strangely immobile as the sick man's agitation increased.

Drew fought the helplessness slowly overwhelming him. He was so hot ... burning up ... and his mind was becoming confused. The madam was right. He was sick, but he had been sick before and he had handled it. He didn't need anyone's help.

But ... what was that?

The sudden boom of cannon fire startled him. He heard glass breaking. He ducked his head at the thuds of splintering beams falling around him.

The Yankees were firing their big guns again!

The barrage was relentless. Wounded men lay all around him in a house where only three walls remained. Some had minor wounds, and some had wounds so severe that he knew the men could not last much longer. He glanced at Willie, who lay on his stomach firing his gun as the enemy continued its unyielding approach.

The enemy would soon overwhelm them.

No, he couldn't let that happen! He knew the fate that awaited these injured men in Federal prisons, where maggots feasted on the wounds of the dying and where Confederate soldiers gradually became unrecognizable as the brave men they had once been.

He looked up at the mustached fellow standing over him. The man was not wearing a Yankee uniform, but he knew an enemy when he saw one.

"Lie still."

He turned toward the other side of the bed, where a woman in red stood. Her voice echoed hollowly in his ears as she continued talking. He could not understand the words, but the mustached fellow reacted by holding him down more firmly.

He winced at the pain. She was the enemy, too. He needed to escape.

He tried to get up. He punched and struck out at the man restraining him. His wounded leg failed him, but he would not give up.

He could not give up!

Tricia snapped free of her immobility when Chantalle was flung back a step by the sick man's thrashing. Stopping only a moment to steady her, Tricia ignored the older woman's protests and moved closer to the stranger's bedside.

She dodged a flailing fist, frowning when she saw the fellow's face for the first time. He was dark-haired, light-eyed, even-featured, and his expression was set. He was a big man who appeared in the prime of life, with muscle enough to perform whatever determination he had manufactured in his fevered mind, despite his injured leg's obvious weakness.

Somebody was going to get hurt.

She couldn't let that happen.

Moving closer, Tricia ordered, "Stop fighting! You'll hurt yourself if you continue."

Drew turned toward the sound of the woman's voice. It was filled with a remembered pain that was similar to his own, and he was drawn instinctively to it.

His struggles halted when he saw her standing beside his bed. Her hair was long and fair. Her skin was flawless. Her eyes were large and filled with the anguish he had heard in her voice. And she was dressed in a flowing dressing gown of celestial blue.

An angel ... an angel had come to help him.

"You'll be all right soon. We'll take care of you."

She touched his hand. Her palm was smooth and cool against his skin.

Her tone reassured him.

Her presence consoled him.

He was safe now that she was here.

Relieved, he surrendered to the darkness.

Tears brimmed in her eyes when the stranger went suddenly still, and Tricia choked out, "Is he dead?"

Tricia's question brought Chantalle to the stranger's bedside in a few quick steps. She checked the pulse in his throat and responded, "He's unconscious again. Something you said to him stopped his struggling cold."

Hardly aware of Chantalle's response, Tricia saw that blood had begun seeping through the stranger's trouser leg—trousers that were a Confederate gray.

Her throat choked tighter. He'd been wounded in a war that had brought sorrow to the nation, but the color of the uniform he had worn made no difference to her. She knew what she must do.

Taking a breath, Tricia looked at the mustached fellow who stood beside the bed and ordered, "Take off his pants."

"Ma'am?"

Obviously uncertain, the man looked at Chantalle for confirmation.

Tricia felt Chantalle's startled stare and she returned it with a determined look.

The fellow with the mustache looked at the older woman and repeated, "Ma'am...?"

His hesitant tone hung in the silence of the room. Chantalle responded sharply as she headed for the door, "You heard her, Jake. Take off his pants."

Chapter Two

Drew awakened. He was hot, his memory was hazy, and the throbbing pain in his leg had returned, granting him no peace. He looked around him at the garish decoration of the room in which he lay. The wallpaper was outlandishly bright, the carpet color hurt his eyes, and the furniture was ornately carved. The setting sun shining through elaborate swirls of red satin at the windows cast the room in an eerily unnatural shade, and the matching red satin coverlet at the foot of his bed nauseated him.

What was he doing lying in this huge, pillow-strewn bed with scented, lace-trimmed sheets—a bed far too large for a single occupant?

A soft sound turned Drew toward a young woman working industriously beside a gaudily upholstered chair on the other side of the bed. She was blond and lovely. She appeared angelic with her exquisite features drawn into deep concentration as she fashioned

27

bandages from rough pieces of cloth. Her surprisingly dark eyelashes were thick crescents against the rise of finely sculpted cheeks, the line of her profile was flawless, and her lips were full and appealing.

The pain in his leg suddenly stabbed more sharply. With it came a flash of reality.

He remembered where he was … and he wasn't in heaven.

And the beautiful young woman in the celestial blue dressing gown wasn't an angel, either.

He needed to get out of there.

Tricia turned at the sound of movement from the bed. The progress of events earlier had been so rapid—her bittersweet reunion with Chantalle, the disturbance in the hallway as she attempted to refresh herself, the big man being transported into a room at the end of the corridor, and his sudden lapse into unconsciousness.

After Dr. Wesley examined him, treated his wound, and left, she had felt somehow responsible for him. Uncertain why, she only knew that she had assured Chantalle that she would look after him while Chantalle took care of house business.

Tricia saw the big man begin struggling to stand. She protested as she approached him, "What are you doing? Your leg is badly infected. You need to rest … to give the medicine Dr. Wesley prescribed a chance to work."

"I've heard that before."

Startled by the fellow's gruff response, Tricia said with a touch of annoyance, "You still have a fever and aren't responsible for your actions, so I must insist that you lie still. The doctor said you shouldn't move. If the infection reaches your bloodstream, the consequences could be dire."

"I don't believe in doctors."

"You don't believe ..." Tricia's voice trailed away. She began again, "As I said, you're not responsible for your actions right now, and I don't want to be accountable for your hurting yourself while you're in this condition."

The big man's light eyes locked with hers fiercely as he said, "I'm the *only* person responsible for me, and I can take care of myself."

Taken aback, Tricia managed, "Can you? Look at yourself. You can't even stand up on your own!"

"That's what you think."

Heaving himself to his feet with a tremendous effort, the big man stood uncertainly, appearing even larger and more intimidating. Suddenly looking down at his short clothes with almost comical surprise, as if realizing for the first time that he was partially undressed, he demanded, "Where are my pants?"

Tricia raised her chin. "They were stained with blood from your wound. I asked Polly to wash them."

"Get them back!" he ordered.

"Why?" Uncertain what point there was in arguing with a fellow who wasn't in full control of his senses, Tricia continued, "You didn't seem so eager to leave when you got here."

His expression darkened. "Get ... my ... clothes!"

"No."

Appearing to swell with anger, the big man took a

threatening step toward her, only to grunt with pain as he leaned against the bed. At his side, she touched his forehead. He pushed her away, but not before she felt the unnatural heat under her palm.

Regretting her annoyance, she said apologetically, "Listen to me, please. I don't want to argue with you. Dr. Wesley said your wound had probably happened in the war. Since the war has been over for months, I can only assume that the infection has managed to get a secure hold. I don't understand how you could have been released from an army hospital in your condition, but since you were—"

"What do you know about army hospitals?" The big man's eyes narrowed into deprecating slits. "A woman like you has probably never even seen one."

Tricia gasped. *A woman like you* ...

Her angry protest died on her lips when he attempted another step, only to have his leg collapse underneath him. Falling, he struck his head on the dresser with a sharp crack.

When he went suddenly still, Tricia crouched beside him. He was unconscious, and barely breathing.

Suddenly panicked, Tricia ran into the hallway, calling, "Chantalle ... someone ... help! He's dying!"

Gunfire and cannon blasts erupted simultaneously, rending the brief, unnatural silence. The smell of gunpowder was heavy on the smoke-filled air as Drew looked at the writhing body of his friend. Corporal Paul Williams was only twenty years old. He would never see his twenty-first year.

Drew was still staring down at Paul's bloodied face when the young fellow took his last breath.

Dead...gone...like all the rest. He supposed he should be used to it. She had left when things got tough...his mother, who had said she'd always take care of his two sisters, his brother, and him. Then his father and his brother had left, too.

But it was he who had left his sisters....

Gunfire again! The Yankees were advancing.

He grabbed his gun and fired. He kept firing ... holding them off ... allowing time for his fellow soldiers to get away.

He waited until the last minute, then, still firing, stood up to make his escape. He gasped when a hot, searing pain struck his shoulder, sending him sprawling into the mud. He could feel the blood streaming from the wound as he dragged himself to his feet and continued on. He could barely walk, but the wound did not cause him as much pain as the thoughts pounding through his brain.

His family was gone.

He had watched his friends die.

His leg throbbed ceaselessly, his head hurt badly, his mind was confused, but one thought remained clear.

He had failed them.

Tricia stared down at the big man thrashing on the bed as she waited for the doctor to return. She heard his mumbled torment as he relived moments of the heartbreaking war that had recently ended. Pain twisted tight inside her. She had seen men similarly haunted before, but despite his seeming opposition to every word she said, this man had somehow touched her.

Unwilling to allow Chantalle to see she was so affected, Tricia glanced up at the older woman, who stood opposite her. Chantalle had responded to her call for help by summoning several men into the room to lift the big man back onto the bed. She had sent for the doctor and had then dismissed the men. Tricia had tried to make the fellow comfortable, but she knew the damage was done. His leg was bleeding again, and his head was grotesquely swollen where he had struck it when he fell. She had insisted that she was capable of caring for him, but she had obviously overestimated her ability. Her care had resulted in the wound that presently complicated the poor fellow's condition.

And she still didn't know his name.

Chantalle broke the silence to question softly, "You say you went through the contents of this man's pockets, Tricia, and you didn't find anything that could help us identify him?"

Tricia responded helplessly, "He was only carrying a money pouch with a few coins in it and a few incidentals that don't mean much."

"Incidentals?"

"What appeared to be a Confederate military button or an insignia of some sort, a damaged piece of old jewelry, and a few other things."

"That's strange. He should have some sort of identification." Chantalle was still dressed in the crimson gown she had worn earlier, signifying that her evening had just begun; yet her expression was weary as she frowned and said, "We need to contact his family ... just in case."

Just in case.

Tricia took a breath. "I don't think he has any family. He said he's responsible for himself."

"There has to be somebody."

"I don't think so."

"No one is *that* alone. He came here with a friend, so there has to be someone who cares about him." Chantalle's expression suddenly brightened. "Of course—I should have thought of it sooner. His mount is in our barn out back. I'll get somebody to search his saddlebags. He's bound to have some paperwork in there—especially if he was recently released from a military hospital."

Not waiting for Tricia's reply, Chantalle turned toward the door. She said over her shoulder, "Doc Wesley should be here any minute. I'll be back as soon as I can."

The silence of the room seemed thunderous as the door clicked closed behind Chantalle. Tricia took a few steps closer to the bed and stared helplessly down at the big man. The swelling on his forehead seemed to have intensified. He was still mumbling incoherently, and her sense of inadequacy increased. What was going to happen to him?

Aching deep inside, Tricia scrutinized the fellow's flushed visage. He was young, she guessed, probably in his mid-twenties. She supposed the average woman would think him handsome, considering his heavy dark hair and those startlingly light eyes that had looked at her so accusingly. His features were strong and chiseled despite the beard beginning to shadow his face, and his lips were pleasantly full.

She wondered offhandedly what it would be like to see those lips move into a smile meant expressly for her. Realistically, she supposed she'd never find out.

Tricia glanced up at the door tensely. Where was the doctor? Why was he taking so long to get there?

Tricia looked back at the dresser where the fellow's money pouch lay. She had been so hopeful when she had gone through his meager possessions in an attempt to identify him, but the effort had been a waste. Could she have missed something?

Frowning, she walked to the dresser and scrutinized the few articles again. A money pouch ... a comb ... a military insignia of some type ...

Tricia opened the money pouch and looked inside. As before, she saw a few dollars and a damaged ring that had originally borne a crest that was hard to distinguish. She could barely make out the sailing ship on it, but she—

"What are you doing?" Tricia jumped as the deep voice sounded behind her.

Tricia dropped the ring back into the pouch as if it had scalded her fingers. She said defensively, "I was trying to find something to identify you. We don't know your name ... where you come from."

"Identification ... in my money pouch?"

"You don't have anything else."

"Stay out of my things!"

Tricia took a breath. He was obviously still not himself. Holding her temper, she responded, "What is your name? If you'd tell me now, I could—"

"Just leave me alone."

The fellow's light eyes closed as he winced with pain. Regretting her brief annoyance, Tricia moved back to the bed and whispered, "I'm so sorry that you hurt yourself again. I should've prevented it, but I—"

Startled when he grasped her arm and pulled her down so close to him that she could feel his sweet breath against her lips, Tricia was unable to protest. Her voice caught in her throat when he stared into her eyes and said with a heat totally unrelated to his fever, "You're available to anybody here who has the right price. That confused me at first, but it doesn't anymore. I may not be in a position to take advantage of what you have to offer right now—but I will be." Drawing her infinitesimally closer, he said in a voice that was more warning than promise, "You can depend on it—angel."

Releasing her abruptly, he ordered, "Until then, stay out of my things."

Tricia struggled to ignore the rapid beating of her heart as she responded, "You have the wrong idea about me. I can't blame you for that, I suppose, but I—"

Tricia stopped speaking when the big man's eyes flickered closed and he began mumbling incoherently again. She touched his forehead and panicked at the heat she felt there.

Where was that damned doctor?

Activity in the bordello below was brisk and the upstairs rooms were busy as the twilight darkened, but Dr. Wesley appeared oblivious to it all as he worked at his patient's bedside. Turning toward Tricia at last, he said, "I can't be absolutely certain, considering his condition, but the bruise on this fellow's head seems to be a superficial wound. It is a complication, of course, but I don't think it's a dangerous one. The infection in his leg doesn't seem to be responding to the medication, however, but without any history on him, I can't do much more than I already have. His fever is obviously still high. Fevers always seem to soar at night for some reason, but I can't blame his on the time of day." He frowned. "If we only knew who he was and where he came from. We need to talk to someone about him." The graying physician stared at her over his rimless glasses as he inquired flatly, "You have been seeing to it that he takes his medicine on time, haven't you?"

"Of course I have!"

"I'm sorry, but I had to ask." Dr. Wesley attempted a smile. "I'm very concerned about this young man. The infection in his leg appears to be worsening rapidly. If his condition doesn't start improving soon, I may be forced to amputate in order to stop it."

"No!" Tricia struggled to draw her emotions under control as she continued, "I mean ... I don't know this fellow well. Actually, I don't know him at all, but I do know one thing about him. He's fiercely independent. He doesn't want to rely on anyone, and he won't want to be put in a dependent position."

"I don't know that I'll have any choice."

"There's always a choice."

"And what would that choice be, my dear?" His expression softening, Dr. Wesley said, "He may die otherwise."

"He should be given a choice—however limited it is."

"He's in no condition to make a sensible decision right now."

"Then someone who is."

"Who might that be? Chantalle had someone check the saddlebags on his horse—to no avail. If we knew where he was staying, we might discover something in his room so we could find out what treatment he's already had or who his kin are, but ..."

Dr. Wesley shrugged without bothering to finish his statement, and tears choked Tricia's throat. Forcing them back, she responded hoarsely, "I know what we can't do, Doctor, but what *can* we do?"

"Meaning?"

"When I worked in the Federal hospital, some doctors asked volunteers to bathe patients with cold water through the night in order to reduce their fever. I know that might be considered unusual treatment, but—"

"And it isn't a cure, my dear. If it worked at all in this case, it would simply mean a temporary reduction in the patient's body temperature. His fever will return unless the infection is broken."

"But reducing his fever will give his body a better chance to fight the infection, won't it?"

"Hypothetically ..." Dr. Wesley hesitated before continuing, "But actually, I think it would be a waste of time and effort."

"It worked in some cases at the hospital."

"And in others?"

Tricia did not respond.

"What was the ratio of success?"

Tricia remained silent.

"I think that's your answer."

Tricia said softly, "There's a slight possibility that reducing his fever will help him. You've already admitted that. What I want to know is if cold water baths could harm him."

"My dear, it's a waste of time."

"Could it hurt him, Doctor?"

Dr. Wesley smiled. "No, not if you're careful not to let him get a chill ... *and* if you continue giving him his medicine on time."

Tricia nodded.

Dr. Wesley's reluctant smile broadened. "Chantalle has spoken to me about you over the years—with much pride, I might add—but she never told me what a stubborn young woman you are. Do whatever else you want to do about this fellow's treatment, Tricia. I repeat that I think what you have in mind is a waste of time, but I must also say that this young man is lucky you've taken up his cause."

Packing his bag minutes later, Dr. Wesley turned back to Tricia, put paper packets into her hand, and said, "I have several patients waiting for my attention right now, so the only other thing I can tell you to do is to dissolve this medicine in water every two hours and make sure this young man drinks it all. Good luck, my dear. I'll be back in the morning."

Tricia released a pent-up breath as the door closed behind Dr. Wesley. She turned back to the big man thrashing in the bed beside her. Her gaze flitted from his bandaged leg to his bruised forehead.

Cold water baths...medicine every two hours through the night...

What had she gotten herself into?

"I'm afraid, Drew."

Drew looked down at his sister, Laura Anne. She was so little—only two years old. He was nine and she looked up to him. It was evening, the family had come to the Galveston beach for a few hours of play before going to bed, and Laura Anne—otherwise so brave— was afraid of the nighttime shadows. But Papa was there and he knew what to do.

Smiling, Papa turned and signaled to Whit to gather some cattails. In a few minutes Whit and he had propped the cattails in the sand and lit them. Tall, bright sentinels that warded away the darkness and turned the beach to shifting gold, they banished Laura Anne's fears in an instant.

Standing beside Laura Anne as she looked at the cattails and clapped with glee, Drew watched Whit approach them. His older brother kneeled down beside Laura Anne and whispered solemnly to her, "Fear is the enemy, Laura Anne. Don't let it win."

Fear is the enemy...

Fear... disappointment... loss...

But there she was again—the angel standing beside his bed. Her hair was a luminous gold, and her gaze glowed like a calm, green sea in sympathy with his pain.

She touched him. She laid her hands on him and the fire that burned his skin lessened. She hushed his protests and ministered to his pain.

"Here, drink this. Drink it all."

She held the cup to his lips so he could drain it, and then whispered, "You're going to be all right."

He reached out to touch her ... to draw her close ... but she flitted away.

Was she really an angel?

He wasn't sure.

He only knew ... that he wanted her.

Chapter Three

He shouldn't have had that last drink.

Simon Gault attempted to sit more erect as his carriage moved through Galveston's cobbled streets. He glanced at the gas streetlights that flickered in the nighttime shadows. Some of them had been damaged during the shelling of the city, but the Yankees had made restoring them a first priority. He supposed that was a positive step, yet he wasn't sure how well it was appreciated in a city where anti-Yankee sentiment ran high.

Simon raised an unsteady hand to his well-groomed head. He had stopped one drink short of becoming inebriated—which was one drink too many. He disliked not being in complete control of his faculties, especially when he was entering territory that was not completely friendly.

He had taken great pains with his appearance so that his condition would not be obvious. It was a point of pride that he was physically trim, that his hair was still predominantly dark, his skin relatively unwrinkled, and that he looked far younger than his forty-odd years. His vanity was unruffled despite the challenges of late, although he was certain Angie would not complain as long as the price was right.

He also knew he had taken to depending upon brandy to soothe his frustrations over the past few months, but he consoled himself that it was the best brandy available in Galveston—indeed, that everything he owned was the best.

Simon snickered softly. The best ... he had seen to that. When he was penniless, he had taken *what* he needed to succeed *when* he needed it. When the war threatened his fortune, he had simply played both sides. He'd had no qualms about the deaths of those who got in his way. He did not believe morality was more important than victory.

That premise was stupid.

Morals were excuses that common individuals used for failure—those who chose guilt over success. He was not among that number.

Not that he was incapable of a sentiment akin to guilt. *Regret,* with characteristics too similar to that common emotion for comfort, had unfortunately become his constant companion of late. Yes, he *regretted* his hesitation in dispensing with Whit Hawk when that arrogant fellow entered Galveston and startled him with the realization that an old vengeance had not been completely served. He *regretted* Jason Dodd's part in thwarting his seduction of the beautiful Elizabeth Huntington—the young woman who still did not know her true name was Laura Anne Hawk. He *regretted* losing Grace Marsh and the son she could have provided him to a simple tradesman like David Taylor—a loss engineered by the participation of yet another Hawk: Jenna Leigh.

He *regretted* the return of the whole Hawk clan. He had thought the family as dead as the father whose life he had ended with no regrets at all. He had believed when consigning the elder Hawk to an unmarked grave in California that it was a fitting burial for the man who had thought to usurp his gold strike. He'd had no regrets at all when he sold the claim and used the money to finance his success in Galveston.

He had learned belatedly that the elder Hawk had left his young children with his sister, promising to return to set their lives right again. Yet he had believed any possible threat to his triumph was gone when the orphanage to which their uncle had consigned them had burned to the ground, supposedly taking their lives.

But the damned Hawk bastards had escaped to grow up and come back to haunt him!

It somehow amused him, however, that even though he had failed to eliminate the grown Hawk siblings when they unexpectedly appeared in Galveston, every last one of them still believed their father had simply *deserted* them.

He was also amused that although the Hawk siblings instinctively despised him as much as he despised them, not one of them knew he had ever come into contact with their father.

Nor had his respectability suffered, despite their efforts. Few people in the city, including the gullible men of the renowned consortium, could make themselves believe a great *humanitarian* such as he was capable of crime. Their gullibility would soon allow him to become the richest man in the state.

Simon consoled himself that his pact with wealthy businessmen in the city of Houston would see to that. He had made great progress in using his influence to convince Galveston's consortium that Houston posed no threat to Galveston's commerce—that Galveston's natural harbor guaranteed its future as the most valuable port in Texas.

Rot!

That untruth would enable Houston to easily supplant Galveston's commercial position in the state with plans that were already under way. Once Houston's future was secured, he would receive his financial reward. He would then move his ships and his business there. With that move, he would gain more prestige than his sadistic father had ever imagined was possible. He would also become wealthier than that vicious man or the duplicitous Harold Hawk had ever dreamed.

Then—when he stood at the pinnacle of his power—he would crush every one of the Hawk progeny who remained.

Simon looked up as Chantalle's house of ill repute came into view. Chantalle, for all her professed disapproval and dislike of him, reserved a room especially for him. Despite his animosity toward Chantalle, he continued to make good use of that room. The reason was simple. He recognized his prevailing weakness: the fact that only with Angie, the perverted whore whom he loathed, was he able to sate his dissolute desires.

When his carriage turned into a dark spot free of pedestrian traffic, Simon ordered, "Let me out here, William. I'll walk the rest of the way." He added, "Conceal yourself in the usual place and wait for me. I'll expect you to be there no matter how long I'm delayed."

Simon did not wait for a response as he stepped down unsteadily onto the street and started walking. He had entered Chantalle's house in obvious anger once before, but he could not afford to make that mistake again or his reputation could suffer at a time when respectability mattered most.

Awaiting his opportunity, Simon slipped into a heavily foliated area and made his way with wavering steps toward the rear entrance of the red brick house where his special room awaited him. Within a few minutes, he was walking up the rear staircase.

Startled when he entered the upstairs hallway to see a beautiful blond woman attired in a blue dressing gown, Simon stood abruptly still. Her attire was all the explanation he needed.

Chantalle had hired a new whore.

His reaction to the young woman was immediate, and Simon started toward her. The beauteous witch would need someone to break her in, and he was just the man to do it.

Not allowing him a chance to speak when he reached her side, the young woman shifted the heavy bucket she carried into her other hand and said, "I'm afraid you have the wrong idea about me, sir. I don't work here. I only live here."

"You *live* here, but you don't *work* here." Simon drew himself up to his full height in an effort to impress as he continued, "You must admit that's a strange circumstance."

"Strange ... possibly ... but that's the way it is."

"May I ask your name?"

Green eyes as clear as a tropical sea met his coolly as the young woman responded, "My name is Tricia Lee Shepherd. I'm Chantalle's daughter."

Momentarily too stunned to speak, Simon said, "Chantalle's daughter ... I didn't know."

A mature female voice from behind Simon responded in the young woman's stead, "Yes, she's my daughter."

Simon turned at the sound of Chantalle's voice as the flamboyant madam added flatly, "Everything else she just told you is true, too. She doesn't work here, but your room is waiting for you. I'm sure Angie will be only too happy to accommodate you there as usual."

"Of course, Chantalle." Turning back toward the stunning young woman, he said graciously, "It's a pleasure to meet you, my dear. I hope to see you again under different circumstances."

Simon turned toward his designated room. As he closed the door behind him, he heard Chantalle say, "Stay away from that man, Tricia."

The young woman had the grace not to reply, and Simon sneered as he sat down on the bed. Chantalle had warned her daughter to stay away from him, but it had taken only one look for him to see that her precious Tricia was an independent young woman with a mind of her own.

The apple didn't fall far from the tree.

Simon's sneer became a smile. He had the feeling that if he played his cards right, he would be able to convince the dear girl to visit his special room—possibly before the week was out.

Simon's expression turned suddenly dark. When that sweet young thing lay beneath him, he'd teach her a thing or two that she wouldn't easily forget, and Chantalle wouldn't be able to do a thing about it. That would put the madam in her place!

He could hardly wait.

A sound at the doorway put a halt to Simon's mental meandering. He glanced up as Angie slipped into the room and closed the door behind her. He felt his groin tighten as the sultry brunette said, "Welcome back, Simon. You may be a bastard, and if I don't miss my guess, you're drunk, but I'll be damned if I'm not hot for you." Opening her bodice with a practiced hand, she stood with her breasts boldly bared as she whispered, "Come and get it ... and I promise you won't get the best of me this time."

He needed no further invitation.

Tricia looked up at Chantalle as the older woman followed her into the delirious stranger's room. Dr. Wesley had left almost an hour earlier. In the time since, the stranger's fever appeared to have escalated, firming up the decision she had reached earlier. Dr. Wesley had said she'd be wasting her time with cold-water baths, that her efforts would have no long-term effect on the stranger's fevered state, but she had known she needed to try or forever suffer regret. She had seen so many valiant soldiers leave the hospital with the loss of limbs because of infected wounds. She hadn't been in charge of their treatment, but despite the fact that she had first met him only a few hours earlier, she appeared to be in charge of this fellow's recovery.

He tossed restlessly in bed as Chantalle said softly, "Simon Gault is dangerous, Tricia. I had hoped to spare you from contact with that kind of man. It's imperative that you keep your distance from him."

"You needn't worry about that." Tricia placed the bucket of cold water on the nightstand as she continued, "It was quite obvious what he had in mind when he first saw me, even though he's old enough to be my father. Besides, he was drunk."

"Drunk or sober, Simon Gault is not a man to be trifled with."

Tricia took a patient breath. "I'm not entirely without experience or common sense, Chantalle. I've been on my own too long not to realize when a man's intentions are less than honorable. Besides ... *he was drunk.*"

"Simon consumes only the best liquor available." Halting Tricia when she was about to respond, Chantalle continued, "I know, a drunk is a drunk no matter how he gets that way, but this man sees a difference. He sees *everything* differently from the way a principled man does. He has his own agenda, and to hell with anyone who's in his way."

Tricia glanced at her patient. His face had started to flush an even darker color, and slow panic began invading her senses. She said impatiently, "I understand that Simon Gault is a dangerous man and you want me to stay away from him. I accept what you say, Chantalle, because my first impression supports your warning. Also, you know him far better than I, but I have one question. If he's as dangerous as you say he is, why do you keep a room here specifically for his ... enjoyment?"

"I should think the answer to that question is obvious, Tricia. *Keep your friends close and your enemies closer* is good advice. Angie isn't to be trusted either, but she brings Simon here. She enjoys his perversions, and because of her, he doesn't bother the other girls anymore—and I'm still able to get a sense of what he's up to."

"Why do you care what he does?"

"Because—"

A call from below turned Chantalle toward the sound. Looking back at Tricia, she said, "It's busy downstairs tonight. I have to be there to make certain things don't get out of hand."

Tricia looked at the brassy, middle-aged hussy standing before her, knowing that despite her appearance, Chantalle treated her customers fairly and with respect. Surprisingly, her customers seemed only too happy to respond in kind. Chantalle also kept her girls in line, and Tricia supposed that was the reason her house had a reputation unlike any other bordello in Galveston— because of Chantalle's sincere, warmhearted nature despite the business of her establishment.

"Don't worry," Tricia whispered. "I heard everything you said, and I'll keep my distance from Simon Gault. It won't be any problem for me at all."

Chantalle glanced at the delirious man in the bed

and Tricia added, "As soon as this fella's on his feet, he's on his way, too. I promise."

Tricia did not speak when Chantalle kissed her cheek unexpectedly and then turned toward the doorway. Instead, Tricia picked up the bucket on the nightstand as the door clicked closed and poured water into the waiting basin.

There was fire all around him and he was burning up. He struggled to escape from the flames, then stepped out onto clear ground at last, but he was still hot.

He looked behind him. There were Yankees everywhere. They were all looking for him. They wanted him to reveal the location of the gold shipment, but he wouldn't tell them even if he knew.

"You'll be all right soon. You'll feel much cooler. Just lie back and rest."

He opened his eyes at the sound of her voice. It was the angel again.

No, she wasn't an angel.

She was opening his shirt and slipping his arms free. She was struggling and he tried to help her but he could not seem to make his body cooperate.

He was free of the garment at last. He gasped as he was enveloped by a sensation so cold that it stole his breath. He struggled to clear his vision and saw that she had tears in her eyes.

No, don't cry.

"You're going to be all right. You'll see."

She spoke to him, and then she smiled.

Her smile was beautiful.

She was beautiful.
He closed his eyes.

Tricia struggled to hold back her tears. This man was so sick, she feared for his life. He was too young and too handsome to die. She looked at the broad, muscular chest she had bared for her ministrations, noting the scar on his shoulder. It was from an old wound. She wondered if he had received that wound in battle also. The war had taken so many lives, but although it was over, it still threatened him.

She touched the scar with silent reverence, then dipped the cloth in the basin and twisted it dry before spreading it across his chest as she had done before. The cloth was frigid against his heated skin, and he gasped another mumbled protest. She repeated the act, allowing the cloth to warm up against his skin while she bathed his arms and face.

The water warmed quickly, and Tricia refreshed it with colder water from the bucket. She performed the process again and again. Concerned when his fever did not appear to be subsiding, she moistened the smaller cloth and ran it across his forehead, then his cheeks and mouth. She felt his lips move underneath it, then started when his eyes opened unexpectedly and his hand grasped her wrist with bone-snapping strength. Her heart pounded strangely while his gaze searched hers for silent moments before his eyelids drooped closed again.

Tricia remained momentarily still when he released her. In that moment of silent communication between them, his message had been clear. He was ill, but he would not surrender control easily.

No, he would not tolerate having someone take his leg without his consent. Neither, she suspected, would he give his consent, no matter what the cost.

An unidentifiable emotion twisted tight inside Tricia. She could not let him lose his leg.

But the cloths were warming and the water in the bucket no longer helped. She needed to go down to the pump in the rear of the yard to draw cold water directly from the well. Yet she hesitated to leave him.

With no other recourse, Tricia leaned close and whispered into his unhearing ear, "I have to go downstairs for a few minutes, but I'll come back as fast as I can." She added earnestly, "Don't worry. I won't desert you."

Sounds of animalistic passion rent the silence of Simon's bordello room as he flipped Angie's naked body over and thrust himself into her roughly from behind. Her pained protest excited him and he pumped hard against her. She was hot for him, was she? He wouldn't get the best of her this time? He'd see about that.

"Stop! Stop! You're hurting me!"

Breathless with his growing fervor, Simon bit Angie's bare back cruelly. He smiled when she whimpered, and he muttered, "What did you say, Angie? You want me to stop?"

"Yes ... yes."

"Are you *begging* me to stop, Angie?"

"Yes, I am."

"Let me hear the word I want to hear."

"Please."

"Once more."

"Please stop!"

His passion accelerating at her tearful plea, Simon continued thrusting recklessly inside her. Grunting his final release, he shuddered to a halt and then withdrew from her at last to say triumphantly, "You lose again, Angie."

Breathing heavily, Angie turned over to face him. She brushed away a tear and managed a pained smile as she whispered, "Who says I lost, Simon? You? I got what I wanted, and in a few minutes I'll be as good as new and ready to go back downstairs."

Not allowing Angie to see that her response had angered him, Simon said snidely, "Or maybe I'll keep you here for another round."

"No! I mean—"

Seeing the fear that Angie had inadvertently revealed, Simon laughed coldly. "I know what you mean."

He stood up and walked toward the washstand.

Unwilling to admit defeat, Angie watched him as she drew herself to her feet, reached for her dress, and said harshly, "No, you don't know what I mean. I mean I have information for you about that blond-haired tart you were salivating over in the hallway."

"Blond-haired tart—"

Angie replied with a hint of irritation in her tone, "I saw you. I was watching in the hallway while you played the fool for that pretentious slut, and I heard what she said. Chantalle backed her up, but I know better. She's no better than any one of us here."

"What are you saying?"

"She's the daughter of a whore, all right, but she's not Chantalle's daughter. Chantalle saved her from this 'fate worse than death' that all we women here are supposed to be suffering, but her blood is just as tainted as ours. She proved it by following that stranger who collapsed downstairs into a room at the end of the hall, and by telling everybody to leave her alone with him while she undressed him. And he's hardly conscious!" Angie gave a hard laugh. "It doesn't matter to her what condition he's in, or that he's a down-and-out Confederate who has nothing to offer but his body, just as long as she can get what she wants."

"How do you know all this?"

"Because I made it my business to find out; because I know it pays well if I do; because I don't like women like her who put on airs; and because I'm tired of seeing men fall for innocent acts like hers."

Simon paused to consider what Angie had said, then responded, "Or is it because you're just a little jealous of that *innocent* young woman who has a man all to herself?"

"I'm not jealous of her!"

Fully dressed, Simon turned toward Angie and said, "Maybe not. Maybe everything you said is true. If so, I'll pay you for the information like I always do."

"It's true, all right!"

Simon said as he pulled the door open, "Let me know what you find out."

Noting that the hallway was empty, Simon surrendered to libidinous curiosity and moved silently toward the room at the end. A tight smile on his lips, he boldly jerked the door open without knocking and looked inside. To his disappointment, Tricia Shepherd wasn't there, but an obviously feverish man lay unconscious on the bed.

Simon entered the room and pulled the door closed behind him. Uncertain, he stared as the man on the bed began mumbling incoherently. He saw the bloody bandage on the fellow's leg and frowned.

Who was this man? What was he doing here? Could Angie be right about the beautiful Tricia Lee Shepherd's reason for spending so much time with him?

Titillated at the thought, Simon felt his groin harden. If it were true, if Tricia enjoyed the diversity of perversion, she might be the source of endless hours of enjoyment for him ... hours they could both benefit from before he left Galveston for good.

He needed to know more.

Certain there would be no interference from the unconscious man, Simon walked to the dresser where the fellow's few belongings lay. He muttered under his breath when he found no identification, then picked up the pitifully small money pouch and looked inside.

A few coins ... a Confederate military button of some kind ... an old ring ...

Simon drew the ring from the pouch to view it more clearly. The enameled crest was damaged, but the sailing ship was heart-stoppingly familiar, as was the Latin motto that was only partially visible.

Quattuor mundom do.... To four I give the world.

Simon stared at the ring incredulously. It couldn't be! Another Hawk sibling could not possibly have come back to haunt him!

Simon glanced again at the man in the bed. He was big and dark-haired, not unlike Whit Hawk, but Simon saw no family resemblance. He was certain of only one thing. Fate had provided him the opportunity to dispense with another possible Hawk both swiftly and quietly, and he did not intend to lose it. He'd worry about ascertaining the fellow's identity later.

Knowing that the unconscious man would provide little resistance, Simon picked up the loose pillow lying on the bed. There would be no marks on the body when they discovered him dead. Everyone would think he had simply died in his sleep, and a potential problem would be eliminated.

Simon lowered the pillow over the helpless man's face.

"What are you doing?"

Simon straightened abruptly at the sharply voiced question. With the pillow still in his hands, he turned to see Tricia Shepherd standing in the doorway. He remained silent as she walked toward him and demanded again, "What are you doing?"

Simon said with a smoothness that belied the pounding of his heart, "I knocked, but no one answered. Angie told me that a customer had collapsed from a fever downstairs earlier today, and that you were taking care of him. I came in to see if I could help. He seemed uncomfortable, and I was attempting to slide another pillow underneath his head."

"He doesn't need another pillow." Her expression tight, Tricia added, "And he doesn't need anyone but Dr. Wesley and me to take care of him."

"My dear ..." Simon's smile was benevolent. "I was only trying to help."

Tricia's replied stiffly, "I should thank you, then ... before I ask you to leave."

"But—"

"Please leave."

Simon took a backward step. "Of course, my dear. However, Angie mentioned that this fellow was formerly a Confederate soldier. My sympathies are with all the poor fellows who served the Confederacy so bravely. Please don't hesitate to call me if you need help in any way."

"Yes, of course. Good-bye."

Ignoring the tight pursing of Tricia lips, Simon drew the door closed behind him and strode swiftly down the hallway toward the rear exit of the house. He did not intend to allow the arrival of another possible Hawk to threaten his plans. He'd find out who this man was, and when he did ...

Not bothering to finish that thought, Simon drew the door open and moved quickly down the outside stairs.

Drew awoke slowly. He looked around him, at the morning light shining through the elaborately draped window and at the gaudily decorated room. He ached all over, his leg was throbbing, and he was so disoriented he could not quite figure out where he was.

A sound at his bedside turned him toward the beautiful blond woman asleep in a chair beside his bed. Her perfect profile was angled toward him, a graceful outline against the gaudy upholstery. Her complexion, although pale, was creamy and flawless; her features were small, fine, and motionless in sleep, and her lips were parted, as if in silent invitation.

Don't worry, you're going to be all right. I won't desert you.

The angel ...

No, that was wrong.

His mind clearing, Drew remembered. She looked like an angel and she talked like an angel ... but she wasn't an angel.

The woman stirred, then came to full wakefulness with a start. Sea-green eyes that had been burned into his memory met his as she said, "Oh, you're awake." She blinked and pushed a strand of fair hair from her cheek, scrutinizing him more intently. She touched her palm to his forehead and said, "You're definitely cooler. I'm glad ... I mean, I think Dr. Wesley will be pleased."

"Dr. Wesley?"

"You don't remember him?" Appearing to think better of that question, she said, "He's the man who cleaned out the infected wound in your leg, applied the poultice, and left the medicine you've been taking all night."

"All night ..."

He searched her expression confusedly, and she glanced away. Doing his best to ignore the renewed throbbing in his leg, Drew said with a trace of impatience, "I know where I am, and I know why I came here. What I don't know is how I got into this room."

"You collapsed downstairs yesterday. You had a fever, and Chantalle had you brought up here so the doctor could look at you."

"Chantalle ... the red-haired madam."

The angel's lips twitched. "Yes, Chantalle—the woman who probably saved your life."

His teeth clenching tight against the raw ache in his leg, Drew said gruffly, "I'm harder than that to kill."

He stared at the young woman in the flowing blue dressing gown. His gaze trailed slowly over her petite frame, assessing every inch, indulging himself and allowing the sight of her to dull his pain. An area of his body far distant from his brain stirred predictably, and he knew that if he didn't feel like hell, she wouldn't be standing beside the bed. She'd be in it ... with him, and he'd be—

Drew took a sharp breath as pain stabbed sharply.

The young woman reacted by saying sympathetically, "Dr. Wesley will be here soon."

Drew blinked when the pain stabbed again, and the young woman said, "I'm sorry. I don't have any more of the powder that the doctor left for you. I used it all up last night, but he'll probably bring more. The powder will continue fighting the infection, and I can ask him for something to lessen your pain if you wish. I don't know what he'll prescribe, but a few drops of laudanum should do."

"Laudanum ..." He had been witness to the easy administration of laudanum to many of his fellow soldiers while he was hospitalized. Remembering clearly that he had also seen many of them become addicted to the drug, he said flatly, "I don't need it."

"The use of laudanum is entirely safe if carefully supervised."

"Is it?" Drew's annoyance increased along with his pain as he snapped, "I know better."

"I beg your pardon … so do I." The young woman's voice lost its patronizing quality. "I saw laudanum used to great advantage when I volunteered my services in army hospitals in New York and I—"

"In New York." Drew went cold. "You're talking about *Yankee* army hospitals—"

"That's right."

"Where you nursed wounded *enemy* soldiers."

Momentarily taken aback, Tricia replied, "They weren't my enemies. Besides, the war is over."

"Not for me, it isn't."

"That's a fool's response."

"No, that's a Confederate's response."

"There is no Confederacy."

Drew's jaw locked tight. He needed to leave.

He was about to throw the coverlet off when memory flashed, and he said, "I asked you to get me my pants."

"I told you, they're being laundered."

"I said—"

A sound at the door interrupted his response, and Drew looked up to see a slight, middle-aged man carrying a black bag.

Tricia felt her heart sink. She had not intended her first conversation with the man in the bed to escalate into anger, but her reaction had been spontaneous. In hindsight, she realized that he must be bitter at the loss of a cause for which he had been wounded and had doubtless seen friends die. She supposed she couldn't blame him. She supposed she needed to be more patient.

Tricia looked at the big fellow, who glanced back at her contemptuously, and her anger flared anew.

Patience had never been one of her strengths.

Dr. Wesley walked to his patient's bedside and said, "My name is Dr. Wesley, and if I don't miss my guess, your temperature is just about normal this morning." Turning back to glance at her, he continued, "It looks like you made a real difference last night, Tricia."

The sick man's eyes jerked briefly toward her as Dr. Wesley touched his forehead and nodded. He appeared to listen intently as the doctor worked at his bedside. "You know my name," Dr. Wesley went on, "but I don't know yours."

"Drew." There was a pause. "Drew ... Collins."

"Coming home from the war, are you, Drew?"

A nod was the response.

"Well, if I'm to judge by the change in your condition this morning, I'd say you can be on your way in a week or more."

"A week!" Drew Collins shook his head. "I'm leaving here today."

Dr. Wesley looked down at him sharply. "No, you're not."

"Yes, I am."

Dr. Wesley hesitated a moment, then shrugged. "Well, I guess you could try."

The big man's gaze darkened. "Meaning?"

"Meaning you wouldn't get far. Whether you realize it or not, that leg is as weak as a kitten's right now. It wouldn't support you any farther than the stairs."

"You're wrong."

"Another 'whether you know it or not' is that the infection you've been ignoring has started to spread, which accounts for your fever. You're just lucky this young lady decided to make you her patient last night, or you might not be in the shape you're in this morning. The infection has the upper hand right now. I told Tricia last night that if it didn't subside, you could lose your leg, and that situation hasn't changed."

Drew Collins's mouth tightened almost imperceptibly as he replied, "Yes, it has."

"My dear fellow—"

Interrupting the doctor without hesitation, Drew said, "Look, Doc, I appreciate all you did for me, but I can take it from here. And like I said, I'm leaving today."

"Fine." The room was uncomfortably silent as Dr. Wesley worked over the wound. Abruptly smiling, the graying doctor said, "Well, I've removed the poultice and changed the bandage on your leg, and that's about all I can do for you right now. I'll leave some packets of medicine for you to take. Just don't expect too much from me the next time you collapse, wherever that is."

Tricia stared at Dr. Wesley openmouthed for long seconds before saying, "You can't mean that, Doctor." Ignoring the sick man's glance, she continued, "You can't be agreeing to allow this man to leave yet. You know how badly infected his leg is."

"I don't see as how I can stop him if that's what he intends to do. You can lead a horse to water but you can't make him drink, Tricia. I learned the truth in that adage a long time ago. Some people have to learn the hard way. Like I said, the packets are on the

nightstand, and I'm on my way to another patient."
Hesitating at Tricia's stunned expression, Dr. Wesley
said more softly, "You know where to find me if you
need me."

The door had barely closed behind Dr. Wesley when
a deep voice from the bed behind her ordered, "Bring
me my pants."

Her name was Tricia.

Drew watched as the beautiful blond woman walked
back into his room with her jaw tight. As strange as it
seemed, she hadn't introduced herself to him or even
asked his name. In fact, she had said very little to him
after Dr. Wesley left. He knew she was angry, but he
wasn't sure of the reason.

Admittedly, his own reaction to her was somewhat
confused. She had obviously spent a considerable part
of the night tending to his wound, but she had done
the same for Yankee soldiers during the war. The image of the consolation she had afforded men who
might have taken the lives of his friends infuriated
him. Yet the sight of her evoked a yearning inside him
that gained strength with every moment.

Drew attempted to ignore the throbbing in his leg as
Tricia placed his laundered pants on the bed beside
him and stood there without saying a word. He realized that she didn't intend to move in order to allow
him privacy in dressing.

Drew was almost amused at his own foolishness. Of
course … he should have realized. He was in a bordello, wasn't he? No matter how angelic-looking this

Tricia was, she was not new to the sight of a man in the altogether or in short clothes.

Refusing to admit how much that thought disturbed him, Drew reached for his pants. Whatever the case, he needed to get out of there. Too many Yankees walked the streets of Galveston and perhaps frequented this establishment. Despite the fact that he'd had the presence of mind to lie about his name when asked, he was a wanted man, and he had learned the hard way that Yankees were not fools. They would discover who he was sooner or later.

Aware that Tricia was still staring at him, Drew threw back the coverlet and dropped his legs over the side of the bed. More light-headed than he had expected, he sat there for a few moments, his expression darkening with his mood. Then he stood up to reach for his shirt. He slid his arms into the sleeves with every bone in his body aching, and clumsily fastened the buttons. He stepped into his pants and was perspiring profusely when he finally managed to pull the garment up to his waist. Seeing that Tricia made no attempt to look away, he boldly buttoned his fly as he held her gaze. He noted the flush that colored her face, and he felt a familiar heat unrelated to fever.

Drew attempted to deny his stomach's churning when he finished pulling on his boots. He ignored the flash of vertigo as he buckled on his gunbelt. He was hot and sweaty, his fingers refusing to cooperate as he tied his neckerchief and then reached for his hat.

Speaking for the first time when he turned toward the door, Tricia said, "You're making a mistake."

He wanted to tell her he knew that was true, but not

for the reason she thought. He wanted to say that he
didn't want to leave—not yet. He wanted to admit to
her that despite her sympathy for the men who were
his enemies, despite whatever reason she had for coming South and putting a price on her beauty, he would
have spent his last penny to have her—because he
wanted her more than any other woman he'd ever
known.

But reality intruded.

Aware that his physical condition was growing
more desperate by the moment, Drew limped toward
the door.

He did not turn back as she repeated, "You're making a mistake."

Somehow he wished she had said more.

Her throat tight, Tricia watched while Drew attempted
to minimize his limp as he walked out into the hallway.
The moments just past had shaken her. She had not felt
even a touch of embarrassment as she had watched
him dress ... as he had slid his powerful arms into his
shirt and buttoned it across his chest with fumbling
fingers ... as he had thrust his long, muscular legs into
the Confederate gray of his pants while concealing his
pain. She remembered that he had looked intently into
her eyes as he had boldly buttoned the closure on his
trousers. She recalled the feelings that had sprung to
life inside her, unnamed feelings that had raised a flush
to her cheeks—feelings that had left her somehow
empty and incomplete when he had turned to grasp his
gunbelt and secure it around his hips.

She had been desperate when he turned toward

the door, and she had called out, "You're making a mistake."

Her eyes grew moist when it suddenly became startlingly clear in her mind that her warning had had nothing to do with the condition of his infected leg.

She followed his unsteady progress down the stairs toward the front door.

She held her breath when he drew it open.

She gasped when he hesitated, then collapsed heavily on the doorstep.

Chapter Four

"I told you the last time you came that I didn't want you to come here again!"

Seething, Simon pulled Angie inside the door of his mansion. It was late, and his very respectable doorstep was all but invisible from the street at that time of night; there was little possibility that anyone had seen Angie there. Even his servants were asleep—but Angie had known full well how angry her coming would make him. He had lost control and had punished her on the spot the last time, in the most intimate of ways—the only way a woman like Angie was capable of understanding—but that seemed to have made little difference.

It occurred to him that Angie's arrival at his mansion tonight was her way of evening the score with him. That thought was more dangerous for the dissolute whore than she could possibly realize.

Simon pulled Angie into his study and closed the

door quietly behind them while maintaining control by sheer strength of will. He had had a long, difficult day. The situation with the consortium had taken an unexpected turn. A few of the men were smarter than he had thought. They were holding out against his advice, trying to convince others that steps were needed to ensure Galveston's future, that Galveston's natural harbor did not assure its commercial success. He had smiled at Jonathan Grimel when the distinguished *fool* formally asked the consortium to consider that concern. Simon had pretended amusement at the supposedly preposterous thought, while inwardly he had raged.

Angie's arrival threatened the respectability that was so important to his plans at this time—and she knew it.

Making no attempt to hide his foul mood, he addressed Angie hotly.

"All right, tell me why you're here. I warn you, it had better be good."

Testing the limits of his patience, Angie replied with deliberate evasiveness, "I suppose that means you're not flattered that I came looking for you when I could be sleeping in my fine little room instead."

"Your fine little room," Simon sneered. "You mean the room where you'll take on any and every man who shows up on Chantalle's doorstep, and where you're never truly satisfied until I visit you?"

Angie shrugged a sultry shoulder, allowing her neckline to gape in a way that displayed her breasts enticingly. "There's some truth to that."

Bitch ... she was baiting him.

His flushed expression revealing more than he wished, Simon said, "Out with it! Why are you here?"

"You insinuated you'd be interested in knowing more about Chantalle's daughter and that fella she's been keeping all to herself at the house. I found out the name he uses."

Angie halted, waiting for his response. He struggled for control as he said, "Well? What is it?"

"He calls himself Drew Collins."

"Collins."

"He's still sick, according to the perfect Miss Tricia, but I have my doubts about that."

"Meaning?"

"Something's wrong there. That big fella was in too much of a rush to get out of that bed when he woke up yesterday. He was lucid—for the first time, to hear Tricia tell it—and he immediately tried to leave the house. It was almost like something or somebody was chasing him."

"Is that right?"

"Staying alone in that room with Miss Perfect all night didn't seem to make a difference, and I'm thinking either she wasn't too good at entertaining him or he was too busy looking over his shoulder to linger any longer."

"And you know all this because …?"

Angie moved her body in a sinuous way that tugged at Simon's groin as she said, "Because you pay me well for information … but mostly because I like to please you."

Resenting the effect the worthless whore had on him, Simon gave a scoffing snort. "You like to please me? I suppose that's why you came here when I told you I never wanted to see you on my doorstep again. No ... you don't fool me." Simon closed the distance between them so swiftly that Angie did not have time to retreat. Gripping her hair cruelly, he hissed, "Stupid— that's what you are if you expect me to believe you! I pay you well, and that's the only reason you do my bidding."

He drew her closer, his grip tightening painfully. He felt her heart pounding against his chest as he amended hotly, "No, that's not right. You *want* me in a way you don't want any other man. You hate yourself for it, but you came here tonight thinking you'd tease me into taking you again. But I'm not going to do it. I'm not going to satisfy you. I'm going to send you home *wanting*, Angie, with only material payment to soothe your carnal needs."

Releasing her so abruptly that Angie staggered a few steps backward, Simon was keenly aware that the greedy whore read his weaknesses well. For all his bravado, he felt an overwhelming desire to throw her across the fifteenth-century marble-topped chest he was so proud of, so he could take her just as he had once before. Instead, he moved back to his desk, removed a wad of bills from a drawer, and threw it at Angie. He watched her for a few moments as she stood breathing heavily, then ordered, "Pick them up. That's all you're going to get from me tonight."

Waiting until she scrambled for the bills, Simon added, "But your work for me isn't done. I have a job for you. Drew Collins carries a ring in his money pouch. It's damaged, but it has some sort of crest with a sailing ship and a Latin motto partially visible on it. I want you to find out where he got it. I need to know. But don't come back here with the information. If you do, you'll receive payment of a far different kind than you're expecting."

The money clutched in her hand, Angie stood shaken and trembling when Simon added slowly, "You serve a very important purpose for me, Angie. Don't spoil it. I'll keep in touch. If you have something to tell me in the meantime, find another way to contact me." He paused to add succinctly, "Your life may depend on it."

Simon led Angie to the rear door of the mansion, aware that she was shaking. Whether it was with fear or unsated desire, he could not be sure, but that was the way he wanted it.

No, she'd never come to his house again.

Simon closed the door quietly behind Angie. He locked it firmly, and then paused in the darkness to further consider what she had told him. So the bastard said his name was Drew *Collins*. He had the same given name as Harold Hawk's younger son. Coincidence? He doubted it, but he needed to be sure so he could take care of this particularly vulnerable fellow and be certain that *this* Hawk would be the *last* one to return to Galveston.

Angie would get the confirmation he needed. With the younger Hawk son taken care of, he could eliminate the others, one by one.

He looked forward to it.

* * *

"I brought you something to eat."

Drew did not respond as Tricia entered the room with a tray in hand. Neither did he smile. He didn't like being stuck in bed, helpless because of a debility that he was unable to dismiss any longer. He knew that with every moment he remained in a city overrun by Yankees, the danger of being recognized increased.

But that wasn't his present problem.

Drew watched as Tricia placed the tray with a bowl of broth on the bed stand beside him. It irritated him that despite the pain in his leg, her fragrance assaulted his senses and her presence alerted him to a part of himself that he had difficulty ignoring.

Morning sunlight streamed into the room as Drew stared at Tricia's turned back. She wasn't wearing the blue dressing gown. Instead, she was wearing a plain, tan cotton dress. Her long blond hair was twisted into a conservative bun at the back of her neck, where a few escaping tendrils fell loose to remind him of its glittering glory.

Her expression was severe.

But she was still beautiful.

And he still wanted her.

Drew's mouth twitched as desire expanded inside him. He wanted to sense her lips softening under his, to feel them part to allow the gentle exploration of his tongue, to taste the sweetness of her mouth. He yearned to draw her down onto the bed beside him so he could indulge the emotions running riot inside him—so he could prove to himself that she wasn't an angel after all, that she was flesh and blood and—

Drew halted the heated progression of his thoughts

with sheer strength of will. Rationally, he told himself that the last trace of fever still haunting him was at fault and that his hunger for this young woman would fade when he was well again—but he knew better. There was only one way to ease what he was feeling.

Drew pulled himself to a seated position in bed. A day had passed since he had attempted to leave the bordello with disastrous results. He had spent another night in the gaudy room with the sound of male footsteps and female giggles echoing in his dreams—and with the angel in blue at his side.

During that time, he had learned through snatches of conversation overheard at the doorway that Tricia Lee Shepherd was not the woman he had thought her to be. She was the madam's daughter, who had only recently returned from up North and she did not participate in the services of the house. Dr. Wesley, obviously prejudiced in her behalf, had rambled on about her, extolling her virtues as he tended Drew's leg. Drew had not bothered to reply that his *angel* had merely returned to her roots.

Tricia turned back toward him, the gold flecks in her clear eyes sending heat shooting through him as she said, "You should eat something so you can maintain your strength."

He replied gruffly, "I'm strong enough."

"But you're hungry."

He was hungry, all right.

"Mr. Collins ..."

Revealing seconds passed before Drew realized she was addressing him, and he said abruptly, "My name is Drew."

He noted her hesitation as she said, "You know my name is Tricia Shepherd, but I hesitate to allow the intimacy of first names between us since we're barely acquainted."

Drew would have laughed if he'd felt the slightest bit merry. Instead, he replied boldly, "You've seen me practically naked; you've spent two nights alone with me in this room while I've been exposed to you as I've never been with any other woman—so I'd say you know me more intimately than most women do."

"That's different."

"Different ..."

"You were sick. You still are. You needed somebody to take care of you."

Right.

"Besides, you still have the remnants of a fever."

More than she realized.

"Dr. Wesley said the infection seems to be improving, but it still could go either way."

Drew's stomach twisted tight as her breasts heaved before she said, "But you're right ... Drew. Formality is a bit absurd at this point." She compressed her lips. "Now, are you ready to eat something? Your hands are probably unsteady, so I'll feed you."

That thought was more than he could bear. "I can feed myself," Drew responded more sharply than he intended.

"But I—"

"I said, I can feed myself."

Tricia did not bother to respond. Instead, she pushed the nightstand closer to the bed and said, "Go ahead."

* * *

Stubborn…unwilling to back down…he was *impossible!*

Those thoughts flitted through Tricia's mind as Drew attempted to spoon the thin broth into his mouth while leaning forward awkwardly over the dish. She did not comment when more of the first spoonful ended up on his shirt than in his mouth. She looked away when he mumbled under his breath and tried again, with the same result. She turned determinedly toward the bandages on the dresser that Dr. Wesley had left for her to roll. Moments later she heard the sound of his spoon striking the tray. "I'm not hungry anymore," he said flatly.

"Oh, no, you don't!" Suddenly angry, she strode back to the bed and said, "I'm going to feed you whether you like it or not, and you're going to finish that broth just like Dr. Wesley instructed—because if you don't, you'll never get well."

Drew Collins's eyes met hers as she demanded, "Do you understand?"

She was uncertain whether she saw a hint of amusement in those depths as she sat down determinedly at his bedside. Annoyed, she picked up the abandoned spoon and ordered, "Open your mouth."

Her heart pounded as Drew's lips parted and she shoved the first spoonful of broth into his mouth. She watched as his lips closed and his throat worked visibly as he swallowed.

She was sitting closer to him than she really wanted to. His light-eyed gaze was almost palpable as it searched her face and gradually settled on her lips. She could almost feel his body heat, and she controlled her trembling at the thought that the heat she sensed was unrelated to his fever.

Hardly able to breathe, she slid another spoonful into his mouth.

Damn ... what had she gotten herself into?

Angie shrugged into her dressing gown and pulled it closed around her. She did not bother to fasten the tie, allowing the gown to gape open to reveal flimsy undergarments that exposed a bounty of intimate flesh as she walked down the hallway toward the bordello kitchen. Chantalle frowned on such a casual manner of dress. She took great pains to impress upon all the women that her establishment was not the average bordello, and that she catered to patrons who appreciated an aura of decorum and delicacy in the public rooms, just as much as they sought full sexual gratification once the bedroom doors closed behind them. Angie was only too happy to supply the sexual gratification part, but she continued to fight Chantalle's restrictions at every turn.

Frowning, Angie flipped back her dark, unbound hair and started toward the stairs. Hesitating, she then turned back toward the office where she knew Chantalle would be working on her books. Memories of her visit to Simon's house the previous night remained chillingly clear in her mind.

Simon hated her almost as much as she hated him— with one difference. He wasn't *afraid* of her.

Angie paused at Chantalle's doorway. She was uncertain when the relationship between her and Simon had changed from the mutual gratification of perverse sexual needs to something much darker. All she now knew was that he paid her an exorbitant sum to keep him informed of every tidbit of information she was able to obtain about Chantalle and the workings of her house. The sums had increased along with his almost frenetic interest in everything going on there since Whit Hawk and his sister, Jenna Leigh, had returned to Galveston.

Angie paused with her fist poised to knock on Chantalle's door. Simon now insisted that she find out all she could about an old, worthless ring that Drew Collins supposedly kept in his money pouch.

As if she cared.

She reminded herself belatedly that it didn't matter if she cared. Simon did, and what Simon wanted, Simon got. If he didn't, someone would suffer, and she'd be damned if it would be her.

Knowing only one way to obtain the information Simon wanted—as quickly as he wanted it—Angie knocked on Chantalle's office door.

Chantalle frowned when her office door opened and Angie walked into the room. There was never a moment when Angie seemed other than the voluptuous whore she was. A matter as small as the teasing way she flipped her unbound hair, her deliberately casual dishabille, and the open fondling she encouraged from men in the public rooms of the establishment—all were blatant declarations. Chantalle also suspected a part of it was Angie's desire to irritate her, as was obvious in the attire Angie had chosen to wear this morning.

If Angie did not serve such a useful function in the house, she would ...

Chantalle forced herself to dismiss that thought. Angie did serve a very valuable function, and the girl knew it—but that did not make Chantalle a slave to Angie's machinations.

Chantalle raised her brow at Angie's gaping dressing gown. Angie hastened to tie it closed—too quickly for Chantalle's comfort. Angie was up to something.

Chantalle did not have to wait long to find out what it was.

Angie smiled and said, "I wanted to talk to you, Chantalle ... about that fella Tricia is taking care of."

Immediately alert, Chantalle responded, "What about him?"

"I feel kind of bad about what I said when he collapsed at the front door the other morning. Now I realize he really was sick."

"He's sick, all right, but Dr. Wesley and Tricia are taking care of him."

Angie shrugged. "I suppose that's fine, but I don't know how that fella expects to pay for all the service he's getting, what with him having only a few coins in his money pouch."

Chantalle questioned sharply, "How do you know what he has in his money pouch?"

"You know me. I listen when people talk. It comes in handy sometimes."

"Meaning?"

"Meaning I heard Tricia tell Polly she didn't even know the fella's name at first because he didn't have any identification on him. All he had was a money pouch with a few coins and an old, damaged ring inside it."

"A damaged ring?"

"With some kind of a crest that has a sailing ship partially visible on it—a piece of junk, if you ask me."

Chantalle felt the color drain from her face. Trying to sound uninterested, she said, "I don't know anything about it ... and what difference does it make to you?"

Angie shrugged again. "I don't know. I just wondered if you all knew something I didn't know about this fella. Is he really worth all the expense and attention he's getting? It's clear to me that if he is, Tricia isn't the kind to make him comfortable once he's feeling good again. I figured maybe I should show him that I'm more of what he was looking for when he came here that first day."

"I thought he made it clear that he didn't want you."

Angie's expression stiffened as she said, "That isn't likely. I'm thinking he was just sick that day. Anyway, I figured you'd have nothing to lose and would tell me the truth about him if I asked."

Chantalle was unable to control the subtle curling of her lip as she said, "You know you're not my favorite person, Angie, but you make us both money here, so I'll tell you this. I don't have any more information about this Drew Collins than you do. As far as the ring is concerned, it sounds like it's just a piece of junk, as you said."

"Then why does he keep it in his money pouch?"

"I don't know, sentimental value maybe." Chantalle's expression hardened as she added, "But it isn't my business, and it isn't yours either. Everybody knows I've got a soft spot for fellas who lost everything fighting for the Confederacy. Whether I cater to Yankees or not, that won't change. As far as this fella is concerned, Tricia is taking good care of him, and she assures me that as soon as he's well, he's out the door."

Chantalle stood up unexpectedly and advanced a few threatening steps toward Angie as she continued, "So I'm telling you now, mind your business and everything will be fine. If you don't, you might find yourself out on the street, just like you were before I took you in."

Angie's face flamed as she scoffed, "You wouldn't do that."

Chantalle's response was coldly succinct. "Try me."

Chantalle watched as Angie flounced out of the room. Waiting only until the door clicked closed behind her, Chantalle went still.

... a crest with a sailing ship partially visible on it ...

Like Whit Hawk's ring ... like the pendants that both Jenna Leigh and Elizabeth Huntington had shown her ...

Could it be? Could Whit's brother possibly have returned to Galveston, too?

She needed to see the ring for herself.

Willie Childers squinted against the bright morning sunlight as he urged his horse along the trail. He breathed deeply of the scents of salt air and marshland that were so distinctive to the area, and then shook his head with disgust. He didn't know what had gotten into him a few days previously when he'd left Drew behind at Madam Chantalle's bar. Knowing Drew as he did, he guessed Drew probably had had a good reason for the condition he was in when Willie had emerged from Mavis's upstairs room.

In the time since he had left Drew, he had returned home to the lovingly tearful welcome of his family. He had slept late, had been treated to many of his favorite foods, and had shaken the hand of every aunt, uncle, and cousin who had shown up at his door. He had even spent a few hours with an old girlfriend, but the misery of his last conversation with Drew continued to plague him. He had gone over it a thousand times in his mind and had arrived at the conviction that Drew was not the kind to disappoint a friend, or to talk to a friend the way he had talked to him. No, there had to be a good reason Drew had sent him back home alone, and he should have realized it.

He had made a mistake, and he was determined to correct it.

Willie turned his horse down the familiar trail. He should be in Galveston by evening. He was aware that Drew might have left the city and could be miles away by this time. He hoped that wasn't true. The only thing he was sure of was that he needed to find his friend and correct their manner of parting.

Madame Chantalle's bordello was the last place he had seen Drew. He would start there.

Tricia turned to look at Drew as he dropped his towel on the bed stand beside him and lay back against his pillow. After feeding Drew the broth as Dr. Wesley had instructed, she had left the room and had stayed away while she struggled to draw her ragged feelings under control. Finally disgusted with her weakness, she had warmed some water and filled a basin to bring back to Drew so he might refresh himself.

Her first mistake.

Drew had removed his shirt to bathe, baring his chest and restoring to her mind the intimacy of past nights as she had bathed the fever from his powerful body. She recalled the times during those ministrations when his eyes had flicked open to link with hers, rendering her temporarily breathless. She remembered the inexplicable tightening deep inside her—a spot that now seemed to spring to life each time she was near him. Attempting to strike those images from her mind, she had glanced back intermittently as he refreshed himself, only to realize as his exhaustion became apparent that he intended to forgo any effort to shave. She couldn't let that happen. She had shaved other wounded soldiers in the past. Surely he did not have so extreme an effect on her that she could not do the same for him.

Her second mistake.

Neither Drew's reaction to her effort nor her own was similar to her experience with the patients she had tended in Yankee hospitals. That fact became obvious when she worked up a lather and, in the absence of a shaving brush or mug, prepared to apply it to his face with her hand.

An inner tremor shaking her, Tricia attempted to ignore the sense of heightened awareness as she leaned closer to her patient. She could smell the freshly washed, male scent of his skin ... could feel his breath against her fingers. She sensed rather than heard his subtle intake of breath when she began spreading the lather across his cheeks. She moved her hand gently across his lips and chin, her heart pounding. She told herself she did not truly feel his lips part to touch her fingertips with his tongue, but her hand trembled as she picked up the borrowed straight razor.

To her surprise, Drew did not flinch. Instead, his eyes remained steady on her face, his gaze as intimate as a caress while she glided the blade over his skin.

By the time she was done, Tricia was shaken to the core by the multitude of emotions assaulting her. Carefully she wiped the excess lather from Drew's cheeks.

He frowned as he said, "I can see you've done this before."

"Yes ... I told you ... in army hospitals up North."

His expression sober, he asked unexpectedly, "Did Yankee soldiers smile at you and whisper their thanks when you were done?"

"Sometimes."

"Did they tell you that you were an angel in disguise?"

"Sometimes."

"How did you answer them?"

"I don't remember."

He paused, and then said more softly, "How would you answer me if I said those things to you?"

The subtle softening of Drew's tone touched a chord deep inside her and Tricia's inner trembling increased. How was this man able to threaten her defenses against him with a few soft-spoken words? Why did her heart race as he waited for her to reply? Why

did she long to respond to his question honestly...
with words she knew she dared not utter?

Aware of the intimate danger of the moment, Tricia
forced herself to respond, "That possibility isn't very
likely, is it? You've made very clear what you think of
me for tending to wounded Yankee soldiers—and the
word 'angel' wasn't a part of it."

Standing up hurriedly in an effort to escape, Tricia
said, "I'm going to remove this basin. Do you want
anything else before I leave?"

Drew's gaze drilled heatedly into hers, quickening
her breathing as her question hung in the silence of the
room. She sensed the words he was about to speak,
and her gaze dropped to his lips as they parted.

Her heart pounded.

A knock at the door shattered the moment, snapping
their attention in its direction. Dr. Wesley entered the
room without waiting for a response. Seemingly unaware of the tense moment he had interrupted, he approached the bed, smiling as he said to Drew, "Shaved,
did you? You did a good job. You must be feeling better." He said to Tricia as she turned to leave, "It looks
like you won't have this fella for a patient too much
longer."

Tricia mumbled under her breath as she pulled the
door closed behind her.

The sun had passed the midpoint in the sky when
Chantalle glanced down at Tricia as she turned out of
sight at the foot of the bordello staircase. She unconsciously nodded as Tricia avoided the public rooms
and entered the hallway leading to the rear of the

house, where the kitchen was located. Dr. Wesley had visited earlier in the day. He had left shortly after changing the dressing on his patient's leg, but not before stopping Tricia in the hallway with a few more instructions as to their patient's care. Drew was now sleeping, and Tricia had informed her when she passed her office minutes before that she was taking the opportunity to go downstairs and help Polly with dinner.

Perfect.

Waiting only until she was sure she could not be seen, Chantalle moved silently down the hallway. She opened the bedroom door at the end and slipped inside. She paused to look at Drew as she closed the door behind her. Asleep and motionless in bed, he was so tall and muscular that he appeared to dwarf the bed. She observed with a strange distraction that, cleanly shaven and with his expression relaxed, he was exceedingly handsome. But although his features were strong and even, like those of the other Hawk progeny, she did not see any particular resemblance. Yet one thing was abundantly clear. He was a formidable man who would be a formidable enemy, and she had no desire to incur his wrath.

Waiting a moment to make certain that he was asleep, she walked quickly toward the dresser where his money pouch lay casually exposed. Her jaw rigid, she pulled it open and took out the ring so she could view it more clearly.

Chantalle caught her breath. Angie's description of the ring was accurate. Despite the fact that the sailing ship and Latin motto on the crest were only partially visible, the crest was too similar to those she had seen before to leave any doubt in her mind.

But ... did the ring *belong* to Drew, or had he found it somewhere along the way? He said his name was Drew Collins. If he really was one of the Hawk siblings, why didn't he use his true name?

Chantalle considered those questions thoughtfully, deciding it was wiser not to tell Jenna Leigh or Clay about the ring for fear of raising a hope that could be dashed if Drew wasn't a Hawk after all. Also, Drew's bitterness about the Confederacy's defeat was obvious. It was possible that he would consider Jenna Leigh a turncoat for marrying a Yankee officer and turn his back on her even though the war was over.

There was only one thing she could do.

Chantalle pulled the door of Drew's room closed behind her and headed for the stairs. She would send a messenger to Whit at his La Posada ranch. Whit would sort it all out. He was the eldest of the Hawk clan and he was a cautious man. He hadn't even written to Elizabeth Huntington in New York to tell her he was a part of the family she had come to Galveston hoping to find, or that she also had a sister who was waiting for her return. Aware that Elizabeth was still recuperating from a gunshot wound and that Jason and she intended coming back to Galveston as soon as possible for reasons of their own, Whit had decided it would be better to wait until he could tell her in person.

If Drew Collins really was Drew *Hawk*, Whit would know how to handle the matter.

Chantalle raised the skirt of her gown to her ankles as she hurried down the stairs. She'd send one of her stable hands with the message for Whit. To guard against a repetition of past tragedies, however, she would insist on the importance of maintaining a low profile when leaving the city for La Posada.

She could depend on Whit to take it from there. It was his family, after all.

Afternoon shadows were beginning to turn into dusk when Tricia opened Drew's door slowly and peeked inside as she had done several times during the long afternoon. This time, Drew turned toward her and she said, "So, you're awake. You were sleeping peacefully every time I looked in before. I hope you're feeling better after your rest."

Drew maintained his silence as she approached the bed and forced herself to touch his forehead. She said with an attempt to deny the fluttering inside her, "You're much cooler. Unless I miss my guess, your temperature is normal."

Still no answer.

"Are you hungry?"

Drew gazed at her meaningfully, and Tricia felt her face flush with color as she said, "Polly made a beautiful stew. She's really a great cook. Would you like me to get you some? Dr. Wesley says you may eat anything you like now that your temperature is normal."

Silence.

"Dr. Wesley said you should put something substantial in your stomach before I get you back on your feet tonight."

"What?" Drew broke his silence to question incredulously, "Before *you* get me back on my feet?"

Tricia's chin shot up. "Dr. Wesley said I should help you take a few steps around the room before he returns tomorrow so he can further assess your progress."

"No, that's not going to happen." Drew's expression darkened. "I'm strong enough. I don't need anyone to help me walk."

"Like last time, you mean ... when you collapsed at the front door."

"I was sick then."

"You're still sick."

"You just said my temperature is probably normal."

"You've been sick. Your leg is improving, but it hasn't healed fully yet."

Tricia gasped as Drew responded by throwing back the coverlet and sitting up on the side of the bed as he reached for his pants.

"What are you doing?"

He did not bother to turn around.

He couldn't look at her. Tricia was standing near the doorway with her hair a golden halo, with her eyes wide and uncertain despite her bravado, and with a fragile look about her that turned Drew inside out with longing. He was only too aware that during the short term of his illness, his desire for her had run the gamut—from seeing her as an angel who was there to save him, to seeing her as a temptress bent on tormenting him. The only problem was that his temperature was now normal, he was completely lucid ... and he wanted her even more.

And he'd be damned if she didn't insist on *helping* him!

He had to get out of there.

"Stop! You're going to hurt yourself."

Drew turned back slowly toward Tricia. She was wearing that plain, colorless dress that only accentuated her pale beauty and the slim, fragile lines of her body—yet he knew how deceiving that fragility was. She had stubbornly bathed away his fever throughout two long nights; had forced down his throat the medicine that had halted the spread of infection in his leg; had fed him; had shaved him. No, he couldn't take another minute of it—

Drew took a breath as Tricia started toward him. He commanded sharply, "Stay where you are. I can walk by myself."

"No, you can't. Not yet! Didn't you learn anything the last time you tried to walk alone before you were ready?"

"You said that Dr. Wesley wants me to get back on my feet. That's what I intend to do."

"He said you should try walking—with help."

Drew's eyes narrowed. "With your help, of course."

"Of course!"

"No."

"But—"

"I said, no."

Drew restrained a gasp as he put weight on his injured leg for the first time. Steeling himself against the pain, he took another few steps before his leg started to collapse underneath him.

"Here, lean on me."

She was at his side in a moment, her dainty shoulder firmly wedged under his arm as she said, "Dr. Wesley said you should take only a few steps at first, just to get your blood moving."

Drew looked down at Tricia. His blood was moving, all right, especially with her body tight against his side and her matchless features turned up to his. What was more, he was drowning in the sea green of her eyes, and he knew damned well there was only one way he could be saved.

Tricia had stopped talking. Her gaze was now forged to his, and the tension between them soared.

Drew inwardly groaned as his heart began thudding in his chest ... as he seemed unable to stop himself from lowering his mouth toward hers.

He felt her sweet breath against his lips. He saw her expression change from uncertainty to an acceptance that he knew instinctively could become so much more.

His lips touched hers.

The taste of her ...

A knock at the door jerked both their heads in its direction.

Another knock was followed by an extended silence that Tricia broke as she called hoarsely, "Come in."

The door opened to reveal a slender blond man wearing Confederate gray trousers so similar to Drew's that Tricia knew it could not be a coincidence. Her thoughts were confirmed when the stranger took in Drew's unsteady posture and uneven breathing and said in a voice touched with self-directed anger, "I knew it! Damn it, man, why didn't you tell me you were sick? You know I wouldn't have left you here if I'd known."

Tricia looked up at Drew to see a brief smile spread

across his lips—a glorious sight that felt a little painful because it was not meant for her. The intimacy of the previous moments disappeared as if they had never been.

"I just wanted to make sure you got home on time, Willie," Drew responded. "Did the reception from your family live up to your expectations?"

"It did, but it wasn't the same without you being there like we planned. Damn it, man ..." At a loss for words, the young man shook his head as he entered the room and said, "Well, it isn't going to happen again. You're not going to send me packing this time. I'm going to stay right here with you—day and night—until you feel good enough to ride out of here with me like we planned."

"Willie—"

His face flushed, the young man said, "Don't argue with me, man! That's the way it is."

Mumbling a few words of thanks to Tricia, Willie took her place at Drew's side and walked him back to the bed.

Tricia left the room as they continued to talk. She pulled the door closed behind her and stood stock still in the hallway, reviewing the swift progress of events in her mind. Willie was obviously the fellow who had accompanied Drew to the house that first day, the same fellow who had abandoned Drew at the bar shortly before he collapsed. It was also obvious that Willie regretted leaving Drew behind, that he had suffered for it, and that he had come back with the intention of finding Drew again.

Tricia considered that thought. Her weak moments a

few minutes earlier would have been a mistake for both Drew and her, but Willie was here now. He said he was going to stay—day and night—until Drew healed.

That was good.

Tricia turned toward her room, telling herself again as she closed the door behind her: That was good.

Yes … good.

Chapter Five

"What's this all about?"

The sun was shining, the birds were singing in the branches above him, and a brisk, moist breeze stirred the trees, but simmering annoyance held Simon unmindful of the beauty of the day. Short on patience, he alighted from his horse and walked a few feet deeper into the wooded copse that he had used to conceal his carriage countless times when visiting Chantalle's house. He disliked riding horseback like the common man. He had progressed past that point. He was a man of wealth and influence in Galveston—the kind of man who rode in a carriage and dressed in clothing that was the height of fashion. Contrarily, because he had not wanted to draw attention to himself today, he was now dressed in a common costume consisting of a cotton shirt and trousers, a broad-brimmed hat, and of all things—Western riding boots!

He had halted his horse when he saw Angie's shadowed figure where she waited for him, and had dismounted, feeling annoyance spark anew at the smile she barely restrained. It had only been a few days since he had last seen her at his house, and his anger had not yet faded.

"What's this all about?" Angie shrugged as she repeated his question. "I thought you would realize why I wanted to meet you here. You gave me strict orders never to come to your house again, remember? You also said you wanted me to find out more about the ring that Drew Collins carries in his money pouch. So, when you didn't show up at Chantalle's for a few days, I went to your office and told Bruce I needed to see you, and that I'd meet you in the woods here. I figured that was a safe enough thing to do. Bruce knows how … close … we are. I figured he'd just think I was setting up a rendezvous someplace that might titillate you more than that little room in Chantalle's house."

She paused to run her tongue along her lips as she added coyly, "There's some truth in that, you know. The smell of the outdoors always did free up my inhibitions."

Simon looked at the smiling whore who appeared so confident of her appeal. Never more aware than at that moment of the physical changes in her since the first time he'd seen her, he scrutinized her more closely. He noted that her breasts, formerly firm and tight, were beginning to sag. Spending so much time on her back had begun to affect her figure, too, if he were to judge from the extra poundage around her hips and backside. The fact that she did not limit the scope of her perversions—nor allow herself to indulge them solely with him—had also become obvious. Rings underscored the dark eyes that had previously titillated him with her glances. Most disturbing of all were the lines that had begun to mark her formerly unmarked cheeks—a road map of a lifestyle that might condemn him by his association with her.

Yes, rapidly aging despite her youth, Angie had become an open embarrassment. Observing her pathetic attempts to seduce him in the harsh light of day, Simon realized he no longer had the slightest desire for her.

That realization curled his lips as he said, "Out with it, Angie. What do you have to tell me?"

Miffed, Angie replied, "You wanted to know about Drew Collins. That's his name, all right, as far as I can tell … and he does have that ring you described in his money pouch. I asked Chantalle about it and she told me—"

Aghast, he said, "You asked Chantalle?"

"You wanted the information as soon as possible, and I figured that was the surest way of getting it. But you don't have to worry. Chantalle thinks I asked just because I was a greedy whore looking for the next fella who might make me rich."

Simon barely restrained a reply.

"Anyway, the first chance she got, Chantalle went to that Collins fella's room to verify what I said. I saw her when she came out. She ran right down to the stable to send Will to La Posada with a message for Whit Hawk."

"How do you know all this?"

Angie raised her brows in silent response.

Simon scoffed. A trip to the stable and a roll in the

hay with Will had no doubt netted Angie all the information she needed.

No, he'd never touch her again.

He said stiffly, "When did all this happen?"

"A few days ago."

"A few days ago! Why didn't you tell me sooner?"

"Because I was waiting for you to come to Chantalle's."

"Fool! That delay could cost me dearly!"

"That's *your* fault, not mine!"

Enraged, Simon turned back toward his horse.

"I've got something else to tell you."

He stopped dead, then turned slowly back toward her.

"The blond fella that first came to the house with Collins? His name is Willie Childers. Well, he came back to see Collins and he hasn't left yet. He told Polly he doesn't intend to leave until Collins is well enough to travel."

"Where is he staying?"

"In Collins's room most of the time. Mavis felt sorry him. She told me she offered to take him on for free during off hours, but so far he said he'd feel guilty about leaving his friend alone again."

"How long has he been there?"

"A couple of days."

"How soon does Dr. Wesley think it'll be before Collins is back on his feet?"

"A couple of days."

"Do you have anything else to tell me?"

Suddenly haughty, Angie replied, "I figured that was enough, but if you think I should've waited so I could tell you more ..."

Simon barely restrained the epithet that rose to his lips. But he needed her. She was his eyes and ears in a place where he had to have information.

Digging down into his pocket, he withdrew a roll of bills and slapped them into Angie's hand with the comment, "Make sure you bring me information in a more timely fashion next time, Angie, or you might suffer for it."

Gratified when Angie's expression froze, Simon turned on his heel and walked back to his horse. Mounting, he kicked the animal into motion and rode directly to his office.

The morning sun steamed the weathered wood of the wharf as Simon dismounted, hardly bothering to throw the horse's reins over the hitching post before climbing the steep stairs to the elegant white stone building that housed the office of Gault Shipping. He crossed the cool interior, the boots he despised clicking on the black-and-white mosaic tile floor that had once been the pride and joy of Harold Hawk. He opened the door of the inner office and strode toward the desk, ignoring the surprise his attire caused on the face of the slight, bespectacled, gray-haired clerk seated there.

If he were of a mind to smile, Simon would have been amused at the innocuous appearance of Bruce Carlton. The man's benign exterior was more misleading than anyone dreamed, and it served him well.

Not bothering with any explanation, Simon snapped, "Come into the office, Bruce."

Simon waited until Bruce followed him inside before closing the door behind him. He eyed Bruce coldly as he said, "I have a job for you that you shouldn't find difficult to accomplish. You still visit Madame Chantalle's for an occasional poker game in addition to the usual convenience she offers, don't you?"

"Sometimes."

"Good. Then you won't find it difficult to get access to the upper hallway while you're visiting one of the women there."

"Probably not."

"A man by the name of Drew Collins is recuperating from a leg wound in the bedroom at the end of the upper hallway. He's presently incapacitated and as vulnerable as he'll ever be. Dr. Wesley says he'll be fit to travel in a few days, but I want you to make sure that doesn't happen."

Bruce squinted over the rims of his wire-rimmed glasses as he said, "Just to be clear, boss, you mean—"

Simon's face reddened. "I mean I want you to make sure Drew Collins takes his last breath in that bed. I don't care how you do it … just do it!"

"Right. I understand."

"I want you to report back to me as soon as it's done, do you understand?"

"Right."

Bruce hesitated, and Simon inquired stiffly, "Do you have any questions?"

"No." Bruce shook his head.

"Then what are you waiting for?"

Bruce shrugged. "Well, a fella can't go to Madame Chantalle's without money."

Simon took an impatient breath and turned toward his desk drawer. He opened the strongbox there, counted out a sum, and slapped the bills into Bruce's hand as he asked, "Will that be enough to cover your expenses?"

"That's fine, boss."

"You only have a few days."

Bruce smiled. "I'll take care of it tomorrow."

Drew fidgeted in bed and looked around at the room that had become all too familiar to him. The gaudy decoration had become increasingly abhorrent as the time he spent there stretched longer. If he were not still unsteady on his feet, if he did not know he would be repeating a mistake he had made before, he would get dressed and leave Madame Chantalle's and Galveston right then.

Or … was he just telling himself that?

He was not oblivious to the debt he owed Chantalle for all but saving his life, even though she obviously preferred to keep her distance from him. Nor could he minimize the part Tricia had played. His debt to them both grew with every passing day. He intended to pay that debt when the time was right and Yankee justice no longer threatened him. Dr. Wesley had assured him that the infection in his leg had been routed, that he no longer suffered the threat of amputation, and that he was the only one who would truly know when his leg was strong enough to support him again.

The ultimate decision was his.

Drew frowned over that thought as he looked at the upholstered chair where Willie dozed fitfully. Willie had been a great help since arriving several days previously. His friend had assisted him as he walked a few steps further each day. Drew was well aware that he would soon be able to bid Galveston good-bye.

Galveston ... and Tricia.

Actually, he'd seen less and less of Tricia since Willie's arrival. Because of Willie's almost constant presence in his room, all opportunity for private conversation with Tricia had ceased—but he needed to speak to her. He needed to explain that their brief moments together had not been the result of the workings of a fevered mind. He needed to tell her that if circumstances were different, if he ... if she ...

Drew's thoughts came to a halt when Tricia entered the room carrying a tray of food. Immediately awake, Willie was on his feet to help her as she settled the tray on the bedstand beside Drew and said, "I thought Willie and you might like some of Polly's chicken soup. It's very good."

The sea green of her eyes met his, and Drew went still. He definitely wanted her.

"You're right, ma'am. This soup looks real good. And me and Drew appreciate your thoughtfulness." Willie responded in Drew's stead, smiling his little-boy smile as he added, "We appreciate everything you've done for us, and we're going to pay you back. It just might take some time, is all."

"Payment was never a consideration, Willie." Tricia's reply was spontaneous. "Chantalle is only too happy to show appreciation in her own way for everything our soldiers did for us."

Speaking for the first time, Drew said with a touch of old resentment, "But the Confederacy lost the war, as you once reminded me."

100

Tricia's face colored as she turned to him and said, "Confederate soldiers fought for their country just as bravely as Yankee soldiers did for theirs. Their viewpoints were the only difference between them ... and that difference was settled by the war, once and for all."

Drew retorted, "It was, huh?"

"Yes, it was."

"You won't convince Drew of that so easily, ma'am." Willie shrugged and added, "Or me, either, for that matter ... but this soup sure looks good."

Tricia watched as Willie cleared a space for the plates. She jumped when Drew touched her hand unexpectedly, turning her back toward him. His gaze spoke of a myriad emotions before Willie unintentionally severed the silent communication between them by looking up from the tray to say, "Thank you again, ma'am."

Tricia left the room with a brief nod and a stiff smile.

Drew picked up his spoon.

Tricia's smile faltered as she pulled Drew's door closed behind her. Sadness brought tears to his eyes. There was no denying that he'd be well enough to get back on his horse and ride out in a few days; she'd probably never see him again. He had as much as told her that, even though his touch had said so much more.

Tricia closed her eyes as she sought to bring her emotions under control. Her feelings for Drew were intense, yet she hardly knew him. All she knew was that her heart jumped a beat each time she saw him, that it hammered in her breast every time his gaze met hers, and that his touch stirred her in ways she had never been stirred before.

But they were hardly more than strangers whose acquaintanceship was coming to an end.

Damn, what was she supposed to do now?

The evening was deepening, activity in Chantalle's upstairs hallway was brisk, and the closet where Bruce was hiding grew hotter with every passing minute.

He took a breath and unbuttoned his shirt as he strained to see the portion of hallway visible through the crack in the doorway. He had come upstairs with Georgia a short time earlier and had enjoyed every minute of the time he'd spent with her in her room. He had made an excuse to leave before she was fully dressed so he could slip into the closet unseen and wait for the perfect opportunity to follow through on the boss's orders—but the memory of his time with Georgia lingered. He had enjoyed himself so much that he had made the decision to stop back to see her again when Simon calmed down. He'd be able to relax a little more then.

A familiar chill moved down Bruce's spine when he recalled the look in Simon's eyes and the flush on his face when he'd said, *Make sure Drew Collins takes his last breath in that bed.*

He took consolation in the thought that he had handled similar situations successfully, without casting any suspicion on either the boss or himself. It amused him to think that he would run out of digits if he counted on his fingers the number of times he had "handled things." Actually, if he were to write them all down and describe the various ways he had accomplished those jobs, he could write a book—a dime novel that would chill readers even more than Simon chilled him.

Bruce raised his chin with a perverse pride in his accomplishments. He did what Simon wanted because he knew the depth of his boss's determination, because he knew the danger of trying to thwart it, and because in doing the boss's bidding, he had found a place in life. He had become the right hand of an important man like Simon Gault, an exalted spot that a common, uneducated fellow such as he seldom achieved. He knew, however, that his position was precarious, and all his achievements could be nullified by a single failure.

But he wouldn't fail. The boss had left the details up to him, just like he always did. Bruce had had some fun with that state of affairs in the past. He remembered the cowboy clothing he'd worn when he rode out into open country and shot old Hiram Charters right off his horse so he wouldn't be able to take Chantalle's message to Whit Hawk. He had made that killing look like a robbery, and nobody had ever suspected otherwise.

He had been indistinguishable from every other sailor on the Galveston dock when he had boarded Captain Randolph Winters's ship and plunged a knife into the captain's back while he worked at his ledger. The authorities had never even looked in his direction, and that killing was never solved either.

Bruce's pride briefly dimmed. He had failed to carry out Simon's orders only once—the situation with Jason Dodd—and the memory of Simon's fury still set him to shaking. The boss had allowed him that one misstep because he intended to give him a second chance when Jason Dodd returned to Galveston. Yes, he was Simon Gault's right-hand man, and that was the way things were going to remain.

Bruce unconsciously wiped the perspiration from his brow. That Willie Childers fella was bound to leave Drew Collins's room sooner or later. When he did, Bruce would simply walk inside and take care of Drew Collins before Childers returned. He'd be careful to leave no obvious marks on Collins's body, so it would look like a natural death, and he'd simply use the rear staircase of the building to disappear into the night afterwards. He was good at that—disappearing into the night. He'd had great practice.

Drew Collins—dead.

That order was as good as accomplished. Bruce's only problem was Willie Childers. It was getting late. He wouldn't have much longer before the evening ended and his chance was gone.

Damn that Childers! He was spoiling everything.

Chantalle moved through the noisy crowd on the first floor of her establishment with a practiced smile. Her clientele was in particularly high spirits this evening, unlike herself. Will had returned only a few hours earlier from delivering the message to La Posada. Will had apologized, saying that he'd only been able to deliver that message to Whit's wife, the beautiful Jackie. Whit, himself, was away on a trail drive and she wasn't sure when he'd be back.

Chantalle smiled absently at a client. If she didn't

miss her guess, Drew Collins would leave Galveston as soon as he was back on his feet. She had read that urgency in his eyes. If that happened, both Whit and Drew would possibly have lost the chance of a lifetime to be reunited.

Chantalle's smile dimmed under the weight of her troubling thoughts.

"What's the matter, Chantalle?"

Angie.

Chantalle looked at the nosy whore, her patience short. Angie was already a little too curious about things that weren't her business. Chantalle didn't want to stir her interest any further.

She forced a smile as she replied, "What makes you think something is wrong?"

"Oh … I don't know. You look like you've got something on your mind. It sure can't be that you're worried about business. There're more fellas here tonight than some of these *ladies* of yours can handle." Angie raised her shoulder in a casual shrug. "Of course, that's never a problem for me."

"I know. I can always depend on you, Angie."

"That's right, and I was thinking that maybe you should be—"

Angie's statement was interrupted when Jack Watton, a cattleman who knew his way around the ladies, walked up and said, "Have you got some time for me, Angie?"

Dismissing her conversation with Chantalle at the sound of Jack's voice, Angie fluttered her lashes and looked at him coyly. Taking his hand, she drew his arm around her waist and leaned against him. She curled his hand around her breast, encouraging him to knead it hard as she said, "I sure do, Jack, honey. I haven't forgotten the last time you came upstairs with me. I get hot just thinking about it. You're something special, and I've been waiting for you to come back. I've got something real special I've been saving just for you."

The erotic effect of Angie's statement was obvious in the bulge below Jack's belt, and Angie laughed aloud. She rubbed up against it and eased him toward the stairs as she whispered, "That's fine for starters, Jack, honey, but just remember ... I can take all you've got to give ... and I mean *all* of it."

Chantalle watched as Angie and Jack ascended the staircase. Jack was practically salivating, and Angie ... Angie was Angie—hot for any man who walked through the doorway.

Shaking her head, Chantalle turned toward the bar as the pair slipped out of sight. There might have been a point in her past when that situation would have pleased her, but now ...

Chantalle forced another smile when a familiar cow-poke squeezed past her ample figure as she walked through the doorway into the next room. That smile disappeared from her lips when she reached the bar and met Jake's knowing glance with the order, "Pour me a drink."

Tricia sat back in Chantalle's office chair and rubbed her eyes. She had been working over Chantalle's books for more than an hour in an attempt to straighten out her accounting. It had only taken her a few minutes to see why Chantalle spent so much time poring over the pages.

The problem was organization. Chantalle didn't seem to know the meaning of the word.

Despite Chantalle's reputation as a businesswoman, bills were listed helter-skelter; monetary advances were issued, noted haphazardly, and apparently forgotten; generous salaries were paid under circumstances that were not warranted; and monumental contributions were made to local charities that had obviously been kept secret from the general populace of the city— contributions that had drained the profit from the house as well as Chantalle's surprisingly modest bank account.

Tricia shook her head. Chantalle not only needed an accountant. She needed a keeper.

Despite those thoughts, Tricia felt the stirring of a new pride in the dear woman. She had always been aware that Chantalle was a far more generous person than anyone realized. Chantalle had taken on responsibility for her as a child when Chantalle had had so little that she needed to sell herself to survive. Chantalle had worked her way up in an atmosphere that was generally sordid, but she had committed many selfless acts along the way.

Tricia sighed as her mind slipped back to the bedroom at the end of the hallway. There was another example of Chantalle's charity. Chantalle had generously ignored the cost of caring for a former Confederate soldier, although at the time she hadn't even known his name. But Chantalle had limited her kindness to impersonal aid, keeping herself a friendly distance from the fellow.

Tricia sighed. She wished belatedly that she had done the same.

Confused by the ache deep inside her, Tricia closed the ledger and sat motionless for long moments. Strangely, the conversation with Chantalle that she had dreaded—the discussion of her future—had been brought up again since she had returned. She supposed the reason was simple. She had spent day and night at Drew's bedside. In the time since Willie Childers's return, he had taken over many of her tasks, but she had spent her spare time helping Polly cook and tending to Chantalle's books. Yet she knew that with Drew's departure, the inevitable would come.

That would be soon—too soon to suit her.

Tricia covered her eyes with her hand.

Damn!

She looked up at the clock on Chantalle's wall. It was getting late. The business of the house would continue for a few more hours, but she would soon retire for the night. First, however, she'd check in on Drew and make sure he and Willie had everything they needed. Seeing to their comfort was her duty, after all.

Bruce dozed fitfully. He was frustrated and hot in the airless closet. The hours had stretched incredibly long. His last look at his pocket watch had confirmed that the bordello would soon finish up business for the night. The doors would then be locked and his chances of escaping unnoticed would lessen. He had crept out of the closet a short time earlier to check whether

Collins's friend had possibly slipped out of the room without his knowledge. A quick peek had revealed that both Collins and his friend were asleep—Collins in the satin-covered bed, and his friend a dozing watchdog in the upholstered chair close by.

Irritated, Bruce had then slipped back into the closet, hoping that Childers would leave the room soon, if only for a few minutes. A few minutes would be all he needed.

The sound of approaching footsteps outside the closet door snapped Bruce fully alert. Drawing back more deeply into the closet, he held his breath, and then released it softly when the light footsteps passed by and came to an unexpected halt. He peeked out into the hallway and saw a beautiful young woman pause with her hand poised to knock on Collins's door. Apparently thinking better of it, she pushed the door open slowly and looked inside. He saw her back up as Willie Childers slipped out into the hallway beside her. Bruce listened as they started to speak.

"I'm glad you're here, ma'am."

Willie had been instantly alert at the sound of Tricia opening the door. He hastened out into the hallway and drew the door closed behind him. Looking at her directly, he said, "Drew told me everything you did for him while he was sick, and I never did get the chance to thank you, ma'am. Drew is like a brother to me. We promised each other that we'd come through the war together. I suppose that was a crazy promise to make, but Providence helped us to keep it. It would've been hard if a single, foolish argument had separated us when we came through everything else so fine."

"I really didn't do that much."

"Yes, you did, ma'am. Drew told me you didn't give up when the doc almost did."

"He told you that?"

"Well ... Drew said some things are kind of mixed up in his head, but one thing he knew for sure. You were there every time he opened his eyes."

"Oh ... well, he doesn't owe me anything, if that's what he thinks. You've both already done so much by risking your lives in battle."

"Thank you for saying that, ma'am." Willie smiled. "That means a lot, especially since you spent the duration of the war mostly up North with the Yankees."

Tricia hastened to say, "Willie, I hope you can understand. I had no enemies during that terrible war, and the wounded soldiers I tended didn't wear any particular uniform. I just did my best to help out wherever I could."

"I understand, ma'am. Really I do. My Uncle Fred and Aunt Chloe told me I was a fool to fight for the Confederacy, but that didn't stop them from welcoming me home with a smile a few days ago."

Tricia stared into Willie's clear, blue eyes, feeling tears well up in her own. He was a dear young man. There was a catch in her voice when she replied, "I know your words are sincere, Willie. I only wish I could make Drew understand as well."

"Drew's different from me, ma'am." Willie shrugged his shoulders. "He doesn't trust easily and he takes things hard. It won't be easy for him to forget that a lot of the fellas we knew and liked won't ever be going home because they fought for something they believed in."

"I'm sorry."

"I'm sorry, too. I guess the difference is that I had a family to go home to … folks that I could trust to make it all seem right again somehow. That's why I wanted Drew to come home with me, so's some of that might rub off on him." Willie's youthful face momentarily fell. "I almost ruined it when I let my temper get the best of me and went off and left Drew here, but now that I've got a second chance, I'm going to make sure I follow through."

"I can understand that."

"Drew's a fine man, ma'am. I know he seems hard sometimes, but there ain't a better friend than he is."

"I believe you." Tricia made an effort to conclude a conversation that was becoming painful as she said, "I just stopped by to make sure you had everything you need tonight."

"We do, but …" Willie frowned. "I wanted to go downstairs to check on my horse. He was limping when I got here and I need to make sure his hoof is being taken care of. It might take me a while to check him over, though, and Drew's sleeping so I can't tell him where I'm going. I was wondering if you'd mind staying here just in case he wakes up. I don't want him to think I ran off on him again."

"I'm sure he'd never think that."

"Ma'am … could you?"

"Of course. I'll stay until you get back. It's no problem at all."

"Thank you, ma'am. I appreciate it. I'll be back as soon as I can."

Tricia watched as Willie walked rapidly down the hallway. She pushed open the bedroom door when he disappeared from sight. She walked softly to the bed and looked down at Drew as he slept. He looked good, better than he'd ever looked before. His color had returned—a healthy color that emphasized the chiseled planes of his face and contrasted vividly with his dark hair and brows.

Drew mumbled something in his sleep, and Tricia moved closer. His lips moved again, and she leaned down to listen. Her breath caught in her throat when she realized what he was saying.

He was mumbling her name.

Tricia backed up, halting when her legs hit the upholstered chair behind her. Her throat was tight as she stared at Drew's sleeping countenance ... as she silently wondered, did she whisper his name in her sleep, too?

Sweating profusely, hardly able to breathe in the closeness of the closet, Bruce swore under his breath as Collins's bedroom door closed behind the woman. She had told Willie Childers that she wouldn't leave until he came back. That meant any chance he'd had of accomplishing the job Simon had set for him was gone for the night.

Damn her! If she hadn't shown up, Childers would have been forced to leave Collins alone while he went down to check on his horse, and Bruce could have finished the job he had come for. All he could hope for now was that he'd be able to leave the house unseen.

Bruce took a breath, scanned the hallway, then stepped out into the open and made his way toward the rear doorway.

Out on the street a few minutes later, he glanced cautiously behind him, then walked to the spot where he had secured his horse a little distance away. He managed to escape without being seen, but he still had to face Simon in the morning.

He wasn't looking forward to it.

Chapter Six

Elizabeth Huntington Dodd moved quietly around Mother Ella's empty bedroom in her New York City mansion. The dear woman was gone. Her strained, uneven breathing would never again sound in the room; nor would Elizabeth ever see her smiling face.

Elizabeth fussed with a few meaningless details in the silent room, consoling herself, as she had throughout the funeral the previous day, that Mother Ella had passed peacefully and with the grace that had marked her entire life.

Elizabeth turned to study the picture of the woman she had loved so dearly. Captured on her wedding day in the glory of her youth, Ella stood beside a sober, equally youthful Wilbur Huntington. The sense of wonder and the loving commitment that marked that day and set the tone for the rest of their lives was written in their expressions. That promise had never waned. Instead, it had expanded to take Elizabeth in.

The gratitude and admiration she felt for both those dear people had grown greater over the years, along with a love that knew no bounds—a love that had been returned in kind.

It did not cease to amaze her that despite Mother Ella's rapid deterioration after Jason and she returned home, the dear woman was never without a smile. She realized that Mother Ella had been happy simply because she had returned *home*; because she had brought Jason with her; because she had given Mother Ella the opportunity to be present when she married the man who would love her and care for her the rest of her life.

A sob choked Elizabeth's throat at the realization that Mother Ella had then been content to go to the better place that had been waiting for her—where Wilbur was ready to welcome her with open arms.

Unable to bear the thought of that loss a moment longer, Elizabeth went to the bedroom door. Out in the hallway, she looked up to see Jason approaching. She took the few steps into his embrace in a rush. Closing her eyes briefly as his strong arms closed around her, she whispered, "I can't believe she's gone, Jason."

"I know." His response was filled with a wealth of meaning that went unsaid.

Elizabeth remained in his embrace for a few minutes before she looked up into the dark eyes scrutinizing her with loving empathy and said, "I'll always love her, and this house will always bear tender memories for me."

"I know that, too," Jason said gently. "Take as much time as you need here, darlin'."

Elizabeth nodded, her throat too tight to speak. She went still when she felt Jason stiffen and saw his expression alter suddenly. She turned around sharply to see her cousin Trevor enter the hallway.

Jason watched as Trevor Huntington started toward them. Elizabeth had tried to convince him that Trevor was a decent young man who had done his best during the difficult circumstances of their youth, and that the torments he had endured because of her had endeared him to her.

Jason watched as Elizabeth left his side to welcome Trevor warmly. Following a few steps behind her, Jason approached them slowly, his expression noncommittal. Trevor was Elizabeth's cousin and the only family she presently knew, yet there were some things that Jason had not been able to make himself forgive. He doubted that he ever would.

Nagging at Jason's peace of mind was the occurrence Chantalle had related to him prior to their leaving Galveston. He knew Elizabeth had originally gone to Galveston in the hope of solving the mystery of her past—a mystery that he believed accounted for her nightmares of a fire. The nightmares continued to haunt her dreams, and he believed that only solving that mystery could free her of them. If Chantalle were right, if Elizabeth's pendant did bear the same crest as the ring that Whit Hawk had shown her, the discovery of Elizabeth's true family might be at hand.

He also needed to return to Galveston because he would be unable to rest until he proved that Simon

Gault had collaborated with the enemy during the war and was responsible for the death of Jason's friend Byron Mosley. For a reason he did not yet understand, Gault was also presently doing his best to negate Jason's efforts to prove to the Galveston consortium that Houston was a threat to its future.

It was time to find out more.

"Jason, I found some papers in Mother Ella's study that I wanted Trevor to go over with me. He says he has some time now and we're going to read through them. "

Jason looked at the thin, pale young man. Trevor returned his gaze equally soberly as Elizabeth stood beside him. Jason noted the way Trevor glanced down briefly at Elizabeth. There was true affection in the fellow's gaze ... an affection that he suspected Trevor had not formerly been allowed to display.

"Jason?"

"Of course, go ahead. I have some things to do in our room." Jason noted Elizabeth's relief and he smiled. He loved every bit of her, from the top of her honey-brown hair to the tip of her leather-clad toes. He wanted her to be happy. He would spend his life ensuring it.

Waiting only until Elizabeth and Trevor had disappeared at the curve in the staircase, Jason started back down the hallway. Entering his room, he closed the door behind him and then walked to the small desk in the corner. Seated there with paper in front of him and a pen in hand, he started to write:

"Dear Chantalle ..."

* * *

Galveston was bathed in early morning sunlight that filtered gracefully through the window blinds of Gault Shipping, but Bruce did not feel the warmth of its rays. Instead, his throat dry, he stared at Simon Gault across the wide expanse of Gaunt's mahogany desk.

"He spoiled everything, boss!" Bruce complained. "I waited in the closet hallway for hours, but that damned Childers didn't leave Collins alone for a minute. He even fixed it so's some woman would stay with Collins while he was gone."

Bruce waited for the explosive reply that he knew was coming. Unable to sleep, he had arrived at the offices of Gault Shipping as the sun rose. He had hoped for time to prepare himself in some way for the report that he knew he must make to his boss, but Gault had been waiting for him. Gault had not spared a moment before calling him into his office.

Bruce took a shaky breath. The boss was enraged. Bruce had never seen his face that apoplectic color before. Nor had he ever before seen Gault shake so violently as he did when he shouted, "I don't want to hear your excuses, do you hear? I want you to do your job!"

"I can't, boss ... not the way things stand. I'm telling you that Childers doesn't leave Collins's side for a minute." He took a breath. "I can take care of Collins for you later, after he leaves Chantalle's house, but making it look like he died of natural causes in bed isn't going to work."

"Why not?"

"I just told you. Childers doesn't leave his side for a minute."

"It's important that Drew Collins's death appear natural."

"But Childers—"

"Get rid of him, then."

"W-what?"

"Get rid of Childers! He's a nobody and nobody will care. Make it look like a robbery. You're good at that. You said he goes to check on his horse in the evening. Take care of him then. It'll be dark. You can take his money pouch and gun—whatever he's carrying of value—and everybody will just assume he was killed by a thief."

"But—"

"I want it done, Bruce, do you understand?" Simon was breathing heavily. "I want Collins out of the way, and if you have to dispense with Willie Childers to do it, that's all right with me."

"But, boss—"

Bruce's protest came to a halt when Simon's face flushed darker. Giving up, Bruce said in a rush, "All right, anything you say, boss. It's as good as done."

"Don't disappoint me, Bruce. As you know, I don't take disappointment well."

"Right. Don't worry, boss. It's as good as done."

Shaking, Bruce left the inner office and walked to his desk. He sat down hard and swallowed.

He knew he wouldn't get another chance.

"I brought your supper." Tricia forced a smile as she carried the tray into Drew's room. Willie stood up immediately and walked toward her. Taking the heavy tray, he said, "This sure smells fine, ma'am. Drew and me are going to get fat eating all this good food and sitting around like we are—but we sure appreciate it."

Tricia was wearing a simple blue dress, but the sight of her had the force of a blow to Drew's stomach. She approached and reached toward his forehead, but he shook away her hand.

"I don't have a fever. I'm fine."

Tricia drew back and Drew cursed silently—but it would have been a mistake to let her touch him. It had been a long day and his impatience with his debility was growing. Dr. Wesley had come to see him that morning. Both he and Tricia had watched as he had gotten out of bed and limped across the room with Willie's help. No one had to tell him that it would be another few days before he'd be strong enough to walk well on his own—just as no one had to tell him that his resistance to Tricia lessened with each passing day.

He had originally believed that Willie's presence would cure his malady, but it had not. The truth was, he missed Tricia's concerned advice, feisty comments, and occasionally angry retorts—but most of all, he missed her. She was young, but she had none of the mindless naiveté of youth. She was beautiful, but she seemed totally unaware of the effect of her beauty. She was inexperienced, but her observations were thought-provoking. They agreed on very little about the war, and she had angered him with several of her comments, but the exchanges had made him realize that there was more to Tricia Shepherd than physical appeal.

As if physical appeal weren't enough.

Drew looked again at Tricia.

A blue dress.

His angel.

Hardly aware that he was staring, he saw Tricia flush and then stammer, "You both seem to be all right, so I think I'll be going. I'll send Polly back for the tray. I'll see you tomorrow."

She was going.

Damn.

Well, maybe it was better that way.

She had to get out of there!

Tricia walked out into the hallway, then stopped to catch her breath. The truth was that she had been waiting for suppertime so she'd have an excuse to visit her former patient. She had worked in the kitchen of the bordello and had spent some time with Chantalle's books, but the hours had passed slowly. Strangely enough, Chantalle still seemed to be avoiding any discussion of her future at the house, and Tricia was glad. She needed time ... space ... something to—

"Ma'am, can I talk to you?"

Willie stepped unexpectedly out of Drew's room behind her, and Tricia turned toward him. Seeming embarrassed, he said, "I need to ask a favor of you, ma'am."

"A favor?"

"Yes, ma'am." Willie took a breath and said, "Drew is my friend. He's like a brother to me, but he's been acting like kind of a bastard—if you can excuse the expression, ma'am."

"A bas—" Tricia took a step back. "What are you trying to say, Willie?"

"I mean I ain't never seen Drew act like this before. But then, I ain't never seen him flat on his back like this either. What I'm trying to say is, he's been sick, ma'am. He's anxious to get back on his feet. Doc Wesley says another few days and he'll be fine enough to mount up and ride off like nothing ever happened. Well … almost, anyway."

"So you're saying?"

"I'm trying to apologize for him like he'd do for me if he needed to. And I'm asking you to excuse his behavior, because I know he'll regret it."

"Of course. I've taken care of injured men before and I understand."

"That's right … in Yankee hospitals."

"Willie—"

"I know, the war's over." Willie smiled his boyish smile as he added, "But if you wouldn't mind staying with Drew when I go down to doctor my horse again later tonight, I'd appreciate it."

Panic touched Tricia's mind and she said, "Couldn't you tell him ahead of time what you'll be doing later this evening?"

"Ma'am, I have the feeling Drew's going to try getting up by himself before the doctor says he can. He's been saying all day that he's all right, that he's well enough to ride out no matter what the doctor says. If he tries it, he might break open that wound again, and we'll be right back where we started. And the truth is, ma'am, I'm kind of anxious to get him home with me.

I figure that crazy family of mine is just what he needs right now to make him see that life goes on."

"Willie—"

"I'd consider it a real act of kindness if you'd do it."

Tricia said softly, "You're a dear friend to Drew, Willie. Of course I'll do it."

"Thank you, ma'am."

Willie's smile broadened. "I'll see you later, then. And thank you again, ma'am."

Tricia stood staring at the door that had closed behind Willie for long moments after he had gone back into Drew's room. She was uncertain of the reason for the tear that strayed down her cheek. Hastily, she wiped it away and returned to her room.

"You did what?"

"I arranged for Tricia to come and stay with you while I go to the stable to doctor my horse."

Drew's eyes narrowed. "I don't need anybody to sit with me."

"Maybe you do and maybe you don't."

"What's that supposed to mean?"

Willie shook his head. "It means I need to go down and doctor my horse because we're going to be leaving here in a few days, and he needs to be healthy when we do. It also means that I ain't as dumb as you think I am."

Drew did not respond.

"Dammit, man, I've seen the looks you've been giving that lady, and I've seen the way she's been trying to avoid them. You've got something to say to her, and it's not going to get said with me here."

"I don't know what you're talking about."

"You don't, huh? Well, then I guess you two won't have too much to talk about when I go downstairs later tonight."

"I don't need to talk to her, Willie."

"Yes, you do."

"No, I don't."

"You need to talk to her, if only to thank her for what she did for you." Willie frowned. "Doc told me how she practically saved your leg. If it wasn't for her—"

"All right, I need to thank her."

"Among other things."

Drew frowned and said more softly, "You know the situation I'm in. I can't stay in Galveston. The longer I do, the greater the chances are that the Yankees will realize who I am. I need to get out of here as soon as possible. Whatever I might say to Tricia wouldn't change the fact that she isn't the kind of woman who would take kindly to a man who is living on the run."

"Well, she'll be here later anyway."

"Willie—"

"Like I said, I need to go to the stable to doctor my horse. The rest is up to you." Willie ended the discussion by adding, "Right now I'm hungry and I'm going to eat while the food's hot."

Drew remained silent as Willie's spoon clicked against the dish. His friend was no longer listening.

Simon paced the elegant confines of his home study. He had already called his servants into the room countless times with countless inane requests so they would remember clearly that he had remained home that evening, just in case they were asked to confirm his whereabouts. He knew that possibility was practically nil, but he was not a man to ignore precaution—most especially since he had sent Bruce on a particularly important mission that night.

Simon glanced out the window at the shadows that stirred in the hot evening breeze. His patience was short. Willie Childers was an obstacle that would soon be removed. Drew *Collins* would be next, and Simon would be free to follow through with his plans for the future. Once he was comfortably ensconced in Houston in a position of greater wealth and prestige than he had ever known in Galveston, he would make sure every one of the Hawks paid the price of their heritage.

But first things first.

Tonight was a necessary step. Bruce was probably in place to follow through on his orders by now.

It wouldn't be much longer.

Willie smiled to himself as he walked toward the stable. Behind him, Chantalle's bordello was ablaze with light, but the far backyard where the stable was located was poorly lit.

Willie stumbled on the uneven path and mumbled under his breath. He supposed the stable hands knew the walkway well enough so they didn't suffer because of the poor lighting, and it probably wasn't very often they had visitors there. But then, the present situation in the bordello's spare room was not the norm.

Willie frowned at that thought. He knew Drew well enough to realize that there was more to the relationship between the beauteous Tricia Shepherd and him than he was ready to let on. He also knew that Drew did not form attachments easily. His friend had demonstrated that fact clearly during the time they had spent together during the war. Willie knew most clearly of all that however Drew wanted to handle the situation, he needed time alone with her before they left Galveston. He'd done his best to make sure Drew had that opportunity. He hoped Drew would take advantage of it—

Willie's thoughts were interrupted by a sound behind him. He turned around.

No one.

Willie paused and searched the shadows for long moments before becoming amused at his own behavior. Sometimes it was hard to forget that the war was over and threats against Confederates had ceased.

Turning back to the dimly lit trail ahead, Willie continued on toward the stables. Thunder would welcome him. The old fella would stand patiently while he tended to his injured hoof. He had no doubt that he would—

That sound again.

Once more, Willie stopped. A sixth sense turned him toward the shifting shadows nearby.

The silence between them was strained to the point of discomfort as Tricia looked at Drew, lying in the satin-covered bed. She said awkwardly, "I suppose Willie is taking care of your needs and you don't want anything from me right now."

Drew looked up at her, but he did not reply. Tricia stammered, "I mean, you seem to be as comfortable as he could make you."

Drew's look darkened.

Tricia took a breath and said in a rush, "You seem to be recuperating well. You should be encouraged by Dr. Wesley's assessment of your condition. He thinks you'll be able to get back on your feet soon."

"I'll be back on my feet sooner than he thinks."

Tricia took a wary step toward him. "I don't think that would be wise. Dr. Wesley knows what he's doing and he says your wound needs more time to heal."

"More time isn't what I need."

Tricia swallowed. Somehow the next logical question stuck in her throat.

Breaking the silence between them, Drew said, "Why aren't you asking me what I do need?" He paused, his gaze locking with hers as he questioned, "Afraid?"

"I'm not afraid," Tricia responded with more confidence than she felt. "I know you've been ill—very ill— and that I was the first, and occasionally the only face you saw. I know you feel an attachment to me because of it."

"Right." He mumbled more softly, "My angel."

"What did you say?"

"I said you're right, I suppose. I do owe you for the time you spent with me those first few nights, even though Dr. Wesley more or less said you'd be wasting your time."

"You don't owe me anything."

Drew replied unexpectedly, "I figure that's true, too, especially since you did the same for men who might have put me in this bed in the first place."

"I don't think that's the right way to look at things, either."

"No? What is the right way?"

"You were sick. I did what I could to help you."

"You would have done the same for any man."

"That's right."

Drew's expression tightened. "Thanks."

"F-for what?"

"For making it clear to me exactly how you feel."

Tricia did not respond, and Drew smiled stiffly. "I guess that says it all."

She realized that all his smile really meant was that it was the beginning of the end.

"Who's there?"

Willie stood motionless on the rough trail, his question sounding loud in the nighttime silence broken only by the chirping of night creatures, an occasional whinny, and echoes of frivolity from the brightly lit bordello behind him. He frowned and reached for his gun, then realized with a mumbled curse that he had removed his gunbelt days earlier and had left it in Drew's room.

Standing stiffly, he called out again, "Who's there? You might as well come out, because I can hear you."

Still no response.

Willie waited a few minutes longer and then glanced

at the stable, some distance away. The hair on the back of his neck stood up straight, an indication that danger was closer than he realized. Making a swift decision, he turned toward the stable and took his first step, only to halt abruptly when a sharp, searing pain pierced his back.

Gasping, Willie turned, his eyes widening when a shadowed figure stepped into view and struck another piercing blow to his chest.

Willie struggled for breath. He could feel himself falling. He heard the harsh thud as his body struck the ground, but strangely he felt no pain. The acrid taste of blood filled his mouth, and he struggled for breath as he looked up at the man leaning over him.

He strained to make out the shadowed figure's features as the fellow struck a third time.

He wanted to speak.

He wanted to ask why.

He wanted to say that he wasn't ready to die … but it was too late for him to say anything at all.

The small bordello room had grown incredibly warm and the silence between Tricia and Drew became more awkward with each passing moment. Drew kicked off the satin coverlet that had lain across his legs, grateful that he had insisted upon wearing his trousers so he would feel less of an invalid. She avoided his eyes and looked straight ahead as she sat on the upholstered chair nearby. She hadn't said a word since their brief, sharp conversation, and regret welled inside him.

He wasn't sure what had gotten into him when he

had spoken to her so gruffly. That had not been his intention when she had entered the room, but she had come in wearing that simple blue dress that made him ache with longing. The tendrils of hair hanging loose at the back of her neck had tempted his touch. The wary gaze of her incredible eyes had knotted his stomach up tight. The slight nervous twitch of her lips had raised a desire in him to soothe her anxiety in the only way that would ease the need building inside him as well. In that moment, he had wanted to get out of that bed and prove to her that he *could* make her feel what he was feeling ... but he did not.

Instead, he had spoken to her harshly, out of frustration.

The minutes ticked by painfully. He was aware how much he owed her—a debt he dared not express. He knew that speaking those words would be the first step in a direction he could not afford to go.

But there was one thing he needed to do. He needed to talk to her without the bitterness that had tinged his former comments. He needed to say that he—

A banging on the door raised Drew's head. A moment later Jake's pale face appeared. Jake glanced around the room and then stepped aside to allow Chantalle to enter. Her face was equally pale underneath the paint of her profession. Chantalle glanced at Tricia in a way that brought Tricia to her feet. Then she looked back at Drew and said, "I have something to tell you, Drew."

Drew's heart pounded as Chantalle advanced toward him with tears bright in her eyes. His breathing seemed to stop when she said, "One of my stable hands just found your friend Willie lying on the path behind the house. He was stabbed. He's dead."

Incredulous, Drew blinked. He couldn't have heard her correctly. He shook his head as if to clear his mind. He saw the tear that slid down Chantalle's brightly painted cheek as Doc Wesley entered the room and moved soundlessly toward him.

Chantalle whispered, "I'm so sorry. I don't know how it could have happened."

Hardly aware of the sharp prick of the needle Dr. Wesley plunged into his arm, Drew said hoarsely, "But why ... how ...?" He took a breath. "I need to see him."

"He's not here anymore. Doc Wesley told some fellas to take his body to the funeral parlor." Chantalle continued in a rush, "It was a robbery. At least, it looks that way because Willie's pockets were turned inside out."

"No." Drew shook his head. "Nobody with any sense would rob a down-and-out Confederate when there are fellas with full pockets walking the street. I have to see him." Drew tried to get up, but his legs refused to obey him. His gaze was clouding, and voices were beginning to echo from a distance as he tried again and failed. Still struggling, he felt Tricia's hand on his arm. He saw the tears that she brushed away as she said, "Relax, Drew. There's nothing you can do."

He said thickly, "It's my fault. Willie came back to Galveston because of me."

"It's nobody's fault except for the person who killed

him, but that person won't get away with it. They'll find him."

"They?" Drew's eyes were drooping closed as he heard himself say, "Not *they*. I'll find him."

"Drew ..."

Drew heard Tricia whisper his name. He saw tears streaking her cheeks. The world was going dark around him as he repeated, "I'll find him."

Chapter Seven

Drew awakened gradually, with a sense of foreboding heavy on his mind. He opened his eyes, uncertain of the reason for his reluctance to start the day. He glanced around the bordello room, at the sunlight beginning to filter through the heavy satin curtains, his sense of apprehension growing. He looked at the upholstered chair nearby and saw Tricia dozing with her head resting against the curved back. He was surprised. He had expected to see Willie there and he—

Drew came to full consciousness with a start. Reacting to his sudden movement, Tricia was suddenly awake. She stared at him silently for a few moments, then moved to his bedside and said, "Are you all right, Drew?"

She brushed away the single tear that trailed down her cheek, and he knew it was true. Willie was dead.

"Why?"

He was unaware he had spoken aloud when Tricia

responded, "I don't know. The stableman found Willie on the path to the stable. It appears to have been a robbery."

"No. That doesn't make sense."

"What other reason could there be? Willie was just in the wrong place at the wrong time. Whoever did it was probably lying in wait for anybody who happened to walk up that path."

In strict control of his emotions, Drew threw his legs over the side of the bed as he prepared to stand. He pinned Tricia with his gaze. "Nobody goes back to the stables except Will and Carlos. Do you mean to tell me somebody was hoping to rob either one of them? It wouldn't be worth the effort."

"Willie's money pouch was gone."

"Willie's money pouch never had much in it. Anybody with any sense could tell that just by looking at him."

When Tricia had no response, Drew asked, "Where is he? Where did they take his body?"

"It's still at the funeral home. Nobody knows where his family is located. They figured—"

"I know where his family is."

Drew reached for his boots.

"Where are you doing?"

"I'm going to the funeral parlor first, and then I'm going to tell Willie's family what happened. They need to know."

"Drew, please ..." Tricia attempted to stay his hands. "You're not ready for all that traveling yet. Just tell Chantalle where his family home is, and she'll arrange for somebody to go there and notify them.

Willie's gone. You can't do anything about his murder right now, and you might end up hurting yourself if you get up too soon."

"I'm fine." The deadening ache inside Drew swelled.

"Drew—"

"I need to see him." Drew's voice grew hoarse. "We had a pact. We made a promise to each other that I intend to keep."

"I know. Willie told me you promised each other you'd make it out of the war alive. He said it wasn't a realistic promise, but it was a promise you both managed to keep. You kept that promise, Drew. It's over and done."

"He didn't tell you the rest of it, then." Staring intently into her eyes, Drew continued, "We also said if one of us didn't make it, the one who was left would get even. I'm going to keep that part of the promise, too."

Not waiting for Tricia's response, Drew shook off her restraining hand and reached for his boots. He sucked in his breath, ignoring the pain when he straightened out his wounded leg and stood up.

"I'm going with you."

Drew looked down at Tricia as she stood beside him. He frowned.

"No."

Tricia's response was equally succinct.

"Try to stop me."

Colonel Clay Madison stood up angrily behind his desk and stared at Sergeant Walker. Assigned to the Adjutant General's Office in Galveston with orders to restore order in a city that had suffered greatly during an extended blockade by Yankee ships, Clay had not expected that his duty there would be so difficult. A Northerner by birth, he'd had little experience with Southern pride, and he had not realistically estimated the resentment he would encounter from the former Confederate supporters who seemed to fill the city. He had learned the hard way that in Galveston, the term "Yankee" was faint praise indeed, and although soldiers wearing Federal blue walked the street freely, an undercurrent of resentment flowed beneath surface smiles.

He'd had good days and bad days during the course of his assignment. Bad days had included periods of unrest and incidents that had caused several riots in the city. Yet it was in Galveston where he had met the young, bright, extremely feisty and beautiful young Southern woman who had eventually become his bride.

That had been a good day.

This day, however, was a bad one.

Addressing Sergeant Walker with carefully suppressed agitation, Clay said, "You're telling me a man wearing Confederate Army trousers was found murdered behind Chantalle Beauchamp's bordello?"

"Yes, sir."

"This isn't the first incident reported there."

"Yes, sir, but no robbery to date."

"What was the victim's name?"

"Wilson Childers, sir. He was a former Confederate soldier who had just returned from the war. He had … umm … business to conduct at Madame Chantalle's, and he was on his way home. He was found with his pockets turned inside out."

"You're certain he's a former Confederate soldier, or are you just making that assumption because he was wearing the trousers from a Confederate Army uniform?"

"Madame Chantalle confirmed the information. She knew him."

"He was a friend of hers?"

"I don't know, but she reported his death."

"Has the news of his death been reported to his family yet?"

"Nobody seems to be sure where they're located."

"Has his death become common knowledge in the city?"

"I don't know, sir."

Clay hoped not. He was intensely aware that if his wife, the former J. L. Rebel, were still reporting on a daily basis in her former position on the local newspaper, the news would have spawned another riot like the one that had rocked the city shortly after she started working there. He was silently grateful that Jenna Leigh had learned that the power of the press could be a dangerous weapon if not used wisely. He was also grateful that marriage had mellowed his wife's former antagonism toward the Yankees.

The death of a former Confederate ... a young soldier on his way home. Clay winced at the thought. Rabble-rousers in the city who supported rebellion against Federal martial law would not be satisfied that his death was the result of a robbery. Nor would they believe that a "Yankee" officer would make an honest effort to apprehend his killer. He could not afford to allow those rabble-rousers any leeway. Serious repercussions could follow. He hated to think that the murder of a poor soldier returning from the war could become the incident that ignited a smoldering truce into flames.

There was only one way to prevent it.

Clay ordered, "I want a military detail ready to travel with me to Madame Chantalle's within five minutes. We need to make sure the citizens of Galveston realize that the Adjutant General's Office will not sanction the killing of a former soldier—no matter the color of the uniform he wore."

"Yes, sir."

"I want our investigation to be visible, Sergeant … very visible."

"Yes, sir."

Clay watched as Sergeant Walker left to follow his orders. The sobering truth was that no matter how visible his actions, only one thing could save the situation. He needed to find the poor fellow's killer fast.

A late morning sun shone brilliantly and the heat of the day was building as Drew took a deep breath and stood still momentarily on the paved walk outside the funeral parlor. Outwardly stoic, he rigidly controlled the agonizing pain that tore at his innards. He had just viewed Willie's body. At his side, Tricia brushed away her tears and raised her chin. It occurred to him as she stood silently beside him that her presence was a comfort and a source of strength that he had not expected.

She had been equally silent as they'd entered the

room where Willie's body lay. She had not made a sound as they'd viewed Willie's motionless form. Looking down at his friend, Drew had felt a sense of unreality envelop him, and he had been momentarily disconcerted. Willie looked so strange. Willie's eyes, formerly sparkling with a joy he seemed to find every day under any circumstances, were closed; his mouth, formerly smiling broadly at the slightest provocation, was colorless and still. Accepting fully for the first time that Willie was dead, Drew had struggled to suppress his grief.

It was at that moment when Tricia had slid her small hand into his. He had looked down to see that she shared his pain, and the knowledge had consoled him. Borrowing her strength, he had taken a deep breath and reaffirmed his determination.

Willie was gone.

But he was not forgotten.

Drew took Tricia's arm as he limped toward their horses.

"Where are we going now?" she asked.

Drew was only too aware that his leg had not returned to full strength. Struggling to hide his physical pain, he replied, "*I'm* going to see Willie's parents. It shouldn't take too long, maybe a day or so."

"I'll be ready whenever you are."

"You're not coming. I appreciate your support, but I don't know the exact location of his family's place, and I'm not sure how long it'll take me. You have a reputation to consider. It won't survive if you travel with me unchaperoned."

"If I was worried about my reputation, I wouldn't have come home in the first place."

"That doesn't mean you have to throw your reputation away."

Tricia's reply was flat and unyielding. "I'm going with you."

Halting beside their mounts, Drew said harshly, "This is my job. Willie was my friend. You don't have anything to do with what happened."

"Don't I?" Tricia's expression was adamant. "Maybe I didn't know Willie as long as you did, and maybe I didn't suffer through all the difficulties you shared together, but I truly liked him. There was an honesty about him, and an optimism that was rare, especially since he had gone through so much. To me, his death isn't just another in a long line of losses like those I couldn't do anything about during the war. It's sadder because he *did* survive, because men like him are the South's strongest hope for renewal, and because he came this far only to lose his …"

Momentarily unable to continue, Tricia reined in her emotions and continued, "I need to be there when you tell his family, Drew. I need to let them know how I feel. It's something I must do."

Drew looked deep into Tricia's green eyes. Underneath the glaze of tears, he saw a sorrow that mirrored his own, as well as a determination that could not be denied.

He responded gruffly, "I'm going to get some supplies for the trail first. I won't wait for you if you're not ready when I'm done."

"I'll be ready."

Drew swung Tricia up onto her horse. He turned his mount back toward the bordello with the realization that Tricia wouldn't have accepted no for an answer even if he had tried.

Colonel Clay Madison halted at the front door of Chantalle's bawdyhouse. He turned toward the military detail behind him and said to the uniformed soldiers, "I'm going inside to speak to Madame Chantalle about the murder that was committed near her stables last night. Now, I don't care how many times you may have visited this house on your own in the past, or how well you know any of the women here. That isn't my concern. What is my concern is the fact that you have accompanied me here on an official, military investigation. You represent the United States of America, and in that capacity, I expect you to behave with the decorum befitting that position." Glancing at Sergeant Walker, Clay instructed, "I expect you to oversee the actions of this detail however long I will be interviewing the persons involved, Sergeant."

Turning back toward the door without waiting for a reply, Clay entered the house. Minutes later, he was facing Chantalle in her office. Obviously affected by the murder, Chantalle was pale underneath the makeup of her trade as she said, "I have nothing to tell you that you don't already know, Colonel. Willie Childers was on his way to the stables to doctor his horse. My stable hand, Will, discovered his body."

"What was Childers doing here?"

Chantalle paused, and then said, "He and his friend came here for the usual purpose. His friend became ill after Willie left, and I had him taken upstairs, where a doctor could see him privately. Willie came back to check on his friend while he recuperated here."

"Mr. Childers was a former Confederate soldier?"

"Yes. He was still wearing the pants and boots of his Confederate uniform."

"Did you see anyone take offense at that?"

Chantalle almost smiled. "Here in Galveston? You'd have more cause to ask that question about someone wearing Federal blue."

"Believe me," Clay responded, "I know."

"Is that the reason for the detail that's waiting on my front doorstep right now?"

Clay paused, and then replied, "You are aware of my situation here, Chantalle. This isn't the first time I've come to you with an inquiry of this sort."

"It's the first time you've come with a full military detail to back you up."

"The difference this time is that a former Confederate soldier has been murdered."

Chantalle's expression stiffened. "The death of a prostitute didn't warrant the same attention—is that what you're trying to say?"

"The death of a prostitute was as deep a concern as the death of this former Confederate soldier, but different measures are necessary to handle the situation. We intend to find the person responsible for Childers's death, just as we found the man responsible for the other murders, but it's necessary for the people of this city to know that the Adjutant General's Office will give the same attention to Willie Childers's murder that it would give to the death of a soldier wearing military blue." He paused and added, "I hope you understand."

Chantalle raised her chin and said reluctantly, "I do, but that doesn't change what I've already told you. I don't know anything more than that Willie was dead when my stable hand found him."

"I'll have to speak to the fellow. If you don't mind, I'll—"

Turning at Chantalle's response to an unexpected knock on the door, Clay frowned at the big man who opened the door and took a few steps into the room. "Is anything wrong, Chantalle?" he inquired.

"No. The colonel is here to make an inquiry about Willie's death." She turned toward Clay to say, "Colonel Madison, this man is Drew Collins. He's the fellow who was traveling with Willie—the man who Willie came back here to see."

Clay extended his hand in greeting. He did not react visibly when Collins did not accept his handshake. "I'd like to express my condolences. I understand your grief at the loss of your friend. To have endured so much during the war, and then to lose him on your way back home is ... tragic beyond words. But I promise you that the Adjutant General's Office will pursue this crime and make sure the perpetrator is punished. I, personally, give you my word on that."

Clay noted that Collins deliberately ignored his comments as he faced Chantalle and said, "I'd like to speak to you when you're done here, Chantalle."

"Of course."

Clay watched as Collins left without speaking to him. He looked back at Chantalle, making no comment. Responding to his silence, she said, "Drew and Willie were close friends as well as fellow Confederates. As you can see, the war hasn't ended yet for Drew."

Saddened, Clay nodded.

"Drew is going to leave Galveston shortly to inform Willie's folks about his death. If you don't mind, Colonel, I'd like to talk to him before he goes."

"Of course." About to depart, Clay turned back to say, "If your friend intends to inform Childers's parents of his death, please make sure he tells them they'll need to get permission from the Adjutant General's Office before they take their son's body home."

"Of course."

"One thing … do you think there could be any other reason than robbery for Childers's death?"

Chantalle shook her head. "Why would you ask that?"

"It was just a question."

"No, I don't think so. Willie was an affable young man. Everybody liked him, including me. I can't think of anyone who would purposely want to hurt him."

The moisture that sprang into Chantalle's eyes confirmed in Clay's mind that she was telling the truth.

He bade her a solemn good-bye. He could not help thinking as he did that the bright paint of Chantalle's occupation hid a painful past that the sad circumstances of Willie's death had somehow renewed in her mind. He had the feeling that if not for the vagaries of life, she might have been a far different woman.

He was walking back down the staircase toward the front door when Chantalle emerged from her office and started hurriedly toward the room at the end of the hallway.

She had said she needed to talk to Drew Collins.

Clay frowned as the tall man's image came back to mind. Collins obviously wore his Confederate pants and military boots proudly. He was a big man, dark-haired and light-eyed, a common enough description except for the fellow's direct manner, which bespoke the cold determination of a military man accustomed to authority.

Nagging at his mind also was the wariness in Collins's eyes at the sight of Clay's Federal uniform. He supposed wariness was to be expected; yet Collins's intensity seemed extreme.

Clay paused at the front door of the bordello. He hadn't learned anything more than he already knew about Childers's death by speaking to Chantalle, but the military presence at her front door had been noted. He had no doubt word would spread quickly that Childers's murder was being thoroughly investigated— which it was.

With a command to the waiting detail as he stepped out onto the doorstep, Clay turned toward the backyard.

"The whole town's talking about it, I'm telling you!" Bruce looked at his boss, inwardly quaking at the growing rage on Gault's face. "I did what you told me. I took care of Childers just like you wanted. It was easy." Bruce almost smiled. "Like I said, Childers wasn't expecting anything. He even left his gun back in Collins's room, so all I had to do was—"

"Spare me a repetition of the gory details!"

Bruce immediately stopped talking. He had shown up at the office early that morning with news that he'd thought the boss would appreciate. After all, he had taken care of Willie Childers just as he'd ordered. With Childers out of the way, it would be easy to slip into Collins's room. It would be just as easy to make Collins's death appear to be an accident. He was an expert at that kind of thing, after all.

He had made his report to Gault, and he had basked in the glory of his boss's faint praise, until—

"How do you know all this?"

Bruce adjusted his wire-rimmed glasses nervously as he replied, "Billy Thurman just came to deliver that bill of lading you were waiting for. He said it's all over town that Colonel Madison showed up at Chantalle's and stationed a military detail at her door while he questioned her about Willie's death. He went back to the stables to question her stable hands, too."

Bruce stared at Gault as his boss appeared to swell with anger. His greatest fears confirmed, Bruce offered meekly, "Do you still want me to take care of Collins tonight, boss?"

"Are you insane?" Bruce felt perspiration begin dotting his brow as Gault continued scathingly, "You are a fool if you think anyone would believe that Collins's death was due to natural causes after all this."

"But—"

"I'll have to change my plans temporarily, that's all. The excitement about Childers's killing will die down, and when it does, you can take care of Collins."

"But what if he gets back on his feet before—"

"I said I'll have to bide my time, do you understand?"

"Yes, boss."

"Neither of us can take the chance that an investigation will lead suspicion our way."

"There isn't any chance of that, boss. I made sure of it."

"You had better." Gault's lifeless eyes studied Bruce coldly as he continued, "I'll let you know when it's safe to follow through with the rest of your assignment. But in the meantime, I expect you to keep your eyes and ears open."

"I sure will, boss."

Gault added subtly, "For your sake, as well as mine."

Bruce nodded and left Gault's office. He stood unsteadily beside his chair in the outer office for a few moments, and then sat down abruptly. The boss was angry. Bruce didn't like it when Gault was angry, because that was dangerous.

Bruce took a breath as he silently added, dangerous for everybody … including him.

Drew kept his horse to a steady pace along the narrow trail. Tricia and he had traveled in virtual silence as they passed through salt marshes, then moved on toward more stable ground. The area became heavily foliated with trees and plants indigenous to the semitropical area, and he experienced a strong sense of nostalgia. Willie had described the trail they were taking many times during lulls in action, when thoughts of home became more vivid. The pictures Willie had drawn as he rambled on were clear in Drew's mind, almost as if those memories were his own. He recalled lamenting that he had not been able to speak of his own home. Those memories were uncertain to him—as indistinct as the images of his mother and father. All that he remembered clearly was the orphanage and the years of routine that his brother, sisters, and he had spent, waiting in vain for their father to return to claim them.

Unfortunately, he remembered with relentless clarity the day he'd returned to the spot where the orphanage had stood and found only burned and blackened rubble. With his sisters dead and his elder brother lost to him, he'd had few memories that he cared to share.

Drew attempted to ignore the pain and the growing stiffness in his leg. He glanced at Tricia. It occurred to him that there was far more to Tricia Lee Shepherd than he had ever imagined at first glance.

At first glance ... his angel.

Tricia's attire was nothing like the flowing, almost celestial garment she was wearing when he first saw her. The wide-brimmed hat she presently wore low on her forehead hid her fair hair except for the long braid that hung down her back. It shaded her heavily fringed, sea-green eyes and shielded her flawless complexion from the heat of the burning afternoon sun. She wore a simple shirtwaist tucked firmly into the brown split skirt that allowed her to ride astride as she kept hand-tooled boots resting firmly in her horse's stirrups. Drew wondered absentmindedly how she had managed to come up with so efficient a Western riding outfit on the spur of the moment. But then,

Tricia was Tricia. He had learned that she did exactly what she wanted to do.

She obviously had done considerable riding, as was demonstrated by her easy control of her horse. It bothered him to think that she probably had not gone riding alone, and that any man with an ounce of blood in his veins, whether a Yankee or not, would take that opportunity to …

Forcing that thought from his mind, Drew concentrated instead on the present. Dressed like an angel or not, Tricia was a formidable young woman. He could understand Chantalle's pride in her, as well as the disapproval she had not hesitated to express when Tricia told her flatly that she would accompany him when he traveled to see Willie's folks.

Drew glanced again at Tricia. His leg was stiffening painfully, but he ignored it as thoughts of the night to come sprang to mind. He had been determined to leave Galveston to notify Willie's family as soon as he was able. He had told himself that he would not allow Tricia's presence to alter his plans, but the afternoon sun was rapidly dropping toward the horizon, and he was well aware that twilight was not long away. They would not arrive at Willie's home before sunset, and they could not travel in the dark.

Drew's brows knitted with concern as he looked at Tricia. Whatever her background appeared to be, she had proved to him that she was a proper young woman. He did not want to spend the night with her on the trail.

Responding to his glance, Tricia said, "It's easy to see that whatever you're thinking isn't good—and that it's directly related to me." She hesitated, her gaze searching his face as she asked abruptly, "What's the matter, Drew?"

"It's getting dark. We're going to have to stop for the night."

"So?"

"Even Chantalle realized what that fact will imply to others."

"I told you, I don't care what other people think. Besides, it's a little late to worry about that now."

Drew did not immediately answer her. She was right. He had been aware of the possibility of gossip when he'd agreed she could accompany him. So why ...?

Drew's mouth twitched with annoyance. He was only fooling himself. What people would think was only secondary in his mind. Foremost were his own thoughts of what the night could bring.

Damn, as if things weren't difficult enough.

But he had made his bed. He would have to lie in it.

Belatedly wincing at his unwitting double entendre, Drew directed his mind elsewhere.

Tricia moved quietly around the makeshift camp that Drew had set up for the night. When she had questioned him about their progress, he had responded simply that they'd probably reach Willie's family sometime the next day. She hadn't pressed him any further, aware of just how difficult that meeting would be.

Tricia watched as Drew hobbled their horses a distance from the fire and limped back toward her.

Limped ...

Tricia said abruptly, "Your leg is bothering you, isn't it, Drew?"

"No."

"You don't have to lie to me, you know."

"I wouldn't bother to lie."

"Why are you limping, then?"

Drew's strong features were tightly drawn when he turned back toward her and said, "My leg isn't my biggest concern right now, understand?"

"I do … and I don't." As adamant as he, Tricia pressed, "You have a painful mission to accomplish, but I saw what your leg looked like when you collapsed. I don't want to take the chance that'll happen again because of neglect."

"What difference does that make to you?"

"What diff—"

Tricia went silent as Drew pinned her with his gaze. She needed to be honest or he would see right through her, but how could she respond?

Could she confess that she was attracted to him in so many ways she could not explain; that because of him, she had begun feeling things she had never felt before; that her concern for him was no longer limited simply to the altruism that had driven her to remain at his side through those long first nights when his leg and his life were threatened?

Lastly, could she tell him that Willie's death had affected her deeply, not only because of her affection for the young man whose endearing smile had touched her, but because she suffered Drew's torment as well as her own; that she wanted—no, she *needed desperately* to lessen his feelings of loss whatever way she could?

She couldn't, because she knew his next question would be, *Why?*

She had avoided facing that question. She continued to avoid it as she responded with the partial truth, "Because whether you realize it or not, my time is valuable to me. I don't like to think that I wasted my effort those first nights while you lay delirious in Chantalle's house, or that you're going to neglect your wound so that it will happen again."

"That's my business."

"Not anymore."

Tricia was uncertain of why Drew did not press her any further, but she was grateful as he instructed abruptly, "Put your bedroll beside the fire and go to sleep. We'll be getting up at dawn."

Tricia followed his directions silently. She caught her breath as he laid his bedroll beside hers. She waited, then released her breath when he turned his back toward her and was soon breathing evenly in sleep.

Mrs. Childers stared at him wordlessly as the hot mid-morning sun beat down on them relentlessly. Drew remained silent, at a loss for words; Tricia stood equally silent beside him.

Drew had spoken little as Tricia and he resumed their journey earlier that morning. Myriad thoughts of the day to come had tormented him, and the sober mission had grown tenser with every mile. Willie's homestead was small and proud. He had described the modest farm so well that it had almost been familiar to Drew as Tricia and he had approached it. In a way, it had almost been like coming home.

Now as he stood there silently, he recalled that he had ridden up to the front porch of the house as a small woman walked out to greet them with a smile; a graying man had approached from the corral. Drew hardly remembered dismounting and then lifting Tricia down from her horse. He only recalled the feeling of dread that had started deep inside him as he walked up the stairs.

What he did remember was that Myra Childers had looked up at him with eyes so reminiscent of Willie's that it had been like a blow to the gut, and that anxiety had flashed briefly there, preceding tears as he said the words forever burned into his heart.

Drew mumbled inadequately as Willie's parents gasped with grief, "I'm so sorry."

Nathan Childers wrapped his arms around his distraught wife, ignoring the tears that streamed down his wrinkled cheeks. Drew felt Tricia's presence beside him and he glanced at her to see that her cheeks were wet as well.

He listened as Tricia softly spoke, heartfelt words that came from the well of sorrow deep inside her.

Drew held his breath as Myra Childers turned toward him again at last. Her lips trembling, she whispered, "You said you're Drew Hawk, Willie's friend?"

Drew did not note Tricia's surprise when he nodded his assent. He listened as Myra continued hoarsely, "Willie wrote us so many times about you. You were like a brother to him."

Unable to say more, he managed, "Yes, ma'am."

"He was worried about you. He said he was going

back to Galveston to find you because you had gotten separated somehow."

Drew could not reply.

Raising her chin, Myra said in a broken rasp, "Willie valued your friendship as much as he loved his family and his country. I only wish that Willie could have been walking beside you when we met you for the first time."

Those words rang over and again in Drew's mind. Remaining at the Childers family farm as long as he could bear it, he finally mumbled an excuse for leaving and took Tricia's arm to lead her back toward their horses.

Turning back to the aging couple, his heart aching for their grief, Drew shook Nathan Childers's hand, and waited as Myra Childers bade Tricia a tearful good-bye before turning toward him. The ache inside him turned to a pain so sharp that it momentarily stole his breath as Myra abruptly hugged him tight against her motherly form. His throat thickened as s he whispered, "Come back to see us, please, Drew. That would please Nathan and me greatly, and Willie would be happy to know that you considered this house your home."

Drew boosted Tricia up onto her saddle, then mounted as well before turning his horse toward the trail back to Galveston.

Twilight had turned the wooded trail into dark shadows that inhibited further travel. Directing his mount into a clear area, Drew pulled back on the reins and said to Tricia, "We'll camp here for the night."

He dismounted, lifted Tricia to the ground, and then turned his back on her, making himself busy setting up camp. There had been very little conversation between Tricia and him after leaving the Childers farm; he had gone over and over again in his mind his conversation with Nathan and Myra Childers.

His throat tight, Drew recalled the emotion that had clouded Willie's eyes each time he had spoken about them. That same emotion had been reflected in his parents' eyes each time they said his name. The love between them had been vividly clear.

Drew inwardly winced as he recalled his own parents—the mother who had deserted the family when their lives grew difficult; the father who had left them promising to return, but who had never been heard from again. In direct contrast, Willie's family had been separated by miles, but their hearts had remained close. Drew would never forget Willie's tales of his hearty welcome home.

He was glad Willie had had that—a welcome home. He'd had so little time afterwards.

It irked Drew that he had needed to tell Willie's parents they must get a release from the Adjutant General's Office before taking Willie's body home. He supposed those were the rules when a murder investigation was being conducted in a city under martial law, but he knew it would not be easy for those two good people to petition a Yankee's permission to bury their son.

Drew's mind moved briefly to Colonel Clay Madison. Despite his dislike of the uniform the fellow wore, the officer had appeared sincere in his determination to find the man responsible for Willie's death. Under other circumstances, Drew might have liked the fellow who had held his gaze forthrightly as he expressed his condolences and promised to find Willie's killer; but as things stood, he had no other thought but to avoid the colonel.

It didn't matter, in any case. Drew would find the person who'd killed Willie, and he would not leave it to Yankee justice to see that the murderer received what was coming to him. The war had been long, and it had taught him many lessons; not the least of which was to take opportunity when it presented itself, for the chance might never come again. He would not forget that lesson when Willie's killer stood in the sights of his gun.

But in the meantime, Willie was dead simply because he had been unable to turn his back on a friend.

That thought suddenly more than he could bear, Drew stumbled, then sat down on a log as grief overwhelmed him. He did not hear Tricia approaching. He did not see the sorrow that briefly convulsed her features before she knelt beside him and slid her arms around him.

So close to him, hugging him tight, she whispered, "Don't … please don't, Drew. I can't stand to see you grieve."

The pain inside Tricia was excruciating as she embraced Drew tightly. His strong body shook with the intensity of his sorrow, and she whispered against his damp cheek, "Your going to Willie's parents … the fact that you traveled all the way there … that you thought so much of Willie that you would not allow anyone else to break the sad news to them, meant more than you realize."

Drew looked up at her, his expression fierce. "I didn't do anything noble. Willie died because of me. It was only right that I should be the person to tell them."

"You weren't responsible!"

"Yes, I was."

"No—Willie would be the first one to tell you that."

"Willie … he was always too generous for his own good."

"Is that the way you see it, Drew? What if I were to tell you that you're a better man than you seem to believe you are—that Willie knew it and understood it, and that was the reason he came back for you?"

"Tricia … please …"

"What if I were to tell you I believe that, too, because I know you better than you seem to know yourself?"

"Tricia …"

Drew raised his eyes to hers, and Tricia's throat choked tight at the sorrow reflected there. Sorrow ached inside her, too. It was a knot of torment that wrung her heart dry as she whispered, "Drew, please, don't talk any more. I can't bear to hear your self-recriminations when I know they're unjust. There's only one thing I want from you right now." Her eyes holding his directly, Tricia whispered a truth she had withheld even from herself as she said, "I want you to hold me … to show me that I'm the only one who can help you through this sadness—that there's no one you want more than me."

Drew went still. His eyes were moist, and the pain inside her clenched tighter. She said earnestly, "Make love to me, Drew. It will never be more right than it is at this moment. I want to be a part of you. I want you to know that whatever you feel, I feel it, too, because I'm linked to you in every way."

"Tricia ..." Drew's voice was hoarse with emotion as he said, "I don't want your pity."

"It's not pity that I feel for you, Drew." Her eyes intense, she added in a whisper, "Of all the emotions you've raised inside me, pity has never been one of them." When he still hesitated, she added, "Maybe this will prove to you how I feel."

Slowly, gently, Tricia pressed her mouth to his.

The touch of her mouth ... the taste of her lips ...

Drew's arms slid slowly around Tricia. He pressed her warmth against him, just as he had dreamed.

His angel ...

His mouth searched hers, desperate to taste its sweetness. His lips moved over the soft contours of her cheeks, her chin, only to move back, suddenly fierce when he covered her mouth with his again. He could not seem to get enough of her. His hunger for her was so intense that he devoured her with his kisses. He fought the restrictions of clothing in his desire to touch her more intimately, groaning aloud when their naked flesh met hotly for the first time.

The firm softness of her breasts against his lips ... the silky smoothness of her intimate flesh underneath his palms ... the moist heat as he slipped his fingers into the crevice at the juncture of her thighs.

158

Holding himself strictly in check, he caressed her intimately and watched with a sense of growing heat the myriad emotions flickering across Tricia's flawless features. He saw her flush. He felt the impact when her eyes glazed over with passion. He shuddered with his own passion barely controlled as the first quaking began inside her.

"Drew ..."

Panic invaded her gaze and Drew whispered hoarsely, "Give to me, Tricia. Help me to believe that you want me as much as I've always ... always wanted you."

Tricia gasped as his seeking caresses moved more deeply into her intimate heat. She raised her body, instinctively allowing him further access as her eyelids began fluttering and she groaned softly.

"That's right, Tricia." His passion almost beyond control, Drew rasped, "Show me ... I need to know."

Tricia's slender body reacted spontaneously to his prompting. Convulsive shudders shook her as her body quaked in loving tribute, and Drew felt control slip away. Her quaking had barely ceased when he slipped himself fully atop her at last. Hushing her response with a whisper, he paused briefly to indulge the sensation as he brushed her moist nest with his male organ. He caught his breath as he entered her slowly, then, unable to further control his passion, thrust himself deep inside her.

Her gasp echoed his own, and a sense of wonder overwhelmed him. Moving with gradually increasing impetus, he plunged more intimately inside her. His movements jerked to a halt when his control slipped away at her impassioned gasp and she joined him in a sudden, consuming rush of fulfillment that held them helpless in its grip.

Throbbing to mutual stillness, they remained joined for long moments with an unwillingness to end the beauty of the moment. Finally breaking the silence between them, Drew spoke in a whisper that came from the heart.

"My angel."

Tricia looked up at him. Her delicate features still colored with emotion, she was more beautiful to him than she had ever been before.

Chapter Eight

"Wake up, Tricia."

Tricia awakened slowly. Momentarily disoriented, she felt the comfort of warm body heat wrapped around her, and she burrowed instinctively closer.

"Tricia ..."

She opened her eyes to the sudden reality that she was lying on a blanket in a forested clearing barely lit by dawn, and that she was looking up into the eyes of the man she loved. Emotion swelled as Drew touched his mouth to hers. She slid her arms around his neck when his kiss deepened, accommodating him with a need that rose to meet his. She felt the swell of his passion as his body moved against hers, and her own passion expanded as well. She gasped when he slid himself atop her. His mouth covered hers, and his male organ sought her intimate heat.

He entered her, and she briefly held her breath at the wonder of the moment. Looking up at Drew, at the passion reflected on his strong features, she encouraged him softly, and the dance of love began. She was breathless when he stilled briefly, as if wanting to say something, but his words went unexpressed in the rush of emotion that thrust them unexpectedly over the brink of passion.

When their bodies grew still minutes later, Tricia felt Drew turn her face up to his.

"Tricia ... it wasn't my intention to wake you up this way, but it all got beyond my control somehow."

Tricia took a breath and glanced away. Reality. They could avoid it no longer.

Drew whispered, "Don't turn away from me, Tricia. I need to have you tell me you're not sorry this happened between us. I need to hear you say it wasn't only sorrow that brought you into my arms, and that you still feel the same way you did last night. I need—"

"Here's my answer to all your questions, Drew." Tricia brought her lips to his for a kiss that said more than words ever could.

Staring wordlessly into her eyes for long moments after she pulled back, Drew said, "You know there are things I need to do when we get back to Galveston ... things that can't wait."

Tricia's gaze locked with his as she whispered, "I understand that last night didn't change any of the bad things that happened before it. Willie was your friend, and you have to do all you can to find the person who killed him. That precedes everything else in your mind."

"Not everything."

Responding to his fleeting smile, Tricia whispered, "I

know, but reality is hard. It intrudes into the most intimate moments and it won't let you forget. No one knows that better than I."

"There's more I need to deal with than you know. My personal past as well as things that happened before the war ended ... they're all mixed up together somehow. I know now that's part of the reason why I came back to Galveston with Willie in the first place. But the thing that sticks in my mind ... the thought I can't avoid ... is the feeling that my past had something to do with the reason Willie was killed. I need to know the truth before I'll feel free to go on."

Hesitating, Drew continued, "I'd explain it all to you if I could, Tricia. There are only two things I'm really sure of now. The first is that I can't forget what happened to Willie and I need to go back to Galveston to get to the bottom of all this."

"What's the second thing?"

Drew froze.

"Drew?" she pressed.

Drew took a breath. "Do you trust me, Tricia?"

"Yes."

"Then trust me to give you that answer as soon as I'm able."

Taking a moment longer, Tricia nodded. She saw relief on his face, followed by determination. Yet his features softened as he stood up and handed her clothes to her.

Tricia stood and dressed. Her fingers worked self-consciously at the buttons of her shirtwaist as Drew dressed, watching her every move.

When she was finally fully clothed, Drew stepped up

close to her and said softly, "I made you nervous. I'm sorry, but I couldn't help staring. I've never seen a woman as beautiful as you are in every way. My eyes couldn't get their fill."

Her throat suddenly tight, Tricia smoothed his cheek with her palm as she whispered simply, "Me, too."

Drew took her mouth with a passionate, soul-searching kiss that stole all thought from Tricia's mind. She caught her breath when he pushed down her split skirt, thrust aside her undergarments, and entered her. She stood still, enraptured and helpless against his loving assault as he cupped her buttocks with his palms, supporting her with his strength as he paid tribute to the intense emotions they shared. Culmination came slowly, heatedly, with a prolonged ecstasy that left her weak-kneed.

Breathing heavily, Tricia was attempting to speak when Drew adjusted his clothes and said in a gruff tone at odds with the sated passion in his eyes, "Wait here and don't say anything or we'll never get out of here."

Able to do little else, Tricia struggled to catch her breath as Drew quickly packed the saddlebags and readied the horses. Turning back to her when he had tied her horse's reins to his saddle, he then swept her up into his arms and placed her on his horse. Mounting behind her, he nudged his horse into motion as he settled her back against his chest and whispered into her ear, "Relax ... sleep a little if you need to. It's going to be a long day."

Turning around to face him, Tricia protested, "I'm fine ... really. You didn't have to worry about me."

The ardor in Drew's gaze halted her dissent as he replied, "If you think I'm going to let you out of my arms a minute before I have to, you're wrong. So just lean back and rest. You can ride back into Galveston on your own horse ... that's a promise ... but until then, I want you near me."

I want you near me.

Drew's words sent tremors of emotion down Tricia's spine. Facing forward again, she leaned back against his chest and closed her eyes as Drew pulled her closer.

Chantalle heard the growing activity downstairs with irritation. The sun was beginning to set, and patrons were arriving at a steady rate. They probably thought it strange that she wasn't there to greet them at the door as was her custom, but she presently had little patience for that task.

Chantalle glanced out the window as the sun dropped rapidly toward the horizon. Tricia and Drew had been gone for three days. They had two long nights behind them, and she was concerned for Tricia in so many ways. Drew had described to Chantalle the approximate area where Willie's family ranch was located, and they'd had plenty of time to reach it and inform Willie's parents of his demise. She knew Willie's parents wouldn't waste time in coming to claim his body, and that Drew would waste even less time in returning to find Willie's killer—providing he did not get distracted along the way.

Chantalle's expression grew tense. She had expressed her disapproval of Tricia's insistence on traveling with Drew, but Tricia had made up her mind. Tricia had insisted they owed Willie that much, and Chantalle had been unable to talk her out of it. What worried her most was the fear that Tricia had lied to herself about her motives. Chantalle had seen the glances that Drew and Tricia occasionally exchanged. If Chantalle had realized how close the two would become, she would have found someone else to tend him during the critical days of his illness.

Aware there was no point in such retrospection, Chantalle forced those thoughts from her mind. Tricia and Drew still had not returned.

Where were they? What had happened to them?

Chantalle took a breath and made her decision. If they didn't come back before sunset, she'd send a search party out to find them in the morning.

With that matter firmly settled in her mind, Chantalle stared out the window. The question Colonel Madison had asked her just before concluding his interview returned again to mind.

Could there have been any reason other than robbery why someone would want to hurt Willie?

She had responded in the negative, and Colonel Madison had appeared to dismiss the thought, but his question had returned to haunt her.

Simon Gault's hatred for Whit Hawk—the man who had thwarted him at every turn and who she had come to believe was possibly Drew's brother—was an accepted fact. She also knew that Angie was not above passing along information to Simon whenever it benefited her.

Was it mere coincidence that the first person she'd asked to deliver an important message to Whit Hawk

166

at La Posada had not lived to deliver it? Was it also a coincidence that poor Hiram Charters's body had been found on the trail with his pockets turned inside out just like Willie's, so that his death, too, was pronounced a robbery?

Chantalle had recently sent Will to La Posada with another urgent message for Whit, telling him she had something important to discuss with him.

She knew Simon well. He was vindictive and would do anything to get revenge on Whit—but would he go so far as to have Willie killed to prevent a possible reconciliation between the brothers?

Chantalle took a shaky breath as a final, chilling question came to her mind. Did that also mean that the threat to either Whit or Drew remained?

Angie's familiar footsteps sounded in the hallway, and Chantalle turned sharply toward the door. She stepped into the corridor as Angie attempted to pass with a grinning, well-sated cowpoke beside her. Forcing a smile, Chantalle said, "If you don't mind, Johnny, I need to talk to Angie. You know the way downstairs. Just tell Jake I said to give you a drink on the house when you get there."

Grinning more broadly, Johnny replied, "Thank you, ma'am. That's right kind of you."

Noting Angie's surprise, Chantalle walked back into her office. She closed the door behind Angie as the sultry brunette followed her inside. She said flatly in response to Angie's raised brow, "I need to know something, Angie. Did you tell Simon that I sent Will with a message for Whit Hawk shortly after Drew collapsed downstairs?"

Angie looked at her blankly. "I don't know what you're talking about."

"Don't lie to me, Angie. This is too important. I know Simon pays you to keep him informed about what happens around here."

"You're crazy, Chantalle. Simon is a regular here, and I'm the only woman who can handle him, but that's as far as it goes." She shivered unexpectedly. "To tell you the truth, I'm not even sure of that anymore. He gives me the creeps."

"But his money doesn't."

"I told you, I don't spy for Simon." She shrugged again and added, "You know me. I keep my eyes and ears open around here. I might've mentioned some things to Simon when we were together, and maybe he showed me his appreciation whenever he could, but that's in the past. Things are different now. He's getting to be more than even I can handle."

Chantalle raised her brows. "I thought no man was a problem for you."

"That's what I thought, too, but Simon ..." Angie hesitated. Her color draining, she added more softly, "I don't know ... the way he looks at me sometimes, I think he'd as soon kill me as he would close that bedroom door behind us."

Angie's paleness seemed to confirm her fear, and Chantalle hesitated. Angie glanced away revealingly, and Chantalle realized that the girl had already begun to regret confiding in her.

Dismissing Angie abruptly, Chantalle watched as the door closed behind the younger woman. She turned back to the window and stared blindly out at the rapidly setting sun. Had Angie lied to her? Maybe. The truth was, she couldn't be sure of anything.

Her body aching from the journey, Tricia rode alongside Drew as they entered the city of Galveston at last. Their mounts' hooves clapped on the cobbled streets as shadows created by gaslights flickered against buildings that had begun going silent for the evening. The traffic of the day had all but stopped on the streets, but Tricia knew that the reverse would be true at Chantalle's house, where the activity of the evening had barely begun.

Tricia glanced at Drew, riding silently attentive to their surroundings. She had felt the gradual stiffening of his posture as they approached Galveston. She had noted the regret in his voice when he finally said, "We'll be in the city soon."

She had known what that meant. She had known how it would look if she rode into Galveston in Drew's arms, and she had no desire to stir up the inevitable talk that would ensue.

As for herself, Tricia cared little about anything anyone said, but she knew appearances were important to Chantalle, who had worked so hard and sacrificed so much for her. Yet the truth was that she missed having Drew's arms wrapped around her. She missed the sensation of his strong chest supporting her back and his hand casually cupping her breasts. His intimate touch seemed somehow so right, and she longed for it … for him.

Tricia glanced again at Drew. He was frowning, and she had noted that he still limped when he walked, but it was obvious that his leg was rapidly growing stronger. She marveled at the sight of him. He wore his weather-beaten hat low on his forehead, concealing the thick, dark hair that had slipped so smoothly through her fingers as they made love. His dark brows were drawn down over light eyes that had shone with emotion when he held her in his arms. There was a tension about the posture of his powerful body as he rode ... an expectancy ... but he was all male and he took her breath away.

Tricia's heart pounded. She had not believed she could love a man the way she loved Drew—yet love had never been mentioned between them. They had been close. They had shared moments of exquisite ecstasy, yet she was uncertain what the next day would bring. She felt strangely uncertain.

As if sensing her perusal, Drew turned toward her. He searched her expression briefly. His gaze then dropped to her mouth before he glanced up at her again with a look almost as intimate as a kiss.

All uncertainty dropped away.

Drew forced his perusal back to the streets through which Tricia and he rode. He had felt this same presentiment of danger before, and it worried him. Uncertain what it meant, he only knew that he needed to get Tricia somewhere safe.

He glanced at her again, relieved to see that she wasn't looking at him anymore. She was a distraction for him ... an intimate distraction that he could not presently afford.

Driven by a sense of urgency, Drew turned his mount

onto the familiar street where Chantalle's house stood brightly lit. He glanced at Tricia to see that she was frowning, and he said, "Chantalle will be glad to see you, but I think it would be wise if we didn't use the front entrance at this time of night."

Tricia nodded, and the brief locking of her gaze with his sent a familiar longing streaking through him. He fought to ignore it. Other matters presently took precedence over the emotions they shared—important matters that he sensed had somehow resulted in the death of a friend.

That thought played heavily on his mind as Drew lifted Tricia down from her horse behind Chantalle's house. He nodded at Will when the stableman took their mounts' reins and guided Tricia toward the back staircase without saying a word. Drew knew what he needed to do, and it would not be easy.

He saw the relief that flashed across Chantalle's face when Tricia and he pushed open the rear doorway to the second floor and unexpectedly met her standing there. He saw Tricia's flush of regret for the concern so obvious in Chantalle's expression, and he remained silent as Tricia stepped forward to hug Chantalle briefly.

They followed Chantalle without a word as she turned toward her office. Drew waited only until the door closed behind them to say, "I'm sorry if you were worried, Chantalle, but Tricia and I accomplished our purpose. We notified Willie's parents, and they'll be coming to Galveston to pick up Willie's body as soon as they can make arrangements at their ranch."

"I'm glad," Chantalle said, then waited for Tricia to speak.

"We're fine, Chantalle." Tricia glanced at him briefly before adding, "Drew's leg is getting stronger every day. I'm sure Dr. Wesley will agree that it'll be completely healed soon."

"It's healed already. I don't need Doc Wesley to tell me that." Aware how gruff that statement sounded, Drew continued, "I'd like to thank you for taking me in while I was sick, Chantalle. I'll pay you back for your expenses as soon as I can, but I'll be going back to the place where Willie and I rented a room for the remainder of my stay in Galveston."

Drew felt Tricia's shock at his unexpected announcement. He had purposely neglected to mention his plans to her because he knew she would object. He needed to make sure she was somewhere safe so he would be free to do what he must.

With that thought in mind, Drew took a breath and continued, "It's getting late and it's been a long day. I need to leave."

"Drew—"

Cutting Tricia's response short, aware that her protest would only make a difficult situation worse, he addressed Chantalle, saying, "Tricia can fill you in on the rest. I have to go."

"But, Drew—"

Drew tipped his hat, ignoring the look in Tricia's eyes as he said, "Thank you, ma'am ... Tricia," then turned resolutely toward the door. He was hastening down the rear steps as quickly as his injured leg would allow when he realized that for the first time in his life, he was running away from something.

Drew reached the base of the staircase, grateful that Will hadn't had time to stable his horse. He mounted up and turned the animal toward the street with the thought that he wasn't running away because of *fear*. No, the emotion that flushed through him as he dug his heels into his mount's sides was far more powerful—and he needed desperately to avoid it.

Tricia caught herself still staring at the doorway through which Drew had exited the office so unexpectedly. She turned back toward Chantalle abruptly, struggling against the tears in her eyes as she said, "It's obvious that I wasn't expecting Drew to leave so soon." She shrugged. "I guess he couldn't stay here indefinitely, especially in light of everything that has happened, but I thought he would give me more warning so I could ..."

Tricia's voice came to a halt, and Chantalle said gently, "You don't need to explain anything to me, Tricia."

"But I do, because I don't really understand ..." Her voice trailed away before she began again more strongly, "I know that telling Willie's parents about his death was probably the hardest thing Drew's ever done. I admire him for his determination to honor Willie the only way he could, but I'm confused." She hesitated briefly before continuing, "Drew identified himself to Willie's parents as Drew *Hawk*, and they seemed to recognize him by that name. They said Willie had told them about him, that Willie considered Drew almost a brother."

"Drew *Hawk?*"

Tricia blinked back her tears. "I know Drew has secrets in his past that he feels it's unsafe to share with me, so I didn't press him. I think he believes that I missed that slip in the stress of the moment ... but I didn't. Now Drew is gone. I'm not sure when I'll see him again ... if ever ... and I don't know what to do."

Chantalle's breathing had accelerated, and Tricia said, "I didn't mean to upset you, Chantalle."

"No ... you didn't." Chantalle took a breath. "I just wish I had an answer for you. Besides, I'm not exactly the right person to come to for advice about things like this."

"Yes, you are." Tricia stepped up to hug her unexpectedly as she whispered, "You're a good person, Chantalle. You've made mistakes in the past, but you've come to terms with them. You've also found Captain Knowles. Despite his absences at sea, you and Joshua have made a lasting commitment to each other. You've made the best of your life." She drew back as she whispered, "You're exactly the right person for me to ask."

"Thank you, Tricia. I appreciate that. Unfortunately, the only advice I have to give is to wait and see what happens. Whatever uncertainties remain about Drew's name, I'm sure he'll clear them up as soon as he's able."

"Wait and see ... somehow that doesn't seem enough." Tricia brushed away a tear, then said abruptly, "I'm going to my room. I'll see you in the morning, Chantalle."

Watching as the door closed behind Tricia, Chantalle went suddenly still.

Drew *Hawk*.

Bruce stood silently in the darkening shadows on the street outside Chantalle's bordello as Drew rode out onto view and spurred his mount forward. Bruce had come to Chantalle's that evening on the spur of the moment, hoping to learn something that would satisfy his boss's rage.

And he had.

Smiling, hardly able to believe his luck, Bruce waited a few minutes as Drew rode down the street. He then followed, keeping a discreet distance behind him.

Chapter Nine

"I saw him and I followed him, boss. He went to a hotel by the rail yard where it was real cheap and took a room there. As far as I know, that's where he stayed the rest of the night."

"The rail yards, you say?" Simon was elated. Due to Angie's sudden proclivity for keeping her mouth shut, he had been late in learning that Collins and Tricia Shepherd had left the city to inform Willie Childers's parents of his death. He had been silently enraged at the thought that with each day that elapsed, the possibility grew greater that Whit Hawk would receive Chantalle's message to come to Galveston. Whit would then learn about the possibility—no, the *probability*—that Drew Collins was in reality Drew Hawk, the brother Whit had searched for most of his adult life.

Simon would then be faced with *both* of the male Hawk progeny, who would undoubtedly join forces against him.

No, he would not allow it! He would make sure that the brothers were eliminated before that could happen—one at a time. Then he would take care of the sisters. He would destroy every last person who had ever borne the Hawk name. Nothing else would satisfy him.

He also knew that nothing would happen ... until he took the first step.

The first step—Drew Hawk.

Simon no longer cared about making Drew Hawk's death appear to be an accident. Nor did he care what Colonel Clay Madison of the Adjutant General's Office deduced after Drew was dead. No one would suspect him anyway.

Taking a breath, Simon looked at his hireling. Bruce's face flushed as Simon said generously, "You did well, Bruce. Willie Childers's death didn't work out the way we planned, but we won't suffer the same fate with Drew Collins."

Again basking in the light of Simon's favor, Bruce said, "That's right, boss. Just tell me what you want me to do and I'll take care of it."

"The answer to your question should be apparent," Simon said. "Eliminate Drew Collins, of course! I'll need him out of the way before the situation becomes too complicated. I expect you to take care of it as soon as possible—the sooner the better. Delay doesn't work to our advantage anymore."

"All right, boss."

"But I need a definite plan in order to avoid any suspicion that might come up." Simon smiled as a thought struck him. "I'm invited to a soiree at Willard

Spunk's house the day after tomorrow. I'll arrive early and stay late, and I'll make sure that I'm in obvious attendance the entire evening. I will be my usual charming, relaxed self. I may even arrange for company in the private, wee hours if I can find a woman there who suits my fancy. You'll be able to take all the time you want to eliminate Collins then, and no one will believe I had anything to do with his death."

"That sounds good, boss."

"So it's settled, then."

"Yeah … sure. You said the day after tomorrow?"

"Yes, the day after tomorrow—Friday evening, you idiot! And make sure you don't fail."

Bruce's broad smile paled in the face of Simon's displeasure. He replied, "It's as good as done, boss."

Simon replied with barely restrained menace, "It had better be."

Tricia walked out into the hallway of Chantalle's house. Unable to help herself, she glanced toward the empty room at the far end, and the torment inside her increased. It had been two days since she had seen or heard from Drew, and she ached with the pain of his absence. She had busied herself as she had done before, working in the kitchen, and later in the afternoon at Chantalle's books, but she had found it difficult to concentrate on either task. She recalled the sensation of Drew's lips against her cheek, her eyelids, and then her mouth. She remembered how his kiss had deepened until she had accepted his loving assault with joy rising inside her. She tried to evade recollection of the touch of his palms against her skin, his fluttering kisses against her breasts, then the ultimate sensation of feeling him deep inside her.

His mumbled endearments echoed in her ears. Memory of his soft groan of fulfillment raised a flush to her cheek, and recollection of the rosy afterglow that had held the two of them in its grasp brought tears to her eyes.

She loved him…but he seemed to have forgotten her.

Could it be that everything between them had been a lie? Could it be that she had merely fallen prey to seduction?

No. Tricia shook her head. She had seen a depth of emotion in Drew's eyes that could not have been feigned. She had heard a tremor in his voice that had bespoken feelings that for some reason he had chosen not to voice. She had sensed the wonder he experienced in the throes of their lovemaking—because she had experienced it as well.

They were meant to be together.

So … why had he left her?

Tricia approached the door of Chantalle's office as evening shadows deepened. She was about to knock when it opened as Chantalle instructed firmly, "Remember, Will, get an early start. Leave at dawn, and make sure you stress that it's imperative for Whit to come see me as soon as possible."

"Yes, ma'am."

"I'm counting on you."

"Yes, ma'am."

Smiling belatedly when she realized Tricia was standing there, Chantalle said, "It looks like you've already finished your work for today, Tricia. Will and I are done talking, too, and Polly must have supper ready by now. We'd better hurry because the traffic downstairs will start getting heavy soon."

Tricia forced a smile in return. It occurred to her that some things changed while others never did. She fell into step beside Chantalle as the older woman started down the staircase. Tricia glanced back at Will as he hurried toward the rear entrance and asked, "What was that all about, Chantalle? It seemed pretty urgent."

"Oh ... it's nothing."

"It didn't sound like nothing."

Chantalle shrugged. "I need to talk to a friend of mine, the owner of La Posada. A mutual acquaintance is in trouble and I need him to help out."

Involved in her own problems, Tricia asked almost in afterthought, "Is it anyone I know?"

"Not really."

Chantalle forced a broader smile and continued on down the stairs.

Drew frowned with frustration as another day drew to a close. He glanced out the window of his hotel room at the shadows darkening the rail yards beyond, but he saw only Tricia's image. He wondered what Tricia was presently thinking. He wished he could tell her exactly why he'd chosen to separate himself from her—that to have her sharing his danger was more than he could bear—but he knew that if he did, Tricia would insist on remaining with him.

Drew's stomach knotted tight as he recalled the

moment he'd walked into Chantalle's office to find Colonel Clay Madison of the Adjutant General's Office talking to her. He knew enough about the Union Army to be certain that paperwork with his name and description on it had been forwarded to Galveston, with details of the charges against him. He was also certain that sooner or later Colonel Madison would go to Chantalle's house to find him. The last thing he wanted was for Tricia or Chantalle to become involved in whatever the Yankees might have in store for him. He knew the Yankees wouldn't believe him when he said he didn't know what had happened to the money—that he had been badly injured in the raid and had barely made it back to safety with his men.

A sense of danger crept up his spine each time he left the hotel. He had often stopped to see if he was being followed. But when he had seen no one, he blamed the feeling on jumpiness resulting from the war—but he knew better. There was more to Willie's killing than met the eye, even though he had been unsuccessful in unearthing the motive or killer.

Drew reviewed in his mind his activity of the past two days since he had returned to Galveston. It had been surprisingly easy to discover the names of Chantalle's best customers, and he had made a point of visiting every one of them to see if they could shed any light on what had happened to Willie. Without exception, they said they had no idea who had killed him and voiced surprise that anyone would lie in wait to rob someone in Chantalle's backyard, where so few of her customers ventured.

Drew unconsciously shook his head. Their com-

ments had confirmed in his mind that the manner of
Willie's death didn't make sense. His conviction that
the murder was related to him in some way was the
second reason why he had separated himself from Tricia. If anything happened to her because of him ...

Drew began pacing in frustration. He stopped
abruptly when pain stabbed sharply in his leg. Wincing, he sat on the side of the bed, removed his boots,
and rolled up his pants leg so he could check the bandage there. He raised the bandage cautiously and saw
that the wound was healing well. He merely needed to
get off his feet for a while. He couldn't afford a physical complication at this point.

Drew lay back and elevated his leg. The image of his
green-eyed angel returned, and he silently indulged it.

Tricia frowned as the driver of her carriage maneu-
vered his way through a part of town where she rarely
ventured. She wondered why Drew had taken a room
at a hotel there, aware that although Chantalle's house
was not respectable, at least it was clean, relatively private, and well kept—all things that she doubted she
would discover when she found Drew's temporary
quarters.

The Easton Hotel ...

That establishment had at one time enjoyed a well-
deserved reputation as one of the best hotels Galveston had to offer, but that time was long past. She
had been surprised when Georgia mentioned the previous day that one of her "visitors" had seen Drew un-
locking the door of his room there.

Tricia's mouth twitched at the memory. She had

almost forgotten that information sifted through a bordello as easily as sand through an hourglass, and that the women working there seemed pleased to be the informants.

She had been grateful to learn Drew's location, but she worried about him. What if his wound wasn't healing properly? What if neglect had caused his leg to become infected again, and he was lying in his cheerless room in terrible pain? What if he was too proud to call anyone because the shock of Willie's death had finally become too much for him and he needed someone to intervene? What if he needed ... her?

Tricia took a breath as the carriage turned another corner and slowed down. Her heart pounded when she saw the derelict facade of the Easton Hotel. All her *what if*s faded from her mind as the truth became abundantly clear.

The truth was that *she* needed *him*.

Stepping down from the carriage when it drew to a halt, Tricia turned back to pay the driver. She shook out the folds of her simple blue gown, ran her hand over the upward sweep of her hair, and started resolutely forward.

As she stepped into the lobby, all eyes turned in her direction, and Tricia realized the riskiness of her situation for the first time. Almost without exception, the occupants of the lobby were male, poorly dressed, and unkempt. Almost without exception, they were either leaning unsteadily against the bar visible through an open doorway or staring at her.

Not to be deterred, Tricia raised her chin and walked toward the registration desk, where the clerk eyed her with a raised brow. She inquired politely, "I'm here to see Mr. Drew Collins, who is registered here. Is he in?"

She was unprepared when the clerk asked, "What do you want to see him for?"

Stunned, she replied, "I beg your pardon?"

"I said, what do you want to see him for?" The clerk leered. "We've got plenty of fellas right here in the lobby who would be willing to help you with anything you've got in mind."

"Really?" Tricia replied with a forced smile. "Because what I have in mind is to see Mr. Collins. Is he in or not?"

The clerk's leer widened as he replied, "He's in, all right, and I'd say he's a lucky man."

"If you'll tell me his room number—"

"It's room number ten, right up them stairs."

Aware that she had gained the attention of the entire establishment as she ascended the staircase, Tricia inwardly shivered. She reached the second floor feeling apprehensive. What if Drew didn't want to see her? What if he was angry because she had come? What if their brief time together had not meant as much to him as it had meant to her? What if …?

Tears filled Tricia's eyes as she asked herself the question she had tried to avoid for two long days.

What if Drew didn't love her as much as she loved him?

Tricia started abruptly forward. There was only one way to find out.

She walked down a hallway stained by years of wear and abuse, and stopped in front of a nicked and battered door marked with the lopsided numeral 10.

YES! ☐

Sign me up for the **Historical Romance Book Club** and send my TWO FREE BOOKS! If I choose to stay in the club, I will pay only $8.50* each month, a savings of $5.48!

YES! ☐

Sign me up for the **Love Spell Book Club** and send my TWO FREE BOOKS! If I choose to stay in the club, I will pay only $8.50* each month, a savings of $5.48!

NAME: _____

ADDRESS: _____

_____

TELEPHONE: _____

E-MAIL: _____

☐ **I WANT TO PAY BY CREDIT CARD.**

☐ VISA ☐ MasterCard. ☐ DISCOVER

ACCOUNT #: _____

EXPIRATION DATE: _____

SIGNATURE: _____

Send this card along with $2.00 shipping & handling for each club you wish to join, to:

Romance Book Clubs
20 Academy Street
Norwalk, CT 06850-4032

Or fax (must include credit card information!) to: 610.995.9274. You can also sign up online at www.dorchesterpub.com.

*Plus $2.00 for shipping. Offer open to residents of the U.S. and Canada only. Canadian residents please call 1.800.481.9191 for pricing information.

If under 18, a parent or guardian must sign. Terms, prices and conditions subject to change. Subscription subject to acceptance. Dorchester Publishing reserves the right to reject any order or cancel any subscription.

JOIN NOW!

Her throat suddenly tight, she paused a moment before she raised her fist and knocked firmly.

Breathlessly, she waited.

Drew stirred at the sound of a knock on his door, unaware that he had been dozing. He stood up and reached automatically for the revolver he had placed on the nightstand. He approached the door, cautious and uncertain. At another knock, he unlocked the door, jerked it open, and then went still.

A thousand thoughts flashed across his mind in the silent moment before he took Tricia's arm and pulled her into the room. His heart drumming, he looked down at her as he pushed the door closed behind them and asked tightly, "What are you doing here?"

"I came to see you, of course."

Breathing heavily under the assault of conflicting emotions, Drew replied, "You know you shouldn't be in this part of town … much less be seen coming to my room alone. You know what people will say about that."

"I told you before, what people say or think about my actions doesn't bother me."

"It bothers me."

"You sound like Chantalle."

Drew responded gruffly, "Believe me, my feelings for you are nothing like Chantalle's."

Tricia took a step closer. The sweet female scent that was hers alone inundated his senses as she looked up at him. The heat of her green-eyed gaze gnawed at his control as she searched his face for a few silent moments, and then said more softly, "How *do* you feel about me, Drew? That thought's been plaguing me for the past two days. I need to know."

"Tricia—"

"Tell me ... please."

In tenuous control of his restraint, Drew replied, "Do you need to hear the words, Tricia? Is that it?"

"Yes."

"I didn't think that was necessary. I thought I had proved to you, the best way I know, that I care about you."

"You *care* about me?"

"Yes ... you know I do."

Drew saw the effect his words had on Tricia, and his inner hunger increased. He wanted her. He needed her in a way he had never needed another woman. Those words hung on his lips, begging to be spoken, but he had no right to say them with his future stretching out before him as darkly as his past.

"You care about me ... in the same way you've cared about other women before me?"

"No."

"You care for me more?"

Drew did not immediately respond.

"Drew ..."

"I've already answered that question."

Tears suddenly bright in her eyes, Tricia said, "Have you? Why are you holding back, Drew? Why won't you say what you mean?"

"I *am* saying what I mean."

"Talk to me ... please, Drew."

"Tricia—"

"I need you to tell me one way or another whether

the emotion between us was special to you, Drew, or if it was just ... ordinary lust."

"Don't even say that!"

"Then tell me!"

Struggling to resist her appeal, Drew whispered, "Don't do this to me, Tricia."

"Do what, Drew?"

Suddenly gripping her tight against him in the only response he could give, Drew covered her mouth with his. He was aware only of the sensations ripping through him as Tricia melted in his arms and returned his kiss. Her body melded to his, responding instinctively, giving kiss for kiss, caress for caress.

Lifting her up into his arms abruptly, Drew carried Tricia to the rumpled bed and dropped his revolver back on the nightstand as he laid her down. Her softness underneath him sent new tremors of need pounding through his veins. He could not suffer the impediment of clothing between them, and he undressed them with fumbling hands.

He tasted her flesh at last, and his emotions soared.

Mumbling loving words that he could not suppress, Drew traveled the length of Tricia's nakedness with his kisses. Finding the warm delta between her thighs, he indulged himself deeply. Undeterred by Tricia's whimper of uncertainty at the intimacy of his ministrations, he savored her sweetness with an ever driving urgency for more. His attentions increased as her impassioned whispers grew more urgent. With a growing elation, he felt the first tremors that shook her slender frame, and he anticipated the glory soon to follow.

As her body erupted with sudden rapturous spasms,

Drew accepted Tricia's honeyed response to his love-making, and his heart sang. He continued his ardor until her quaking ceased and she was breathlessly silent and still in his arms.

Raising himself above her at last, he murmured in a throbbing voice, "This is how I feel about you, Tricia. This is how much I want you ... as much as I've always wanted you."

Drew thrust himself inside her. He then paused momentarily to enjoy the moment of complete possession as brilliant sparks of silent jubilation filled his mind. He began moving with rapidly increasing vigor until emotions formerly held in check exploded into a fiery ecstasy that carried them both to shuddering release.

They were still joined with the moist heat of mutual passion when Drew looked down at her again. Waiting until her heavy eyelids rose with sated languor, he whispered, "I couldn't show you any more clearly how I feel about you, Tricia. It's the way I'll always feel."

Drew watched as the power of the moment choked off Tricia's response. He saw her lips tremble with words she could not seem to voice. Sharing those feelings more deeply than Tricia could know, Drew surrendered to the sensation still holding them captive in its thrall.

Slowly, gently, he covered her mouth with a kiss that said all they had been unable to say ... and the dance of love began again.

Bruce moved silently through the hallway of the Easton Hotel. The streets outside had darkened, and the pedestrian traffic of working men and women who favored that time of day for the pursuit of their amusements had grown more disorderly with the passing hours. Again dressed in the clothing of a common wrangler, totally unlike the more formal apparel he usually wore in his position at Gault Shipping, he had been all but invisible. He had tied up his horse in the deserted alleyway beside the hotel and had made his way to the rear of the building. He had been smart enough to wait for a later hour, making sure that the boss had time to firmly establish his presence at the high-class party he was attending.

Bruce had checked the stable to make sure that Collins's mount was there, and had returned to the deserted alleyway in order to use the rear entrance of the hotel. He had not found it difficult to ascertain Drew Collins's room number on a previous visit, and he knew exactly where to go.

The hallway was deserted as he had expected, and Bruce smiled. The boss had made it easy for him this time. He hadn't placed any restrictions on the job other than to get it done as quickly and efficiently as possible. He would, of course, go through Collins's things in an attempt to make it appear that Collins had been robbed, but he doubted he would find anything of value. He would probably have to be satisfied with taking a souvenir of the outing, as he had done many times before.

Bruce paused in front of room number 10. He saw no light shining underneath the door. Collins must be asleep. Bruce had already decided that if Collins happened not to be in his room when he arrived, he would simply wait for him to return and take care of business then.

Taking a slender tool out of his pocket, Bruce worked silently at the lock. He was good at picking locks. It was one of the many unheralded talents that he had used liberally before coming to work for Gault years earlier, and it had served him well.

Listening acutely for the soft click that indicated the mechanism had turned, Bruce pushed the door open a crack and then paused again to listen. He smiled when he heard the sound of slow, even breathing.

Collins was asleep.

Perfect.

He withdrew his gun from his holster and pushed the door open far enough to allow him entrance.

The subtle click of the lock had awakened Drew abruptly. Immediately alert, he saw the shadow of a man standing motionless in the hallway outside his door. He reached for the revolver on the nightstand and stood up, shielding with his broad frame the bed where Tricia slept. He held his breath as the door was pushed open a crack.

Aware that his eyes were accustomed to the darkness of the room—an advantage the intruder did not have—he waited until the figure slipped inside before he said, "Put your hands up right now or I'll shoot!"

The sequence of events that followed was too rapid for his mind to immediately digest. But Drew acted on instinct and pulled the trigger as a gunshot flashed in the darkness. He stood motionless at the thud of a heavy body hitting the floor.

"Drew ... what happened?"

He felt Tricia's seminaked warmth at his side and thrust her behind him as he reached toward the lamp and lit it. He went still at the sight of the man lying on the rug just inside the door, his gun only inches from his hand.

Drew knelt down beside the fellow as Tricia asked, "Is he dead? Who is he?"

One glance, and Drew responded, "He's dead, all right ... and I have no idea who he is."

"But what did he want from you ... from us?"

"Again, I have no idea."

"Get dressed, Tricia," Drew instructed cautiously as he stood up and reached for his pants. "We're going to have to report what happened. But first ..."

Kneeling down again beside the dead man, Drew searched his pockets. He frowned at the absence of identification of any kind, then went still when he reached into the fellow's shirt pocket and withdrew an ancient gold coin.

"What is it? What did you find, Drew?"

Drew was momentarily unable to respond.

"Drew?"

Drew stood up, then looked down at the lifeless man. He felt Tricia's hand on his arm as he squeezed the coin tightly in his fist.

Tricia looked up at him expectantly, and he opened his fist as he replied, "Willie said this was his good luck charm. His father gave it to him. He carried it with him during the war; he never let it out of his sight."

Incredulous, Tricia managed hoarsely, "What you're saying is—"

"What I'm saying is that this has to be the same man who killed Willie."

"So that means—"

"That means that for some reason, this fellow wanted both Willie and me dead."

"But … why?"

"I don't know." Drew's light eyes went dark with determination as he said, "But I'm going to find out."

Chapter Ten

Simon fought to suppress his agitation as he closed his office door. The uniformed Yankee officer presently leaving the luxurious building that housed Gault Shipping and Exchange had come to make official inquiries about Bruce Carlton, his office manager and clerk, who had been killed in a foiled attempt to commit a robbery in the early morning hours of that day.

A foiled attempt to commit a robbery.

His jaw locking tight, Simon slammed his fist down on his immense mahogany desk. He had barely been able to sustain the incredulous expression he had feigned at the news. His pretended sorrow at Bruce's death, as well as the shock he had expressed at the "dark side of Bruce that he had never suspected," would have been deserving of an ovation if he had been on the stage. Instead, it had merely sufficed to satisfy the Yankee investigation.

The incompetent fool! The only thing Bruce had

done right was to follow the order to wait until he was involved in the evening's festivities at the Spunk soiree before making his attempt to kill Drew Hawk, thereby assuring that he was free of suspicion.

Simon strained to bring his anger under control. He had known as soon as he arrived at his office and found Bruce absent that something was wrong. Had Bruce succeeded in what he had set out to do the previous evening, he would have been waiting there, beaming with pride.

The ignorant toady!

Instead, Bruce's stupidity had forced Simon to tell the warehouse manager to send Billy Jerome out to take Bruce's place at the desk in the outer office. It had been Billy Jerome who had ushered in the uniformed officer who had announced Bruce's fate. Despite Billy's obvious eagerness to assume Bruce's position, however, Simon did not fool himself that Billy was dependable enough to assume Bruce's more secretive duties as well.

Simon frowned at that thought. He supposed he should be glad that it had not been Colonel Clay Madison of the Adjutant General's Office who had come with the news. That simple fact indicated the Adjutant General's Office had not yet made the connection between Willie Childers's death and the attempted robbery of Drew "Collins"—the only fortunate aspect of the whole disastrous episode.

His expression rigid, Simon walked to the window of his office and stared out at the open sea. The morning sunlight glittered on the placid expanse—diamonds on a sea of undulating silver—but he was blind to all but his rapidly expanding rage. Hawk had escaped him, but not for long. Simon had been forced to learn the hard way that the only person he could count on was himself.

He was resolved: Drew Hawk's time was limited.

Chantalle's house was unusually silent in the early morning hours when Drew awoke with a start in his former room at the end of the hallway. He squinted against the newly risen sun shining through the windows, then threw back the coverlet and reached for his boots. The unexpected intrusion into his room at the Easton Hotel had left him restless and on edge after he had brought Tricia home. Yet his mind was acutely clear as he stood up, ran his hand through his tousled hair, and turned toward the door.

Drew glanced at the upholstered chair beside the bed in passing, and was struck by a rush of memories. He had awakened from his delirium shortly after arriving in Galveston to see Tricia— his beautiful angel— dozing exhaustedly there after nights of caring for him. He had learned belatedly, however, that Tricia was not the beauteous seraph that he had thought her to be. Beautiful, appealing, irresistibly feminine—she had proved to be all those things—but she was also a flesh-and-blood woman with a mind of her own, one with a dedication of purpose and strong opinions that often conflicted with his. She had tested his patience, inspired his respect, and taught him to feel a depth of love he had not believed himself capable of giving.

He recalled that Willie had returned to Galveston and had taken Tricia's place on that upholstered chair, determined not to leave him again until he had recovered. The attempt on his own life the previous night had confirmed his suspicion that Willie's concern for him was the cause of his death rather than robbery.

But the question remained. Why?

A chill ran down Drew's spine at the thought of the danger Tricia had been exposed to the previous evening because of him. Had he not awakened at the sound of the lock turning, had the intruder's first shot not gone wild—

That unfinished thought knotted Drew's stomach tight as he pulled open the door and started down the hallway toward Chantalle's office. He slowed his step as a uniformed Yankee officer whom he did not recognize emerged and started back down the steps toward the front door. Drew waited only until the lock had clicked closed behind him before approaching Chantalle's office. Tricia had been badly shaken when they'd returned the previous night after the scene at the Easton Hotel. The look on Chantalle's face when he told her what had happened and when he described the intruder to her, had been revealing, but he had not wanted to press her in Tricia's presence. He had been somehow certain that Chantalle knew their attacker, but she had not commented. Then she had followed Tricia to her room, giving him no opportunity to question her further.

To her credit, Chantalle had not asked why Tricia was in his room at the Easton Hotel at that late hour, and neither he nor Tricia had attempted to explain the obvious. He wished he could tell Chantalle the truth depth of his feelings for her daughter—but he could not. He wished he could tell her that what he wanted most in the world was to have the right to hold Tricia close in his arms for the rest of his life—but he would not. Tricia deserved neither the uncertainties nor the danger his love would bring her.

Drew knocked on Chantalle's door and entered when she responded, but he was not prepared for what he saw. Her face, devoid of the makeup of her trade, revealed the difficulties of past years clearly; her unbound hair showed streaks of gray usually hidden by her elaborate coiffure; her generous proportions, unbound by a corset in the simple flowered robe she wore, were thick with middle age. For the first time, she looked the part of Tricia's mother, but she also had the appearance of a woman supporting the heavy weight of concern for her child, and Drew was strangely affected.

He said instinctively, "What's the matter, Chantalle? What did that soldier say?"

Chantalle stood up and responded softly, "He came here to make some inquiries and to leave a message for you that the fellow who tried to kill you last night was identified by one of the men at the Easton Hotel. His name was Bruce Carlton. Bruce was one of my customers ... and he worked for Simon Gault."

"Simon Gault ..."

"Simon is one of my customers here, too." She scrutinized his expression. Appearing to make a decision, she said abruptly, "Close the door and sit down, Drew. There are some things I need to tell you."

Drew went still. He somehow knew this was the moment he had been waiting for.

He pushed the door closed behind him.

Chantalle stared at Drew tensely as he sat down stiffly on the chair facing her. She could no longer bide her time and wait for Whit. Things had gone too far and the situation was getting too dangerous. She had to tell Drew.

She started slowly. "You have a ring in your money pouch, Drew." At Drew's surprised expression, she said, "You know Angie. You can't miss her around here. She's the brunette who met you at the door that first night, the woman you turned down when you went to the bar instead. To Angie, that was the ultimate insult. She'll never forgive you for it."

Chantalle paused briefly before continuing, "Angie is Simon Gault's favorite in this house. She's the one who told me about the ring. She said she heard Tricia telling somebody about it—which I don't believe for a moment, but that's beside the point. She was searching for information that I couldn't give her, but I went to your room afterwards to confirm what she said. You were still ill, and while you were sleeping, I looked in your money pouch. I saw the damaged ring."

"That happened during the war." Drew shrugged. "I couldn't wear it anymore in that condition, and I didn't want to throw it away. My money pouch seemed like the logical place to keep it."

"It has a sailing ship on it and a banner with the Latin words *Quattuor mundum do*."

His expression suddenly dark, Drew asked, "How

do you know the full inscription? The Latin words were partially lost when the ring was broken."

"I know because I've seen it before." Chantalle ignored the increasing rigidity of Drew's posture as she continued, "But the man who showed me his matching ring didn't have the family name Collins. His family name was Hawk—Whit Hawk."

"Whit ..."

Drew's face paled revealingly as Chantalle continued, "Whit showed up in Galveston a few months ago. Just about the first thing he did was to ask me if I'd ever seen a ring like his before. He told me his brother had one, too, that they'd lost touch with each other years earlier, but he was still hoping to find him. I studied the crest, and when I saw your ring ..." Chantalle paused before continuing in a rush, "But you said your name was Collins and you didn't even bother to mention that you had a ring or a missing brother. I wasn't sure who you really were or what I should do."

Chantalle noted Drew's difficulty in swallowing before he said hoarsely, "Where is he? Did he leave Galveston?"

"He has a ranch not far from here called La Posada, where he lives with his wife."

"His wife ..."

"Whit and Jackie were recently married." Allowing Drew a moment to absorb that information, Chantalle then stated softly, "Like you, Whit is a handsome man, Drew, but with the exception of your physical stature, you don't resemble each other at all. I was confused. Because I'm fond of Whit, I sent a man to La Posada to tell him to come here as soon as he could. I knew how Whit felt about finding his brother and I didn't want to stir up any false hopes, so I wanted to tell him about you calmly, and in person. He's a good man. I knew he'd do the right thing."

"When is he coming here?"

"I don't know. Whit was on a trail drive when Will reached La Posada the first time. When he didn't come, I wanted to make sure Jackie had stressed how urgently I wanted to see him, so I sent Will back again."

"And Whit's still not here."

"I can only assume he hasn't returned to the ranch yet. I know Whit. He'll come as soon as he gets my message."

Agitated, Drew stood up as he said, "But that has nothing to do with what happened last night."

"Let me finish, Drew." Chantalle watched as Drew sat back down. She noted that his hand trembled as he pulled the chair closer and she continued, "Simon Gault—Bruce Carlton's employer—is a very dangerous man. He hates Whit, Drew. I don't know why, but he hated him from the first moment he saw him. After they had a few run-ins, things got worse. Simon pays Angie to keep him informed about what's going on around here—we all know it, although Angie denies it. Angie serves her purpose in this house, and her connection to Simon never seemed important to me before this. The point is that I think Angie and Simon were in cahoots about your ring somehow, and since Whit didn't make a secret of his search for his brother, I think Simon drew his own conclusions."

Openly skeptical, Drew interrupted, "You're telling

me Simon Gault hates Whit Hawk so much that he wants to kill me on the chance that Whit is my brother?"

Chantalle hesitated, and then asked flatly, "*Is* Whit your brother, Drew?"

"I had a brother once." A smile touched Drew's lips as he said, "I had a family, too, but that was a long time ago."

Chantalle repeated, "*Is* Whit your brother?"

Drew's expression hardened. "I don't know. I don't know if I want to believe he is, either."

"Drew—"

"Too many years have passed. We've all changed."

"Is that why you kept the ring—because you wanted to forget your family?"

Drew stiffened. "I never said I wanted to forget them. I could never forget them."

"You're talking about your sisters now."

Drew's expression grew grim. "What do you know about my sisters?"

"I know Drew Hawk probably thinks they're dead … that they died in a fire. But actually they're alive and well."

"W … what?"

"They're alive, Drew … both of them."

"That's impossible!"

"They lived through the fire and were adopted. Jenna Leigh moved here to the city a while back. She's a reporter on the *Daily Galveston*. She recently married Colonel Clay Madison."

Drew went briefly silent. He then asked, "Colonel Clay Madison—that Yankee officer I met in your office?"

"The war is over, Drew."

"Not for me, it isn't!"

"Jenna Leigh felt that way at first, I think, but she learned that she can't live in the past."

"You asked, and now I'm telling you. No sister of mine would ever marry a Yankee—and Jenna Leigh isn't my sister if she did!"

"Drew—"

"You said both sisters were alive."

"Laura Anne came to Galveston, too." Chantalle watched his reaction as she said the name. She noted his flush when she added, "Laura Anne's name is Elizabeth Huntington Dodd now."

Drew looked at her confusedly.

"It's a long story. Elizabeth was in New York for a while, but she's on her way back to Galveston with her husband, Jason Dodd, who is also a close friend of mine. She doesn't know anything about her sister or her brothers yet."

Drew shook his head. "This is wrong ... all wrong."

"If your name is really Collins, it doesn't matter, does it?"

"My name is Collins as far as the Yankees are concerned."

"What are you saying?"

Drew replied coldly, "My name is Drew *Collins*—because Drew *Hawk* is wanted by the Union Army for something that happened during the war."

"But ... the war is over!"

"I told you, it isn't over for me."

"Drew, you know why I told you all this, don't you?" When he did not reply, Chantalle continued, "I told you because of what happened last night. All I can think is that if Simon Gault really is behind it all, he won't stop. I know him. He's vindictive, cruel, and relentless."

"If that's true, why do you tolerate him here?"

"He's also an important man in this city. I needed to accept him if I wanted to survive here."

"What about Tricia? What have you told her about all this?"

"She doesn't know anything."

Drew stood up, his expression tightening. "You kept all this a secret from her, too?"

"I didn't have a choice. Whit needed to know first."

"And Willie could be sacrificed."

"I had no way of knowing that would happen! At first, I had no reason to believe Simon had anything to do with Willie's murder; but the minute you described Bruce to me, I knew I had to say something."

Silence followed, and Chantalle felt a stab of fear at how Drew was going to respond.

Drew stared at Chantalle in silent incredulity. Whit was alive? Jenna Leigh and Laura Anne were, too? But ... Laura Anne wasn't Laura Anne anymore. She was Elizabeth Huntington Dodd, and Jenna Leigh was married to the same Yankee who was investigating Willie's death—who was bound to see the wanted notice about him sooner or later—and who would then arrest him.

Drew's expression grew taut. No, he couldn't afford to believe any of what Chantalle had told him. He *wouldn't* believe any of it until he saw Whit in person ... until he stood eye-to-eye with the man claiming to be his brother.

As for his sisters, they were dead, and he was the person responsible for their deaths. He had borne that guilt for so many years that it was a part of him. He would not surrender it now, only to discover belatedly that Chantalle was wrong, and to be forced to suffer all over again.

He took a breath as he looked at Chantalle's anguished expression. His inner anger gradually faded when he realized that whether she was right or wrong, she obviously believed she had needed to tell him. She obviously cared.

Drew said softly, "If you're right and Simon is determined to do me in because he thinks I'm a Hawk, Tricia won't be safe in my company."

Chantalle blinked, and then said, "I hope you don't mean—"

"Chantalle, please ..." Drew halted her protest. "You know what I have to do. Please tell Tricia I'm sorry. Tell her I need to clear this all up before we can have any thoughts about going on. Tell her I can't abide putting her in danger. If anything happened to her—"

"You can tell her yourself, Drew."

"No." A shadow of a smile touched Drew's lips as he said, "Tricia won't take no for an answer. Last night proved that to me. Last night also proved that I have trouble maintaining my convictions under her persuasion, and I can't let her distract me from what I need to do."

"She won't like it, Drew."

"But she'll be safe."

Chantalle did not respond. Her expression of sad acceptance touched him deeply. Leaning forward impulsively, Drew kissed her pale, lined cheek. He said simply, "Thank you ... for everything."

Then he limped out the doorway and headed for the street.

"Drew isn't in his room. Where is he?

Tricia had awakened at mid-morning after a mostly sleepless night. Still lying motionless, she had recalled the terrifying attempt on Drew's life in the wee hours that same morning, and a cold chill traveled down her spine. Drew had insisted that they return to Chantalle's house to assure Chantalle that Tricia was all right. She had agreed, aware that news traveled with lightning speed in a bordello, and that Chantalle might become aware of the attack before the local authorities were informed. She had not taken into account that Chantalle would accompany her to her room afterwards, or that Drew would retire to his former room at the end of the hallway.

She had gone to that bedroom as soon as she'd awoken this morning—only to find the bed made up as if no one had been there.

Panic still pervaded her senses as she presently faced Chantalle in the confines of her office and asked again, "Where is he, Chantalle?"

Dressed in a surprisingly conservative gown, Chantalle replied, "He's fine, Tricia. I don't know where he is right now, but he's fine."

"When is he coming back?"

"I don't know."

"What do you mean?"

"I mean I don't know when he's coming back here."

"What are you saying?"

"Drew has a lot to mull over, Tricia … and he's worried about you."

"About me?"

"He said he couldn't bear the thought that you might've been hurt during the attempt on his life."

"But I wasn't. Drew took care of it. I'd put my life in his hands anytime. He knows that."

"He knows it … but the danger to you was more than he could bear."

"Was …?" Tricia's blood ran cold. "Say what you mean … please."

Her expression strained, Chantalle whispered, "I don't know when he'll be back … maybe not until this whole situation has been cleared up."

"But if someone wants to kill Drew, he's the one who is in danger. I need to be with him so I can—"

"He doesn't want that."

"How do you know what he wants?"

"Because he told me." Chantalle continued softly, "You said there were dark spots in Drew's past that he kept secret from you. They've come back to haunt him, and he doesn't want you to be a casualty of the circumstances."

"I don't understand."

"And I wouldn't want to be the person to explain it all to you, even if I could." Pausing, Chantalle then said, "I have only one question to ask. Do you love him?"

Unaware of the tear that spilled down her cheek, Tricia replied, "Yes, I do."

"Then trust him. Believe in him. Let him work all this out."

Tricia shrugged uncertainly as she asked, "And in the meantime?"

Tears overflowed Chantalle's darkly kohled orbs. Silent, appearing unable to reply, she closed the distance between them and gathered Tricia into her motherly arms.

"Why didn't someone inform me about this sooner?"

The report of the attempt on Drew Collins's life lay on his desk as Colonel Clay Madison stood up and faced Sergeant Walker. The stiffness of his military posture betrayed his annoyance as he said, "My investigation into Willie Childers's death is common knowledge in this office, and the link between these two attempted robberies is plain to see."

"Sir, Lieutenant McMasters received notification of the crime during the early morning hours. He didn't note a relationship to the Childers investigation at that time and he—"

"He didn't? Not even when he went to the scene of an apparent robbery attempt and saw that Drew Collins was wearing Confederate Army pants and boots just like Willie Childers? He must have realized that Collins was probably a former Confederate soldier, which should have led him to connect last night's attack to the murder at Madame Chantalle's—*which* I am very publicly investigating. If he had read the notification I passed around in order to keep all officers abreast of the situation, he also would have realized that I had actually interviewed Drew Collins in connection with the Childers case. Collins was the fellow who accompanied Willie Childers into Galveston. He also should have realized that this attempt on Collins's life could change the whole direction of my investigation."

"Sir, it wasn't until this morning that this report from Lieutenant McMasters came across my desk."

"Two days after the fact?"

"There's been a change in personnel down the line, sir. Some miscellaneous paperwork has been held up for even longer periods than this."

"Is that so? We'll take care of that situation later." His expression angry, Colonel Madison continued, "In the meantime, have Lieutenant McMasters report to me immediately. I want to know everything he's done so far in his investigation. I don't intend to embarrass the Adjutant General's Office any further with my ignorance of the affair."

"Yes, sir."

"I want to see all that 'miscellaneous paperwork' you mentioned that's been held up 'down the line,' too, and I want to see it immediately."

"Yes, sir."

"Make sure Lieutenant McMasters reports to me within the hour. I've already lost two days in this investigation. I don't want Galveston's confidence in *Yankee justice* to erode any further."

"Yes, sir."

Leaving with a solemn salute, Sergeant Walker returned minutes later, carrying a thick file.

His brows drawing into a knot, Colonel Madison asked, "What's that?"

"This is the miscellaneous paperwork that was held up, sir. It was also forwarded to me this morning."

Colonel Madison's lips twitched with annoyance as he accepted the file and ordered, "Find McMasters!"

Hardly aware that Sergeant Walker had left his office, Colonel Madison opened the file and started reading.

Simon was beside himself. He paced his spacious office, unable to concentrate on the forms Billy had placed on his desk for him to sign hours earlier. He walked to the window as he had done countless times, his thoughts in turmoil as he stood staring out blindly at the expanse of sea beyond.

Two days had passed since Bruce had been killed in Drew Hawk's hotel room. The authorities had shown no interest in Simon beyond notification and a few questions that first day, but he had received reports from his informants in the city that Drew had been everywhere, making inquiries about him. Simon didn't like it. The man's questions were raising eyebrows, and Simon was uncertain what answers had been secretly given to Drew in the more common quarters of the city. He needed to find out more, but with Bruce gone and Angie no longer making any attempt to contact him, his sources were limited.

The thought enraged him. Time was growing short. He needed to convince the Galveston consortium to sign the agreement that would eliminate any change to the present conformation of the port by committing the only available funds elsewhere. Individual investors in Houston would secure his future there when their own futures were assured. Everything hinged on his ability to positively affect the signing of that agreement. He could not afford to have Whit Hawk return just now for fear of the complications that might result, but he sensed that Drew Hawk's questions were part of the reason that agreement was not yet signed.

It irritated him that Drew Hawk had not come to him for information so he, Simon, could claim his innocence. Instead, the bastard seemed content to stick his nose into every past venture he had ever been involved in. He was unsure how much the fellow knew or what his intentions were. He was virtually in the dark.

Yes ... he needed to know more about what was happening.

Despising the need, Simon knew Angie was the only person he could depend on to get him the information he wanted. He would have to visit her again on the pretext of seeking out her sexual expertise. He would appeal to her lascivious nature. It would not be difficult to make her hungry for what only he could offer her, and once they were on familiar footing, he would put her on Drew Hawk's trail.

Yes, he would do that.

His body reacting predictably to the picture he had created in his mind, Simon gave a low snort and turned toward the door. It occurred to him that he might actually enjoy himself while putting that sultry tart in her place again.

The thought amusing him, Simon walked through

the outer office with a mumbled word to Billy as he headed for the exit.

Chantalle greeted Barry Potts effusively as he entered the house and closed the door behind him. Barry was thin and balding, an elderly gentleman who was one of her regular customers. She knew he had often experienced embarrassing difficulties during solitary times with her girls. Mavis had been particularly patient with him, and he had expressed his gratitude for her kindness in the most generous of ways. But Chantalle knew that even if he had not been in a financial position to express his appreciation, she would not have refused him entrance to her house. She liked him and understood his situation, and that was enough.

Chantalle summoned Mavis with a wave of her finger. She watched as the smiling prostitute took Barry's arm and led him inside. Mavis was particularly gentle with him. She seemed to realize that conversation was almost as important a part of their relationship as sexual favors, and that the elderly man needed to believe that Mavis's interest in him went beyond—

Loud, angry voices on the upstairs landing interrupted Chantalle's thoughts. She didn't abide that type of behavior in her establishment. Her thoughts stopped cold when she glimpsed Simon Gault. A moment later, he slipped out of sight, dragging Angie with him.

Her face flushing hot red, Chantalle ascended the staircase in a rush. She reached the upstairs corridor just as Simon attempted to open the door to his special room. His expression rabid, he turned toward her and demanded, "Is this door locked? If it is, I demand a key."

"Do you?" Sparing a short glance for Angie, Chantalle noted that the sultry brunette appeared terrified. She replied, "In answer to your question, yes, the door is locked. It will remain locked until I decide when and for whom to unlock it."

"Is that so?" Maintaining his grip on Angie's arm, Simon said with a poisonous glance, "May I remind you that your ability to do business in Galveston is dependent on the goodwill of the city, and that I am in a position to affect that goodwill any time I choose."

"I don't think so."

"Oh, you don't!" Simon released Angie's arm. Chantalle noted that Angie took the opportunity to slip back down the staircase as Simon turned his full attention toward her, continuing, "You have a very short memory, Chantalle. If not for me, you would not have reached the station you have attained in this city."

"That's what you've always told me."

"It's the truth, and I suggest that you heed it. It is only my friendship with you that has allowed you to—"

Chantalle interrupted hotly, "Don't waste your breath, Simon. You and I have never been friends, nor will we ever be. We have been business associates, and the time has come for me to sever that relationship. To put it plainly, you're no longer welcome in this house. Please leave."

Were she a lesser woman, Chantalle knew she would have been cowed by the fury that transformed Simon's features before he said in a measured tone, "I will give you time to rescind that request, Chantalle. I understand that you may have become upset at the attempt on the life of your daughter's lover, but I—"

Rage flushed Chantalle's senses at his hypocritical tone, and she interrupted, "That's it. You've said enough! Get out of here and don't come back—and you may rest assured that there is not a single person in this household who will lament your departure."

Seeming to swell with wrath, Simon took a threatening step toward her. "Harlot! Take that back or I'll make you take it back."

"Is something wrong, Chantalle?"

Chantalle glanced at the stairs as Jake stepped up onto the landing. She saw Simon's eyes narrow as the big man with the full white mustache approached them, his fists balled. She saw Angie duck out of sight at the base of the staircase as she responded, "Nothing is wrong now, Jake. Mr. Gault was just leaving."

Simon glanced at Jake as the big barkeep neared. He took a backward step and said in a voice throbbing with promise, " You win this time, Chantalle. I'll leave. I have no desire to make a scene, but you'll regret this day. I promise you that."

Inwardly quaking, Chantalle did not reply as Simon turned abruptly toward the rear staircase.

When Simon had disappeared from sight, Chantalle looked gratefully at Jake. His tone was gruff when he said, "You shouldn't have talked him into leaving, Chantalle. I've been wanting to throw that fella out since the first time I saw him here."

Chantalle's smile belied the tremor in her voice as she said, "I'm sorry to have deprived you of that privilege, Jake. I doubt very much if Simon will return." Slipping her arm through his, she said more softly, "Come on. Let's go downstairs so you can pour us both a drink. I don't know if you need one, but I sure do."

Her continuing smile masking her concern, Chantalle started down the stairs with the memory of Simon's threat lingering in her mind.

Colonel Clay Madison looked up from the folder on his desk. His brows tight, he read the official notification again, more slowly. He glanced at the date on the top of the sheet and mumbled brusquely before standing up, snatching his hat, and turning toward the door.

In the outer office, he told Sergeant Walker, "I'm going out for a while. I'll be back shortly."

"Sir, Lieutenant McMasters has been located. He'll be here soon."

"Tell him to wait here for me."

Closing his office door behind him with more emphasis than necessary, Clay untied his horse from the hitching post and spurred him into motion. Arriving at the small house where he and Jenna Leigh resided while their new home was being renovated, he dismounted and approached the door. He paused for a breath as he pushed it open.

Jenna Leigh emerged from the kitchen, obviously surprised to see him there, and he was momentarily silent. He supposed he would never become fully accustomed to his wife's extravagant natural beauty; to the glorious blond hair that spilled free of her normally upswept coiffure, and the mesmerizing, amber-eyed gaze that revealed her quick mind. He attempted a smile when she said, "What are you doing home this time of day, Clay? I was just cleaning up and I—"

Her voice abruptly stilled. A shadow passed over her face as she said, "What happened?" She took a breath. "It's not Whit. He hasn't been hurt, has he?"

"No, it's nothing like that." Closing the distance between them, Clay slid his arms around Jenna Leigh and drew her close. Inwardly marveling at the multitude of emotions that simple intimacy stirred inside him, he whispered reassuringly, "As far as I know, Whit's fine." He went on, "I just read something in a file of military papers that crossed my desk, and I figured you'd want to know."

"What is it?"

Knowing that Jenna Leigh's keen mind would quickly sort fact from fiction, he said, "I received a memorandum this morning that was passed down through military channels months earlier but was somehow held up along the way. It stated that the Union Army is conducting a search for a former Confederate Army officer who led a raid on a Union Army payroll just days before the war ended. It said that although the Confederate commander responsible for the raid surrendered, the money was not found. The commander claimed that the officer who headed the raid never made a full report to him, that he has no record of the payroll ever reaching the hands of the Confederate Army, and that the payroll was probably stolen by the men conducting the raid."

"Yes ... so?"

"The name of the officer in charge of that raid is Drew Hawk."

Jenna Leigh gasped. Clay felt the tremor that shook her as her eyes widened and she strove to catch her breath. He said in the hope of lessening her shock, "We can't be sure he's your brother. We don't know if this fellow just happened to have the same name or—"

"What does he look like?"

"The report describes him as approximately six feet two inches tall; black hair; hazel eyes. His birth year is recorded as 1840."

Jenna Leigh swallowed. Her eyes filled as she said in a breathlessly hopeful tone, "1840—the year our Drew was born. Can it be, Clay? Can I possibly be fortunate enough, after all these years of suffering their loss, to find *both* my brothers?"

"I don't know." His expression solemn, Clay continued softly, "I'm especially uncertain because this Drew Hawk appears to be on the run. He could be anywhere in the country, especially if he knows where that payroll went—or if he kept part of it."

"My brother wouldn't do that! My brother was honest and high-minded. He'd never steal anything that didn't belong to him."

"Jenna Leigh … this Drew Hawk did."

"But that was during the war! Whether this Drew Hawk is my brother or not, he was merely following military orders."

"That would be true if the payroll had ever been turned over to his superiors."

"There could be a hundred reasons why it wasn't!"

"And one of them could be that he stole the money."

"I don't believe that."

Clay felt Jenna Leigh's stiffening, and he said softly, "I'm just trying to tell you the way things presently look. Further investigation might prove otherwise."

"Further investigation ... meaning if you discover his whereabouts, you'll arrest this Drew Hawk and question him—put him in the brig for as long as it takes to confirm the accusations of your superiors, who *assume* he is guilty."

"Jenna Leigh—"

"Hasn't he suffered enough? Whether he's my brother or not, this man's dreams were shattered when the Confederacy collapsed, and now you intend to bring him to *Yankee* justice?"

"I'm only telling you what the report states."

"You already believe he's guilty."

"That's not true."

Regretting her attack when pain registered in her husband's gaze, Jenna Leigh halted abruptly. After a few moments, she said more softly, "You know my feelings run high on these matters, Clay, and now that this debacle seems to concern the brother I believed lost to me ..." She took a breath before continuing, "You know I'll do everything I can to find out what happened ... and to find him, don't you, Clay?"

"Yes."

She asked with a frown, "Have you sent word to Whit about this?"

"No."

"I'll handle it, then. I don't want to raise his hopes while everything is still uncertain."

"Jenna Leigh ..."

Looking at her husband with both determination

and affection, Jenna Leigh whispered, "You do know I love you."

"I know."

"And no matter how all this turns out, I'll always love you."

Clay stilled. Deep emotion touched his expression the moment before he lowered his head to cover Jenna Leigh's lips with his in a passionate kiss.

It was a response that came from his heart.

It was also the only response he could give.

Chapter Eleven

Whit Hawk rode toward Galveston at a steady pace. Tall and erect, his broad, muscular shoulders bespeaking controlled power, he sat his mount easily. From all outward appearances, he was relaxed and comfortable as he entered the city and turned toward a familiar area of town—but appearances were deceiving. He had returned to his home at La Posada and to his wife, the lovely red-haired Jackie, only hours before securing a fresh mount and heading out on the road again. He had been exhausted, but the rest that he had been avidly anticipating became secondary to the urgent messages he received from Chantalle summoning him to Galveston.

Whit guided his mount steadily through Galveston's traffic as the afternoon sun slipped from its zenith. He was fond of Chantalle. He had felt a connection to her that first day when they had spoken plainly about their lives without pretense of any kind. Despite her occupation, he respected her in a way he respected few others.

Chantalle had proved her friendship in the weeks that followed, and Whit was keenly aware that although she was the consummate businesswoman, he owed his happy home with the woman he loved in part to Chantalle's generosity and her instinctive trust in him. That trust was mutual, which was the reason he knew that Chantalle's urgent summonses meant that whatever she wanted to discuss with him was urgent indeed.

Whit turned the corner and Chantalle's red brick mansion came into sight. Gray moss clung to the branches of the live oaks arching over the walkway, and the brilliant pink of the oleander hedges lining the brief lawn was a colorful welcome that he remembered well, but they did not lighten his concern as he dismounted and tied up his horse. He was keenly aware that Simon Gault was his enemy—and that the help Chantalle had given him after his arrival in Galveston, thwarting Gault in the process, had made a sham of the friendship Gault pretended for her.

As for Chantalle, she merely tolerated Gault for financial purposes, which only added to Gault's resentment.

Whit's frown darkened as he strode toward the front entrance of the house. Both weary and worried, he gave only polite responses to the women who welcomed him as he entered. Then he headed directly for Chantalle's office on the second floor, where he had been told he would find her.

He knocked on her office door and responded to the call to enter. He smiled with relief when he saw Chantalle seated at her desk with no visible changes in appearance or demeanor. But his relief was short-lived when she stood up and said with thickness in her voice. "Whit … I'm so glad you're here."

Whit slipped his arm around Chantalle's shoulders and said comfortingly, "I came as soon as I got your messages. What's wrong?"

Chantalle sagged momentarily against his side before she straightened up and looked into his eyes. "It's not so much what's wrong. It's what's right, in a way."

"Chantalle …"

Chantalle took a breath. She dabbed briefly at her heavily kohled eyes and adjusted her expression, then took a backward step that released her from his comforting grip. "I suppose you should sit down, because what I've got to say can't be said in a few minutes."

Whit did not move, and Chantalle said hesitantly, "Whit … I think I've found your brother."

The wind knocked out of him, Whit could not immediately reply. Having prepared himself for anything but that, he scrutinized Chantalle's expression for long moments before he managed, "Explain what you just said, please."

"I saw his ring. He doesn't wear it, so I didn't see it at first when he came and collapsed downstairs."

"Collapsed?" Whit swallowed, hardly able to breathe.

"From a war wound that became infected. My daughter nursed him back to health."

"Your daughter?"

221

Whit's incredulity continued as Chantalle's gaze begged his tolerance. "You didn't know I had a daughter. That's a long story, too—too long to explain right now, but he was delirious at first. We didn't know who he was, and when I looked in his money pouch, I saw the ring. It was damaged. The ship and the Latin inscription were hardly visible."

"Then you couldn't be sure it was Drew."

"It's Drew, all right, even if he wouldn't come right out and say it."

"Why wouldn't he tell you what his name is?"

Chantalle's voice dropped. "He's a wanted man, Whit. He fought for the Confederacy, and the Union Army wants him for questioning about something he did during the war. He didn't elaborate, but evidently, whatever it was, the Yankees aren't about to forget it."

Confused, Whit shook his head. "How do you know all this?"

"I know because Drew told me."

"Where is he now?"

"I don't know. He left after we talked—after I told him about you and Jenna Leigh—and I haven't seen him since." Chantalle added apologetically, "I wanted to wait for you to decide where and when to tell him about yourself and Jenna Leigh. He's your brother, after all, but things got complicated and I was afraid for his life."

"Afraid for his life!"

Whit's face whitened, prompting Chantalle to say, "Let me start from the beginning so I can bring you up to date."

Nodding, knowing he had no choice, Whit sat down abruptly as Chantalle started to speak.

Drew walked reluctantly along the Galveston docks. He had previously avoided that particular area with a sense of dread that was overwhelming. He knew the reason was because he had no desire to look into the face of the past when he saw the building that had once borne the Hawk family name.

But it was time.

He had spent the past few days talking to everyone who knew or did business with Simon Gault. The people he spoke to had hesitated to respond to his questions. Once they began talking, however, they expounded with great negative heat about him. Those persons included the captains who commanded Gault's ships, the sailors who labored on them, the merchants who handled his shipments and sold his wares, and the women who had no defense against his unwelcome attentions—more women than he had at first considered believable. Without exception, he had learned that Simon Gault was feared rather than respected; that the patriotism he had displayed in supporting the Confederate cause during the war was suspect; that it was generally felt his concern for the city was actually concern for his personal wealth rather than for the welfare of the city, and that his exalted position in society was undeserved.

Through all the conversations, however, not one person had a shred of proof to back up any of the negative things they said about him.

Drew limped along the wharf, his steps slowing as he approached the two-storied warehouse and office building at the end of the dock. Its steepled roof was high and imposing, just as he remembered it; the white stone that his father had imported from England had weathered the years well; the wide, steep staircase leading up to the first floor where his father's office had been located was still daunting.

The building was now boldly marked with the sign, GAULT SHIPPING AND RECEIVING, and he was unable to advance further as painful memories inundated his mind. His family had been complete and happy during those years when the sign had read HAWK SHIPPING COMPANY. He remembered vividly that his father had brought their happiness to an end with gambling that drove the family business into bankruptcy. Their mother deserted them after that, and their father left them with their aunt and uncle, promising to restore everything they had lost when he returned—which he never did.

His brother Whit was nine years old—just a year older than he—when their aunt died and their Uncle Nolan delivered them to the orphanage where they spent the next nine years. He recalled that Whit had automatically taken charge of Laura Anne, who was three years old, and that Jenna Leigh, then only two, had clung to him, Drew, desperately. Strangely, that day when they realized they had no one left but themselves had been a turning point; and although neither he nor Whit ever discussed it, the sense of responsibility they felt for their sisters grew with each passing year. It also made them stronger.

Until ...

He had left the orphanage at eighteen in the hope of finding either his father or Whit. He had been barely twenty when he returned to the orphanage for his sisters. He recalled his shock when he discovered only the charred remains of the proud old manor house where they had lived. That shock had been multiplied a thousand times over when he was informed that his sisters had not survived the fire.

Did he now dare believe after all the years that had passed that his brother lived on a ranch only a few miles distant from Galveston, and that Whit was expected to come to the city as soon as he received Chantalle's summons? Could Drew allow himself to accept Chantalle's statement that his sisters had survived the fire at the orphanage, and that Jenna Leigh was actually residing in Galveston—*married to a Yankee?*

Drew stared at the sign on the impressive building that had once borne the Hawk family name.

Simon Gault, the man who Chantalle believed hated Whit enough to order the killing of his brother, was the same man who was despised by all who worked for him—the same man who was respected by the highest level of Galveston society. He was also the man who had assumed Drew's father's business.

His mind made up, Drew turned and started back toward the seedy hotel where he'd taken a room. The past and its many betrayals were behind him. He was helpless to change what had happened, but he was determined that he would not add to that list of betrayals. He had a promise to keep. He knew what he must do.

* * *

Whit approached the house where Jenna Leigh was presently living with her husband. It was a small cottage on the estate that Clay had bought for Jenna Leigh as a wedding present. Pleasant and comfortable, it had a thatched roof reminiscent of an English country cottage and a secluded location that the newlyweds doubtless valued. Jenna Leigh had planted flowers along the walk leading to the front door in an obvious effort to add her own touch to the place.

Because responsibilities for his ranch took up most of his time, Whit had not seen as much of either Jenna Leigh or Clay as he would have liked in the time since their reunion; yet the bond between Jenna Leigh and him was strong. He was proud of the stalwart, intelligent woman she had grown up to be, and of the fact that she had become a good wife without sacrificing any part of herself. He genuinely liked the man she had chosen for a husband, too—even if Clay was a Yankee.

Whit's lips curled in a brief smile at the thought. Clay was one of the Yankees primarily responsible for maintaining martial law in the former Confederate seaport of Galveston. Yet Clay was also all the proof Whit would ever need that despite the wide divisions that still remained between North and South, their country and its way of life would survive.

Dismounting, he tied up his mount and approached the front door of the cottage. He was about to knock when it opened and Jenna Leigh greeted him with a startled smile that warmed his heart. She hugged him tight and then drew back. He noted that her smile slipped a little when she said, "I was just thinking about you, Whit."

He cocked his head as he studied her riding outfit and replied, "Funny, it looks to me like you're dressed to go out riding."

Jenna Leigh quipped in return, "That doesn't mean I wasn't thinking about you." She asked, "What are you doing here, anyway? I thought you were supposed to be on a trail drive."

"I was, but when I got back home, I found a message for me from Chantalle." He paused, his expression sobering as he said, "I need to talk to you, Jenna Leigh. I need to tell you something I just found out."

Jenna Leigh paled. Taking her arm, he attempted to draw her back inside as he said, "Maybe you should sit down. What I have to say may surprise you."

Refusing to budge, Jenna Leigh responded, "It's about Drew, isn't it?"

Stunned, Whit replied, "How did you know?"

"Clay told me about it not more than an hour ago ... but how did you find out so fast?"

"Chantalle told me. That's why she sent a message asking me to come to Galveston. As soon as I found out, I came here."

"How did *she* know?"

Whit took an unconscious step back as he said, "Wait a minute. How did Chantalle know what?"

"That Drew is wanted by the Union Army for questioning about a Union payroll that he and his squad commandeered a few days before the war ended. Clay received the bulletin to be on the lookout for him just this morning."

Whit went still. "I didn't know the details, but Chantalle found out Drew was wanted because *he* told her. He was recuperating in her house from an infected war wound. When he left, he told her he was using the name Drew Collins because he was wanted by the Union Army."

"You're telling me that Drew has been in Chantalle's house ... that he was so close, and I never knew?"

"He didn't know about you, either, Jenna Leigh. He thought you were dead."

"So how—?"

"Chantalle saw his ring—a duplicate of mine."

Jenna Leigh's hand flew to her chest, where her pendant lay under the bodice of her dress.

"Chantalle said no one else knows what his real name is," Whit explained. "Drew doesn't wear his ring because it's been damaged."

Tears filling her eyes, Jenna Leigh said, "It's all true, then ... this Drew Collins really is *our* Drew, and he's here in Galveston?" She took a breath. "Clay doesn't know Drew's here in the city. He said he wasn't even certain that the Drew Hawk who was wanted by the Army was actually our brother. He said it could be a coincidence—that it could be another fella with the same name—but I knew it was *our* Drew. I had a feeling."

"You and Drew always were especially close."

"We were all close, Whit. And the years in between haven't changed that. Not for me."

The truth of Jenna Leigh's statement registered deep inside Whit. Distance and years had separated them, but nothing could change their commitment to each other. "You're saying Clay doesn't know about Drew's assumed name, or even that he's in Galveston?" he asked.

"He doesn't know *yet*." She asked abruptly, "Does Drew know about me?"

"He knows you're in the city."

"What did he say?"

His expression growing pained, Whit said, "Drew's had a hard time of it. Chantalle said he was still recuperating from his wound and he was just passing through Galveston with his friend when the infection acted up again. Chantalle and her daughter took care of him while he was sick, but his best friend, a Willie Childers, was murdered when he came back to see Drew. A little later, an attempt was made on Drew's life, too."

"W why?"

Whit frowned. "I don't know."

"He's all right now, isn't he? I mean, he's safe."

"He's safe enough, I guess. Chantalle doesn't know exactly where he is except that he said he's not going to leave Galveston until he finds his friend's killer. He's bitter, Jenna Leigh. He blames most of what's happened on the Yankees."

Jenna Leigh's expression stiffened. "Clay is a Yankee officer. He's also duty bound to find Drew and bring him to justice. Does that mean Drew blames me, too, because I married Clay?"

"I don't know."

"But he's in Galveston."

"I can't be sure."

"I wouldn't be able to bear it if we lost him again, Whit, especially if I were the cause."

"Don't worry. We won't if I have anything to say about it."

"What are you going to do?"

"I'm going to find out what's going on, why Drew's friend was killed and why an attempt was made on Drew's life." His brow furrowing, Whit said, "But I don't want you to get involved, Jenna Leigh. There'll be too many complications with Clay and all—and I don't want to have to worry about your safety."

"You don't have to worry about me, Whit."

"I don't have to ... but I do."

Jenna Leigh studied Whit's sober expression for long moments before she nodded. "All right. I won't take any chances."

Whit's eyes narrowed. "I meant what I said, Jenna Leigh."

"I told you, I won't take any chances."

"You'll stay right here and let me take care of it."

"If that's what you want."

His gaze narrowing further at her quick acquiescence, Whit cautioned, "Jenna Leigh—"

"The same goes for you, too, Whit. I don't want you to take any unnecessary chances."

"I never take unnecessary chances." Turning toward the door, Whit continued, "I'll keep you informed. That's a promise."

"All right."

His hand on the doorknob, Whit turned back to say, "Behave yourself, Jenna Leigh."

"Yes, sir."

Doing his best to ignore the worry that Jenna Leigh's obedient manner inspired, Whit mounted up and turned his horse toward town.

He did not see Jenna Leigh watching him to make certain he was gone before she walked out the rear exit of the house to the spot where she had a horse saddled and waiting. Nor did he see her mount up and ride off as fast as she could.

Jenna Leigh drew her horse up in front of the *Daily Galveston* office and dismounted. Her expression sober, she could not stop herself from breathing deeply of the familiar smell of printer's ink as she walked inside. It reminded her of the years she had spent with Irene Prescott after the fire, while Irene had functioned as her surrogate mother and as one of the most well-respected women in the newspaper business. She could not help smiling at the clanging of the presses. It was music to her ears and indicated that although the afternoon edition had been printed and distributed for the day, owner and editor Noah Dickerson had obviously gotten enough advertising to warrant the printing of an individual sheet to be inserted in the next day's edition—a financial windfall for a newspaper whose financial status had known its ups and downs.

Knowing better than to attempt to be heard over the din, Jenna Leigh nodded in greeting to the men working at the presses as she approached Noah's office. She had proved her value as a reporter on the *Daily Galveston* before marrying Clay. She had continued to contribute to it on a regular basis since her marriage, but without the demanding schedule she had formerly upheld, a situation that suited both her boss and her. Her visit that afternoon, however, did not concern her column.

Jenna Leigh entered Noah's office and closed the door behind her. She sat down on the stiff, cane-bottom chair and looked into the man's face when he glanced up at her. Noah was a bear of a man with a demeanor that might frighten even the most avid of suffragettes, but she wasn't cowed. She liked him because he liked her and respected the work she had done for him. They had long since passed the formal stage in their relationship; yet she hesitated as she said without preamble, "I have a favor to ask of you, Noah."

Noah raised his hairy brows and adjusted his thick glasses. Jenna Leigh knew what he was thinking. She had never asked a favor of him, and he was intrigued. Not desiring to keep him in suspense, she said, "I'd like you to tell John to make the entire past year's issues of the *Daily Galveston* available to me so I can go over them."

"You would, huh?" Noah scratched his thick, muscular neck as he looked at her quizzically. "It'll take John a considerable amount of time to dig them out for you. Would you like to tell me why you want them?"

"It's personal."

"Oh ... personal! Meaning mind your own business, Noah."

"That isn't exactly what I meant, but I suppose my response could be taken that way."

"What did you mean, then?" Noah's gaze drilled her through the thick lenses of his glasses. "You know I don't like mysteries."

Jenna Leigh responded cautiously, "There's no mystery about it. It's personal because I learned this morning that my younger brother—the one Whit and I couldn't seem to locate—was a Confederate officer during the war, and he had some problems during the last few weeks before Lee surrendered. Something about a Union payroll that he and his men had been ordered to capture."

"The war's over, Jenna Leigh. That's old news."

"Not if that payroll was never recovered and if the Union Army is still searching for him in relation to the raid."

"Humm …" Noah frowned. "That must've been a pretty big payroll. What are you looking for?"

"Anything I can learn about the robbery."

"Why?"

Annoyed by the tears that sprang unexpectedly to her eyes, Jenna Leigh replied, "Because Drew is my brother and Clay is my husband, and Clay is also the Union officer who's been charged with finding and arresting Drew."

Showing no reaction to her tears, Noah said, "The robbery obviously didn't happen in Galveston. What makes you think the story will be in our paper?"

"As you said, it must've been a pretty big payroll for the Army to still be interested in getting it back. That might've made it news in Galveston, especially since this newspaper had Confederate sympathies, and the Confederacy was starved for positive news by then."

Staring at her a moment longer, Noah pulled his great bulk slowly to his feet as he said, "All right, I'll tell John ... on one condition. If a story comes out of this, I want you to write it up."

Jenna Leigh hesitated.

"That's the condition."

Jenna Leigh responded, "I won't break any confidences and I won't write up a story until this whole affair is settled—that's my condition."

After another moment's silence, Noah said, "That's all right with me."

Seated at a vacant desk beside the plate-glass window sometime later, Jenna Leigh reviewed the dusty editions of the *Daily Galveston* surrounding her. Her concentration intense, she examined each page patiently. Her reporter's instinct told her that there was more to the story about the payroll robbery than was generally known, and something inside her made her feel that she—

An uneasy feeling caused Jenna Leigh to look up abruptly. A tall, dark-haired man was gazing at her through the window.

Tall, dark-haired, and muscular, with unusual hazel eyes that were stunningly familiar, he was handsome in a way that she remembered well.

Jenna Leigh stood up shakily. Could it be?

She caught and held the fellow's gaze for a brief moment before she called out, "Drew—is it you?"

He was gone in an instant.

Stumbling over a chair in her haste to reach the street, Jenna Leigh called out, "Drew, is it you? Please, Drew, don't leave!"

She emerged out onto the street to find that he was nowhere in sight.

She was still standing there, frozen to the spot when Noah touched her arm and said, "What's wrong? You look like you've seen a ghost."

Hardly able to breathe, Jenna Leigh was momentarily unable to respond. Finally regaining her breath, she said softly, "I thought I did, but I guess I was wrong."

Still shaken, Jenna Leigh turned back to the office.

His determination renewed, Drew walked boldly across the familiar black-and-white tiled floor in the outer office of Gault Shipping and Receiving. He did not answer the slight, blond-haired, bespectacled young man when the fellow asked his name. Nor did he stop as the fellow removed his glasses and stood up uncertainly, then tried ineffectively to block his entrance into Simon Gault's office.

Gault glanced up as Drew pushed open the door. Standing behind his massive mahogany desk, he watched as Drew approached.

Hardly aware of the clerk who stood making excuses in the doorway behind him, Drew halted opposite Gault. The clerk's ramblings ceased, and Drew waited until the door closed behind him before he broke the silence by saying coldly, "You're Simon Gault, aren't you?

"Of course I am. Who are you, and what do you want?"

Drew assessed the man silently. Expensively clothed,

fit, and well groomed despite his age, he was the owner of a shipping company that brought him respect and social acceptance that were vastly undeserved. He was the epitome of everything that money could buy.

Drew studied him more closely as Gault returned his stare with eyes that were black with hatred, cold and conscienceless. Drew knew instinctively that the man's innocence was all an act. Gault knew who Drew was. Everything Chantalle had told him was true. He was looking at the man responsible for Willie's murder, and for the attack on him that had endangered Tricia's life as well. He couldn't be sure if the man bore hatred for everyone with the Hawk name, but he could not afford to take the chance that he did. One glimpse of Jenna Leigh seated near the window of the *Daily Galveston* had released him from the strange inertia that had been holding him in its grip. It had proved to him that whatever he thought of Jenna Leigh's marriage to a Yankee, she was still the little girl he had protected most of his life. He would not allow anyone to hurt her.

Drew began slowly, "You asked who I am, but you know the answer, Gault. What you don't know is that I'm a fair man, so I'm going to make some things very clear to you. You don't like my brother or me. That's fine, because the feeling is mutual. But don't think you're going to even up your score with him by taking it out on the people closest to him. I won't let that happen."

"I have nothing to say to you." Simon's dead eyes held his. "This is my office. I don't want you here, so get out!"

"In good time." The threat in his soft tone unmistakable, Drew continued, "Just so we understand each other—I know you somehow saw the ring that I carry in my money pouch, and I know what conclusions you drew when you saw it."

"You're crazy!"

Ignoring his protest, Drew continued, "So I'm warning you now, I'll prove who killed Willie Childers. I'll prove who sent Bruce Carlton to kill me, and I want you to remember that if anything else happens to anyone dear to me in the meantime, I won't waste my time *talking* to you."

"I told you—"

"Just listen!" His control beginning to slip, Drew continued coldly, "There won't be any place you can hide from me, do you understand?"

"You're talking to the wrong man, I'm telling you."

"Maybe." Drew gritted his teeth in a smile as he said softly, "You have nothing to worry about if I am ... but you'll remember what I said, won't you?"

Gault did not reply.

Drew took a hard step closer and demanded, "Answer me."

Gault's hand snaked toward his desk drawer. Leaning across the desk in a blur of movement, Drew slammed the drawer shut, catching Gault's hand in it. Holding it tightly shut while Gault groaned with pain, he insisted, "Answer me!"

His eyes bulging, Gault gasped, "I heard what you said!"

Releasing the drawer, glimpsing the handle of a gun

as Gault pulled his hand free, Drew added, "Now all you have to do is remember it."

Gault was cursing under his breath when Drew walked out of his office.

Drew stepped down onto the dock and started back in the direction from which he had come. Jenna Leigh was a woman now, and he would make sure she did not suffer because of her relationship to Whit or him. He had lost Willie for that senseless reason. He did not intend to lose anyone else.

Tricia's image flashed into his mind, and Drew suffered an almost debilitating surge of emotion. He loved her. Separation from her grew more difficult every day, but coming face to face with the evil in Gault's gaze had proved to him that he had done the right thing by separating himself from her. Danger followed him in too many ways. It shed its shadow on everyone dear to him. He needed to keep Tricia free of its darkness—at any cost.

Simon stood at his office window, clutching his throbbing hand as he watched Drew Hawk limp away.

Bastard!

He had been right all along. The Hawks were poison for him—every one of them—and the Hawk men were even more dangerous than he'd believed.

Simon cursed under his breath as the pain in his hand heightened. Drew Hawk believed he had won this time, but he would soon discover that small victories meant little when the game was not yet over.

The need to maintain propriety until he was able to

bend the consortium to his will handicapped him. It held him back from a full-fledged assault to attain final triumph over the Hawk family, but it would only take a few more days to convince a few stubborn holdouts. Then he would be free to follow through.

The Hawks had no idea what was coming.

Shuddering with pain, Simon nodded. But in the meantime, he would allow himself the small satisfaction of settling a score that had waited too long.

Tricia paced her bedroom impatiently. Another day was coming to an end ... another day of uncertainty. Where was Drew? What was he doing? Was he well, or was he ignoring a possible resurgence of the infection in his leg?

Tricia's pacing came to a halt. And she needed to know—did he really love her? Was he thinking about her? Did he ache inside at the thought of her, as she did each time she thought of him?

He had said he was concerned for her safety.

She was concerned for his.

He had said he couldn't concentrate on accomplishing what he needed to do when she was near.

She couldn't concentrate on anything she was supposed to do because he *wasn't*.

His absence had caused an impasse that she was not prepared to accept.

She loved him. She needed to be near him. If he loved her, he would need to be near her, too.

The sudden importance of that two-letter word loomed in her mind.

If

It occurred to her that Drew had never actually said he loved her. He had demonstrated in so many ways that she was a part of him he did not want to lose, but he had never voiced the words.

Did that mean he would never say them?

Her throat tight, Tricia took a breath. She needed to find out.

Making a sudden decision, Tricia turned toward the doorway of her room. Moments later, she was moving rapidly down the staircase to the first floor.

Whit dismounted, tied the reins to the hitching post, and hurried up the walkway toward Chantalle's house. Another long day had come to an end. He had spent it combing the docks for anyone who had seen Drew or who might know where he could be found. Drew seemed to have been one step ahead of him all day long, and he had missed him every time.

His brief visit with Jenna Leigh had done little to settle his mind. For all her grown-up beauty and intelligence, she had changed little since she was a child of ten. She still had a mind of her own and was determined to do what she felt she must. The success of the newspaper column she presently wrote as the crusading reporter J.L. Rebel was proof of that fact. He feared that despite her assurances, she would embark on an investigation that would get her into trouble.

As if that were not enough, he had received a message from Chantalle—who seemed to have had no trouble finding him—that she needed to see him right away. That message had brought him to her house on the run.

Whit opened the door of the bordello and frowned at the activity inside. He glanced at the clock in the foyer, aware that when the average citizens of Galveston started preparing to retire for the night, Chantalle's house started to come alive.

Momentarily uncertain, he watched Mavis enter the foyer. The soft-spoken prostitute smiled as she said succinctly, "She's upstairs."

The realization that Chantalle's women knew Chantalle had summoned him caused him to take the stairs two at a time. He reached Chantalle's office and knocked firmly on her door.

He pushed the door open in response to her reply and walked inside. He stopped abruptly at the sight of a slender, blond young woman standing near Chantalle's desk. The angelic quality of the woman—her fair hair and features and a stature so delicately formed as to seem almost ethereal—contrasted vividly with the determined look in her sea-green eyes as she stared at him.

Uncertain, Whit turned to Chantalle and said, "You wanted to see me? Will told me it was urgent."

Standing up, Chantalle approached him soberly. She halted halfway between the lovely young woman and him as she said, "I'd like you to meet my daughter, Tricia Lee Shepherd."

Tricia Lee *Shepherd*.

Whit extended his hand toward the young woman and said, "I'm pleased to meet you, ma'am, but I admit to being confused at your family name."

"She's my adopted daughter, Whit, which is the reason she doesn't carry my family name." Chantalle paused, and then added, "She's also the young woman who was with Drew when he was almost killed in an attempted robbery."

"But that was at night in the Easton Hotel, if I remember correctly. How was she—?"

Whit halted when the answer became clear to him.

Filling in the silence, Tricia said, "I'm pleased to meet you, Whit." She looked at him closely. "Strangely, if I had seen both you and Drew on the street, I would never have taken you two for brothers, despite your similarity of coloring and stature."

"We never did look alike." Whit added, "But we thought alike. I suppose we still do. You're a very beautiful woman, ma'am."

Tricia's cheeks colored at his compliment. "Please call me Tricia ... and please don't tell me you think I look like an angel. Believe me, that's far from the truth."

When Whit smiled in reply, silently acknowledging his reaction to her appearance, Tricia was temporarily unable to speak and moisture filled her eyes.

Chantalle took up the conversation, saying, "Tricia asked me to send for you, Whit. She has some information she was anxious to give you."

Turning toward Tricia, Whit frowned. "Anything you can tell me that will clear up what's been happening would be a help."

Tricia replied, "How about if I could tell you where to find your brother?"

Whit went still, and Tricia continued hesitantly, "As you've probably realized, Drew and I are … were … close, but he left without saying good-bye. He told Chantalle that the attempt on his life made him fear for my safety. If I'd had the chance, I would have told him that I feel the same way about him … that I fear for his safety, too, and that I won't feel content until I know he's all right."

Whit replied softly, "I tried to find Drew most of the day without success, Tricia. I'm anxious to see him, too. As far as I know, he doesn't realize I'm in Galveston."

"I'm sure he doesn't." Tricia paused, then added softly, "He's staying in a small hotel in the seedy part of town. It's called the Hotel Chalfonte."

"The Chalfonte?" Whit shook his head. "You're sure?"

"I got that information from the most reliable sources in town—the women downstairs." Tricia gave a short laugh. "I learned early on that news travels fast in a bordello, and pillow talk is usually the most reliable. Both Mavis and Lily said they heard from their regulars that Drew's been busy the past few days looking into Simon Gault's activities on the waterfront."

"Dammit, that's dangerous! Gault is a vindictive bastard, and he won't like it."

"I don't think Drew much cares about that. He said he's going to find out why Willie was killed, and if he gets any proof that it's related to the attempt on his own life—"

Whit interrupted tersely, "If he's staying at the Chalfonte, I'll find him, and then we're going to have a talk."

Tricia smiled. "Good luck if you think you're going to change his mind."

Whit halted at the look in Tricia's green eyes. He said, "Let me assure you, Tricia, if I find him, we'll have that talk. So, if there's nothing else, I'll be going now. I don't want to take the chance of missing him."

When there was no reply, Whit tipped his hat and said, "Many thanks. It means a lot to me to be able to find my brother again. And if you don't mind my saying so, Tricia, he's a fool if he doesn't come back to you."

With a farewell to Chantalle, Whit turned toward the door.

Simon seethed as he hid in the heavily forested area behind Chantalle's bordello, looking at the bright lights that seemed to dance in the windows. If he were not so determined ... if he did not feel compelled to satisfy at least a part of the fury burning inside him, he knew he would not be standing in the shadows as the nighttime dampness deepened, wearing the clothes of a common cowpoke as insects feasted on his tender skin.

He had prepared for this moment very carefully. He had left his office shortly after Drew Hawk's visit, and had gone directly to see Dr. Bellow. The reserved, aristocratic physician who catered to the high-toned members of his social set had raised his eyebrows when Simon had presented his mangled hand for treatment, saying simply that he had caught it in a drawer.

Simon grimaced at the memory of Dr. Bellow's painful examination. The unsmiling physician had straightened out each one of his fingers and had then announced that none of the digits appeared to be broken—only badly bruised.

Simon glanced at the bandage that covered his hand, aware that it stiffened his movement severely. He had gone straight from the doctor's office to his home, where he had made his presence felt by demanding numerous attentions from his servants. He had then pretended to go to bed, had waited until his servants had retired for the night, had dressed with great difficulty in the common clothing he was presently wearing, and had left without being seen on a horse from his stable that he had saddled himself. He patted the gunbelt on his hips. Fortunately, he was almost as good a shot with his left hand as with his right. He had no worries there.

Neither had he feared that he would arrive too late to accomplish his purpose. He knew exactly what was going to happen. The routine at the bordello rarely varied.

As if confirming that thought, the light at Chantalle's back door went dark. It would not be much longer now.

Simon smiled when the back door finally opened a crack and a familiar figure slid out onto the steps— and after a swift look around, moved down the stairs and into the shadows among the trees. Within a few moments Simon saw the flicker of a match being struck, then the glow of a cigarette in the darkness.

Simon snickered. Although cigarettes of *that type*

were not allowed in Chantalle's house, he knew several similar houses where they were tolerated. Those houses, of course, were not of the caliber of Chantalle's, but the habit, once formed, was difficult to break. He relied on that fact, and on the smoker's distracted state that would soon follow.

Simon moved silently through the darkness until he reached the spot where the cigarette glowed in the shadows. He saw the dark-haired slut who lounged against the tree there, and his jaw clenched tight. He was beside her in a moment, jamming his gun against her side, ignoring her gasp as he said softly, "Fancy meeting you here, Angie. Are you enjoying the night air?"

Angie turned toward him, her eyes wide with fear. He saw her gulp as she dropped her cigarette, doing her best to ignore the gun he kept tight against her ribs as she said, "Simon ... I ... I was wondering when I'd see you again now that Chantalle's barred you from the house. I've been missing you."

"Missing me?" Simon snickered again. Her face was lit with a shaft of moonlight, and her fear was obvious as he replied, "I find that hard to believe, since you're the one who called Jake down on me to make sure I would leave the house the last time I was here."

"No, I didn't, Simon. I didn't have anything to do with it."

"I saw you at the base of the staircase, watching as Jake came up to threaten me."

"No ... no! I tried to stop him. I tried to tell him that he shouldn't interfere."

"How did he know Chantalle was trying to make me

leave? He was behind the bar. He couldn't hear anything from there."

"Somebody must've told him."

"Somebody? That somebody was you."

"It wasn't me." Angie took a breath and said unconvincingly, "You know how I feel about the fun we have together. I don't have any other regulars like you."

"You don't have me anymore, either, Angie."

Angie's smile wavered as she moved her hand toward the gun at her ribs and said, "If you put that thing away, I'll show you how wrong you are, Simon—right here where nobody will bother us."

"Really?" Simon paused. "That sounds good. Let me see ... take down your bodice and we'll get started."

Angie nodded stiffly and raised a hand to her shoulder. In a flash of movement, he slapped her hard and she fell a few staggering steps backward. Her eyes were wide, and he smiled at the sight of the blood that streamed from the corner of her mouth. "You didn't move fast enough, Angie. Hurry up."

Angie slipped one shoulder free and Simon struck her again, knocking her back against the tree behind her. Sobbing, she looked up at him as blood began streaming from her nose and he said, "I'm waiting, Angie."

Angie pushed her other shoulder free. Her bodice slid downward as Simon punched her in the stomach, sending her reeling onto her back. She was crying between gasps for air when he ordered, "Get up! Get up on your feet or you'll be sorry."

Watching as Angie stood up unsteadily, he hissed, "Bitch! You were the one who ran to get Jake. If not for you, I would have backed Chantalle down as I've done countless times before, and I would have been spared the humiliation of slinking away like a whipped dog."

Angie swayed weakly and Simon stared at her. Her formerly upswept hair was disheveled and littered with twigs and leaves. Her dress was similarly littered and stained with dirt. Her nose and mouth were swollen and bleeding profusely. The side of her face was bruised, and it looked to him like her front teeth were broken, adding to the gushing red streams that ran down her neck to streak her bared breasts.

"Who feels like a whipped dog now, Angie?" When she responded with only a whimper, Simon said, "Answer me!"

"I'm sorry, Simon." Angie's eyes rolled strangely as she said, "I didn't mean anything. I was mad, that's all. I won't do it again, I promise."

His grim smile fading, Simon whispered, "You're right, Angie. You won't do it again, because you won't dare—because I'm going to teach you how it will be next time."

Raising the gun in his bandaged hand, Simon whipped it hard across Angie's jaw, sneering as the blow lifted her off her feet and sent her sprawling backward.

He heard the crack when her head hit a sharp object. He saw her go still. He waited for her to move, but she did not.

Simon leaned over her. Her eyes wide open, she lay motionless. She wasn't breathing.

The witch was dead!

Simon took a backward step and straightened up with a look of contempt. Damn her, she had cheated him of total satisfaction, after all!

Simon took another step away, then turned around and walked toward his horse.

So she was dead.

Nobody would lament her passing.

Drew moved quietly around the shabby hotel room as he prepared for bed. He was tired and his leg ached. He'd had a long day confronting portions of his life that had been too painful to review.

The first thing he had accomplished was to come to terms with the painful memories that had swamped him as he climbed Gault Shipping and Receiving.

The second thing was that in doing so, he had confirmed in his mind that Simon Gault was everything Chantalle had claimed him to be—and more. He had only to look into Gault's eyes to see the man's guilt openly displayed.

The third was to have seen Jenna Leigh again.

The fourth ... Drew's strong shoulders momentarily sagged. He would have said he had confirmed his determination to keep Tricia safe by keeping his distance from her, but as night fell, the last thing in his mind was to stay away from her. He wanted to talk to her, to be near her, to hold her close.

Straightening at the sound of a knock on his door, Drew reached for his gun and said, "Who is it?"

"A friend."

A friend?

Drew walked cautiously toward the door. He had

plenty of enemies but very few friends, especially any who would hesitate to give their names. Standing clear of the entrance, he jerked the door open, then stepped back wordlessly when he saw the tall man standing there.

Drew swallowed. His heartbeat thundered and a roaring began in his ears when the fellow spoke in a deep voice that registered familiarly in his mind.

"I've been looking for you, Drew. It's been a long time with a lot of miles in between, but I'm damned glad that I finally found you."

His breathing choked, Drew did not immediately respond.

"It's really me, Drew. It's Whit."

Drew blinked. He took a breath. He was uncertain which of them made the first move as they hugged each other roughly, mumbling incoherently for a few moments before they stepped apart in an attempt to gain control of the powerful emotions of the moment.

Drew's glance was touched with incredulity when he managed gruffly, "Truth is, I never expected to see you again, Whit. Even when Chantalle said you were alive, I couldn't make myself believe her."

"I know." Suddenly grinning despite the glaze of moisture in his eyes, Whit slapped him heartily on the shoulder and said, "Damn, it's good to see you—even if the circumstances that bring us together aren't so fine." He halted, then said cautiously, "About Jenna Leigh ..."

Drew's grin dimmed. "I saw her. She's as beautiful as I always knew she'd be."

"She hasn't changed, either."

"I don't know about that. I didn't talk to her."

"What?"

Suddenly sober, Drew responded, "I'd like to say that things haven't changed, but they have, Whit. I'm not the same boy you left at the orphanage all those years ago. Things happen to change a man when he matures."

"You mean the war."

"I fought for the Confederacy—proudly, I might add—but I saw too much to forget those soldiers who fought beside me and didn't come home."

"A lot of Yankees didn't go home, either."

Drew's expression hardened. "That's right. Some of them came here and married our women."

"It wasn't like that with Jenna Leigh, Drew. Clay— Colonel Madison—is a fine man even if he is part of the martial law in Galveston." Whit's expression grew pained as he said, "I didn't fight in the war. I couldn't seem to choose one side over the other like some fellas did. I figured I wouldn't make it my war."

Drew responded stiffly, "I had no trouble choosing the color of the uniform I wore."

"Maybe so, but the war's over."

"Not for me."

"You mean because you're wanted by the Yankees."

"You know about that?" Drew paused. "I suppose Jenna Leigh does, too."

"She knows. She also knows you're in Galveston, but her husband doesn't."

Drew did not respond.

"It isn't easy for Jenna Leigh, Drew. She was ecstatic

when she learned you were alive and she was determined to clear you of all charges … but Clay is her husband."

"A Yankee."

"A Yankee who knows what it is to have lost somebody in that war. Clay's brother fought for the Confederacy. He was one of your fellow soldiers who didn't come back."

Drew remained silent.

"Clay is a Yankee, but he wants the war to be over and done. He's determined to restore normalcy in Galveston so he can resume the legal duties he was trained for, but it hasn't been easy for him, either. Jenna Leigh was one of his most outspoken opponents when he came here."

"It looks like he won her over, though."

Drew's frigid tone drew a frown to Whit's face as he said, "You can hold on to your anger if you want, Drew, but right now we've got a bigger problem to face, whether you know it or not."

"I know. His name is Simon Gault."

Whit stared at him for a silent moment before responding, "I don't really know if Gault hates me personally, or if he just hates everybody bearing the Hawk name."

"I talked to him today, you know."

"You what?"

"I went to see him in his office—the office that used to belong to our father."

"Pa lost that office … he lost that shipping business all by himself. Gault had nothing to do with it."

"I know, but I can't help thinking Pa's influence has

something to do with the way Gault is acting right now."

"Maybe."

"That's what I was thinking when I decided I needed to meet him and find out for myself if he was the kind of man who could be responsible for everything bad that's happened."

Whit stiffened. "What did you decide?"

Drew gave a low snort. "It wasn't hard. That fella hated me from the minute he laid eyes on me—maybe even before. I didn't need any more than a few minutes with him to see that. The fact that he tried to pull a gun on me spoke for itself, too."

"He pulled a gun on you?"

"I said *he tried*. It didn't work out."

"Meaning?"

"Meaning he's going to have a sore hand for a while. I took that opportunity to give him fair warning that if he ever touched anybody important to me again, it would be the last time."

Whit nodded, and then said, "That's all well and good, but Gault's vicious. He's also determined."

"Like I said, I've given him fair warning."

Whit straightened up. Linking his hard-eyed gaze with Drew's, he said, "Well, I figure two Hawks are better than one when it comes to defending the family name."

Drew smiled at that. His smile faded when Whit added, "In the meantime, there's somebody you need to talk to about where she stands right now."

Drew stopped Whit before he could go any further. His gaze was unyielding when he said, "I'm not your little brother anymore, Whit. What's between Tricia and me is our business—but I'll tell you this just so you'll understand. My best friend was killed a little while after we arrived in Galveston, and it'll be a cold day in hell before anybody can convince me that his connection to me had nothing to do with it. I won't take the chance that somebody will try to get to me through Tricia. I won't take that chance with her safety."

"That's her decision."

"No, it's mine."

Whit shrugged his powerful shoulders. "Well, you're going to have to tell her that, then, because she's waiting outside in the hall to talk to you."

Silent, unable to move when Whit turned and walked out the door, Drew was still staring in that direction when Tricia stepped into sight.

"Are you glad to see me, Drew?" she asked softly.

Still motionless, Drew did not respond. Was he glad to see her? He wondered if she knew how she looked framed in that shabby doorframe with the light from the hallway glinting on her fair hair, and her exquisite features drawn into an uncertain expression. He wondered if she knew how desperately he wanted to close the distance between them and take her into his arms to reassure her ... how he wanted to feel her close ... how he wanted to shut that door behind her and bury himself inside her.

He also wondered if she knew that despite all that he was determined to keep her at arm's length.

When he did not immediately respond to her question, Tricia took a step toward him and whispered, "It wasn't hard to find you, you know. Fellas talk real freely in a bordello and everybody knows you've been questioning people on the docks about Simon. I can understand what you're trying to do … to find out. What I don't understand is why you left me without saying good-bye."

Suddenly aware that they were becoming the object of inquisitive looks from passersby in the hallway, Drew took Tricia's arm and pulled her inside as he closed the door behind them. "You shouldn't be here. People will get the wrong idea."

"What do you mean?" Tricia challenged him boldly. "They'll think Chantalle's daughter is going into business on her own, or maybe that she's a determined whore out to get her man?"

"Don't talk like that."

"Why not, Drew? That's the way I feel right now." Taking a step closer, she said more softly, "But you could change all that with just a few words.

When Drew still did not respond, Tricia said hoarsely, "You're going to have to say it, Drew. I need to hear you say good-bye or I—"

Unable to bear a moment more of Tricia's uncertainty, Drew scooped her into his arms and covered her mouth with his. He heard her soft gasp when their lips touched—or was it his gasp? He felt her melt against him, and his kiss surged deeper. He was lost in the wonder of all that Tricia was. He was quivering with wanting her when a sudden thud in the hallway preceded the sound of voices raised in a drunken argument, and reality returned.

Breathless as he pushed Tricia away from him, he whispered, "This isn't the way I want things to be for us, Tricia. I don't want you here in a place where your safety is protected by a flimsy lock on the door. I want you surrounded by people who value you, who will protect you with their lives. I want to know you're as safe as you can be."

Her voice turbulent with emotion, Tricia replied, "I'll be safe if you take me with you."

"That's not true. I can't even assure my own safety at present, but with Whit … with the two of us walking side by side or fighting back to back, we will be as safe as we possibly can be." Drew saw the tears that filled Tricia's eyes as he whispered, "But if you need to hear the words, here they are. Yes, even though I'm angry that you came, I'm glad to see you. Yes, I want you. Yes, it's the hardest thing I've ever done to keep my distance from you at this minute, but I also know it's necessary if I'm ever going to get to the bottom of what's been going on since I arrived in Galveston." Pausing, he whispered, "Do you understand what I'm saying, Tricia? Just like you, I need to hear the words, and I need to hear them now."

Drew noted the moment when Tricia's expression started to change. Sobering, she raised her chin. Her eyes filled with love, she whispered, "I understand. I don't like it, but I understand that this is something you and Whit need to do together." A quivering smile moved across her lips as she said, "I admit that I feel better knowing that Whit will be watching your back and you'll be watching his. I figure that the two of you are a formidable force, and I couldn't ask for more—except for it to be over."

Nodding, Drew took Tricia's arm. "Come on, I'd better take you back to Chantalle's right now ... before I change my mind."

Tricia did not reply when Drew steered her toward the door.

Whit started toward them with an uncertain expression when they stepped down into the lobby. Drew said, "I'm going to take Tricia back to Chantalle's, where she'll be safe. If you want to use my room for the night, we'll have a chance to talk when I get back."

"That's fine with me." Whit tipped his hat to Tricia and started up the staircase as she and Drew moved toward the door.

A short time later, Tricia was pushing open the door to her room as Drew commented, "Your door is unlocked. You should lock it."

"Why? I'm safe here."

"Tricia, please ... make sure you lock it from now on."

Nodding, Tricia entered and turned up the lamp. He saw the tears that glinted in her eyes as she said, "Thank you for bringing me home, Drew. I know you worry about me, but I don't want that. I'm safe here, so you can do what you have to do. I'll be waiting."

Moving closer to her, he looked down into her pale face. He brushed away a tear that had slipped from the corner of her eye as he murmured, "You said you needed to hear the words. I need to say them, too." He took a breath and whispered, "I love you, Tricia. You're my angel. You always will be."

Tricia replied in a trembling voice, "I love you, too, Drew ... so very much."

Drew enveloped Tricia's slenderness in his embrace.

The last remnants of his control slipped away when she raised her mouth to his and he kissed her passionately, lovingly ... and nudged the door closed behind them.

Chapter Twelve

The constant click-clacking of the wheels continued in the predawn darkness outside the train window. Lying wakefully in a small stateroom as the train made its way unerringly toward Galveston, Jason looked down at Elizabeth. She was dozing in his arms, having been lulled to sleep by the steady rocking of their coach, but he had not been similarly affected.

As the sun began to rise, Jason studied Elizabeth's emotionless expression, hardly able to believe that she wore his ring and bore his name, and that she was now officially his to love for the rest of their lives.

Their wedding in New York had been a simple affair attended by Mother Ella's servants ... and Trevor. It had been intended to be conducted in the elegance of the downstairs parlor, but was held at the last minute in Mother Ella's bedroom when she became too ill to be moved. To the old woman's obvious joy, Elizabeth had worn Ella's ecru bridal gown. Jason cherished the memory of the woman's joyful smile when Elizabeth and he exchanged their vows, and he knew he would never forget the moment when Ella drew him down toward her and whispered, "You're a good man, Jason. I can rest now that I know you'll take care of Elizabeth and she'll never have to suffer alone the nightmares that plague her. Thank you for that. Thank you for giving me peace."

It had been difficult to say good-bye.

Elizabeth stirred, and Jason frowned. So many uncertainties awaited them in Galveston. Elizabeth still had no memory of her childhood. If Chantalle was correct and Elizabeth's pendant did bear the same crest as the ring that Whit Hawk had shown her, Elizabeth might soon be reunited with a member of the family that she had gone to the city seeking. Jason had not yet said anything to Elizabeth about that possibility fearful of raising a hope that might cause her more pain if it were dashed.

He had written to Chantalle, telling her the approximate date of their return and had asked her to arrange to have his quarters readied for them. He could only hope that the mystery of the crests would have been settled by the time they arrived.

Weighing heavily on Jason's mind, however, was his certainty that Simon Gault's collaboration with the enemy during the war, had resulted in the deaths of dozens of innocent seamen—his dear friend Byron Mosley included. He had sworn that he would expose Gault and achieve justice for his victims, however belatedly, and he did not intend to forsake that vow.

His congenial relationship with the men of the Galveston consortium had also led him to believe that, for some reason, Gault was trying to convince them that Houston was not a threat to Galveston's commercial future—when he knew the exact opposite to be true. Jason needed to find out why before it was too late.

Jason watched as Elizabeth stirred again. She opened her eyes slowly. The gold and green sparks in their depths came to life when she asked, "What are you thinking, Jason?"

Overwhelmed by his love for her, he whispered, "That's a secret."

"A secret?" Elizabeth's gaze dropped briefly to his lips. "I thought we didn't have secrets from each other anymore."

"You're partially right. It's no secret how much I love you, but the *mystery* of the many ways that I intend to prove my love still remains."

Chuckling when Elizabeth flushed, Jason continued, "We can look forward to solving that mystery over the years to come, Elizabeth, but right now we need to think about getting our things together. We'll reach Galveston in a few hours."

"Galveston ..." Elizabeth's expression became uncertain. "I have a strange feeling ..." Elizabeth forced a smile before continuing, "I'm glad you maintained contact with Chantalle while I tended to Mother Ella's affairs. I'm happy that we're returning to the city, but—I can't explain why—I feel a strange sense of dread, almost as if one wrong move and our future together will be threatened."

"Elizabeth—"

"It's foolish, I know."

"No, it isn't foolish, but I'll make you a promise." Earnest, Jason whispered, "You don't have to worry about the unknown, because I'll be at your side whatever happens—and I'll protect you with my life."

"I'm not asking that, Jason! I don't want you to risk your life for any reason."

When Jason did not reply, Elizabeth continued as earnestly as he, "Jason ... you're the most important person in my life. The future would stretch out black and cheerless for me if you weren't there to share it with me."

"Elizabeth—"

"It isn't *my* future that I look forward to. It's *our* future."

Our future.

Those two words rang in Jason's mind as the train continued rocking along the tracks. Emotion a hard knot in his throat, he was momentarily unable to voice a response. Strangely enough, a sense of dread similar to the feelings that Elizabeth had described had been the cause of his wakefulness through the night, but he did not dare to confess that thought to her. He had no desire to add fear to her list of uncertainties.

Those concerns foremost in his mind, Jason drew Elizabeth closer. He loved her. Now, while she lay in his arms, he wanted to show her that he'd meant every word he'd said.

Wordlessly, lovingly, Jason covered Elizabeth's lips with his.

* * *

Drew came abruptly awake at the sound of movement in the hallway outside Tricia's bedroom door. Momentarily disoriented, he reviewed the events of the night past—his highly emotional reunion with Whit, and then the long hours of loving he had spent with Tricia in his arms.

At the sound of footsteps racing past the door, Drew threw back the coverlet and reached for his clothes. He glanced at the window, where an early morning sun was shining brightly, then hushed Tricia when she sat up in bed questioningly. He dressed quickly, reached for his gun, and looked back at Tricia as she drew her wrapper closed around her. He motioned her out of harm's way as he unlocked the door silently and pulled it open.

Startled to see Chantalle standing there in her flowered robe, he asked, "What's going on, Chantalle?"

Chantalle swallowed and responded hoarsely, "I was just going to knock. I thought you were here. I heard you come in with Tricia last night." She paused, and then said in a rush, "It's Angie, Drew. Will just found her body in the woods beside the house. She's dead. Somebody killed her."

Expressionless, Drew asked, "How do you know it wasn't an accident?"

"She was half dressed, and somebody had beaten her badly."

Drew heard the sound of distress that escaped Tricia's lips. She rushed to Chantalle and hugged her tightly. He heard her whisper, "I'm so sorry, Chantalle. I know Angie was a problem sometimes, but—"

"But she was one of my girls and I let her down."

Dislodging herself gently from the consolation of Tricia's embrace, Chantalle said self-accusingly, "It was my duty to protect her, and I failed."

"It wasn't your fault, Chantalle." Trembling as they approached, Georgia, Lily, and Mavis halted teary-eyed beside Chantalle. Mavis continued, "We all knew about Angie's nightly ritual—that she sneaked out the back door and slipped into the woods to smoke her *cigarettes* every night before she went to sleep. We tried to tell her she was crazy to take the chance, that it wasn't safe—especially after Willie was killed—but she said nobody ever saw her."

"Why didn't you tell me?"

Mavis replied apologetically, "We knew your rules, and we knew how Angie was. None of us wanted to make her mad, because we were sure she'd make us pay somehow."

"Have you notified the authorities about Angie's death?" Drew asked Chantalle.

She nodded. "I sent Will directly to the Adjutant General's Office. Colonel Madison should be here any minute with his men. I left Carlos with Angie's body in the meantime."

Drew mumbled, "First Willie ... now Angie." He said tightly, "You can't leave the rear entrance of the house open anymore, Chantalle."

Chantalle nodded. She swayed uncertainly, and Drew slid a steadying arm around her. "Come on, I'll take you back to your room."

"No, I'm all right."

Drew scrutinized Chantalle's determined expression

and inwardly marveled. She would not allow herself to give in to weakness.

Tricia moved closer to Chantalle to provide support, and Drew said softly, "You know I can't be seen here when Colonel Madison comes, Chantalle. I can't afford to give him a reason to look into my background."

"I understand. Do what you have to do to keep yourself safe. I'll take care of everything here." She turned toward the women beside her and said, "Come on, girls."

Chantalle started back down the hallway with her women, and Drew turned toward Tricia. He said brusquely, "I need to bring Whit up to date on what happened. We'll get to the bottom of this, Tricia. I promise you that." His expression tight, he whispered, "In the meantime, I want you to lock your door behind you when you enter your room, and lock it when you leave, do you understand? I don't want you to leave it open—ever."

"You don't have to worry, Drew. Chantalle will lock the rear door just as you said."

"I want you to lock *your* door, too. Promise me!"

"All right, I promise."

"I have to leave now." Drew hesitated, and then whispered hoarsely, "Never doubt that I love you, Tricia, or that I'll be back for you."

His head snapping up at the sound of a military command being issued in the backyard, Drew kissed Tricia swiftly. He looked down at the key that Tricia had pressed into his hand.

"It's a key to my door, but it works on the rear door, too." Tricia continued softly, "Chantalle had an extra one made for me a long time ago. She may have forgotten, but I never did. It made me feel like I belonged to somebody, and I've never been without it ... until now." She swallowed and then whispered, "Come back whenever you can, Drew. Whenever you do, I'll be waiting."

Kissing her swiftly, Drew moved down the staircase toward the front door with a silent vow to return.

Simon sat still and silent in his customary place at the graceful mahogany table in Willard Spunk's office conference room. He didn't like the fact that the Galveston consortium meeting had been called so early in the morning—especially since he hadn't received notification until the last minute. He noted that although bright shafts of morning sunlight lit the office cheerfully, the room was unnaturally silent as the members took their places without the casual small talk and greetings normally exchanged around the table. As far as he was concerned, that was fine. He didn't feel like talking either.

Willard, short, balding, middle-aged, and with an occasional eye for the ladies that went ignored by most, was a conservative "city father" who was generally well respected. Simon had always enjoyed an amiable relationship with Willard, who considered him one of the city's foremost businessmen. That fact was evident in the deference shown to him and his opinions, and in the manner in which Willard and the other members normally accepted his advice—advice Simon gave gladly and with a feigned modesty that appeared to impress every one of them.

Yet he could not escape the feeling that today was different somehow.

Simon looked at the consortium members as they assumed their customary places at the table. Joseph Weatherby, Jonathan Grimel, Douglas Forbes, Winston Lyle, Horace Greene, Martin Long, and James Carter—all seemed to avoid his eye as Willard convened the meeting—but Simon laid his unease to his own discomfiture. He had awakened that morning exhausted and sleep-deprived because of his visit to the wooded area near Chantalle's house in the middle of the previous night. Angie's unplanned demise annoyed him. He had intended to use her further, and she had cheated him of the evening's full enjoyment. He disliked having his plans disrupted for any reason, most especially by a wanton whore who had proved unworthy of his attentions and trust.

It also annoyed him that because of his injured hand and Angie, he had arrived at Spunk's office irritable and out of sorts. The need to conceal his ill humor and to pretend a cheerful attitude did not improve his mood. He was unprepared when Willard turned toward him, his round face devoid of its usual smile, and announced that the consortium had decided against taking his advice and would not sign an agreement allocating municipal funds to cosmetic changes in the city while there was still a possibility that improvements to the harbor might be necessary.

Simon forced himself to smile. His tone gracious, he responded, "Surely you aren't concerned about the rumor presently circulating that because the facilities of Galveston harbor are limited, Houston might take over its shipping business. That's preposterous. You know very well that Galveston's natural harbor is an asset that Houston does not have and that—"

"Yes, we know all that, Simon." Willard maintained his sober demeanor as he continued, "But the consortium met at an emergency meeting yesterday and we made our decision then. We do not intend to sign any commitment that may limit our direction in the future."

"An emergency meeting to which I wasn't invited ..."

"We thought it best that way."

Simon stiffened. "Signing the agreement is a way of proving our confidence in the city ... a way of dismissing the negative rumors. I cannot stress enough—"

"You're wasting your breath, Simon. We've made our decision. This meeting was called today only to inform you before we made our decision public." Willard glanced at the forum and said abruptly, "The motion stands that we should not sign an agreement limiting changes in Galveston harbor. Does anyone second it?"

Two *yeas* sounded.

"All in favor?"

There was a chorus of assent.

Willard slapped down his gavel and said, "The motion is passed and the meeting is adjourned."

Startled by the swiftness of proceedings that totally ignored customary protocol, Simon watched as Willard headed for the door. When the other members followed, nodding wordlessly in his direction, Simon stood up slowly. The room was empty when he made his way toward the door, inwardly raging at the speed and efficiency with which his counsel had been overridden.

Houston businessmen were depending on him to facilitate the agreement that would guarantee their investment in Houston's commercial shipping. The grandiose future he had engineered for himself, and which he had believed he was only a few steps from achieving, had been snatched from his grasp—and he didn't know why!

Simon started toward Spunk's private office. Ignoring the clerk who attempted to block his entrance, he pushed open the door and said, "I demand an explanation, Willard! I think you owe me one, and I don't intend to leave until I get it."

"I don't know what you're talking about, Simon." Willard looked at him coldly. "We've all sought your advice on the future of our city, and in most cases have taken it—but not this time."

"You do realize that you and the consortium are revealing a lack of confidence in Galveston, and that lack of confidence will be transmitted to companies seeking to locate here, thereby limiting Galveston's future."

"Possibly."

"Then why do you refuse to sign the agreement?"

Willard stared at him across his massive desk. A small man, Williard appeared dwarfed by the impressive piece of furniture, but his voice was not lacking in authority as he said, "The answer to your question is simple—the members have become suspicious of your motives."

"Suspicious of—" Simon felt the blood rush to his

269

head as he said, "Could you tell me what has caused this sudden *suspicion of my motives?*"

"Talk is rife on the docks about you, Simon ... disturbing talk."

"I don't know what you mean."

"I think you do. It appears that inquiries have been made over the past few months about your activities before, during, and after the war. Negative reports have reached our ears recently that disturb us greatly."

"Rumors? Is that what you're talking about?"

"More than rumors."

"Anything that is claimed without proof is a rumor."

"Perhaps ... and perhaps proof is on the way." Willard's round face did not lose its stern expression as he continued, "The consortium prefers to err on the side of caution. We will not sign anything that might limit Galveston's future."

"Foolishness!"

Hesitating, Willard began slowly, "I think you should know that these inquiries to which I refer have loosened tongues in areas that might surprise you. Individuals who will remain unnamed by me at this time have levied some rather shocking charges against you, including collaboration ... intimidation ... unfair practices that have in some cases affected innocent lives."

"As if some of those charges have not been made against every member of the consortium at one time or another!"

"Perhaps ... but never with such uniformity and rancor."

"This is ridiculous, Willard." Changing his tone, Simon smiled as he said, "You know me well. You know

I would never stoop to the level of committing those crimes."

"Then you have nothing to fear, do you, Simon? When the Adjutant General's Office concludes its investigation, the charges will be dismissed and—"

Simon interrupted coldly, "You're telling me that someone has actually made a substantiated complaint against me and has asked the Adjutant General's Office to investigate it?"

"That appears to be the case. Actually, I was informed yesterday that the complaint would be presented first thing this morning. The members of the consortium were notified in advance, which necessitated the emergency meeting I spoke of. The complaint has been signed by men with whom we are all familiar— businessmen, captains of ships that service this port— including some of your own captains and various men and women working on the docks who have had dealings with you or your company in some way."

"Dealings with my company ... well, we both know that a man I trusted with the processing of my affairs, Bruce Carlton, was found to have a dark side of which I was not aware. Perhaps he is to blame for the problem."

"I'm afraid no one believes that, Simon. We are all aware that Bruce never made a move without your permission."

"So, what you're saying is that the sins of one of my employees have begun shading my reputation!"

Willard stood up abruptly. "Look at it this way, Simon. If you are found innocent of the charges when the investigation is completed, everyone in Galveston will owe you an apology. You'll be able to write your own ticket."

"Of course. There is always a bright side, isn't there?" He stared at Willard coldly. "I suppose there is nothing more for us to discuss."

Not waiting for Willard's reply, Simon stomped out of the office with his head high. His postures stiff, he climbed into his carriage and ordered sharply, "Take me home."

The carriage snapped into motion as Simon silently railed at his realization that life as he knew it in Galveston was beginning to crumble.

But he wasn't finished yet.

Colonel Clay Madison stood with military erectness in the backyard of Chantalle Beauchamp's bordello. He glanced at the madam, who stood silently nearby, her beautiful daughter at her side as his men searched the area. Without her customary makeup, Chantalle's face was pale and her matronly frame was wracked with intermittent shivers. He had already interviewed her and the members of her house, but he had gained little pertinent information. One thing was certain. She and the members of her house had been shocked and frightened by Angie's death, but Chantalle was determined to stay and learn all she could about it.

The backyard went abruptly silent as Clay's men brought forward a fellow they'd found sleeping off a drunk behind several crates in the rear of the yard.

Clay asked with a darkening frown, "What is your name, sir?"

"Charlie Frisk." Seeming confused, Charlie turned

toward Chantalle and said, "You know who I am, Chantalle. There ain't no law that says a man can't get some sleep where and when he feels like it. You didn't need to go calling in the army."

Clay responded before Chantalle could speak, "You're right, there's no law that says a man can't get some sleep where and when he wants to, except when he's trespassing on private property. But that's beside the point right now. What I'd like to know is what you're doing in Chantalle's backyard. Chantalle doesn't cater to excessive drinking in her establishment, so you probably didn't get drunk in her house."

"That's right, I didn't." Charlie continued, "Chantalle won't let me in her house if I've had a few too many, but I don't hold no grudge against her for that. Hell, she don't bar me from the place when I'm sober, and I understand her rule."

"So, what are you doing here?"

Charlie shrugged. "I started out drinking with a few friends last night, and before I knew it, I wasn't in no condition to walk in Chantalle's front door. I guess I figured I'd sleep it off for a few hours and go in later." He winked. "I think that sweet Lily girl has a weakness for me, you know? Anyways, it didn't happen. When I woke up, the lights in the house were out, and I realized it was too late to pay Lily a visit. I started to doze again when the back door opened and Angie slipped out. She went into the woods to smoke."

"And?"

"She was smoking one of *them* cigarettes that Chantalle don't abide. That didn't bother me none, though, and I was thinking of joining her, but then that other fella showed up."

"What other fella?"

"He wasn't dressed in one of them high-falutin' outfits he usually wears. He was dressed in plain cowboy duds—you know, travel pants, a cotton shirt, and a trail hat. He was even wearing a gunbelt. He looked like a common cowpoke—except that his hand was all bandaged. Anyways, when I saw him, I figured Angie and him had arranged to meet, so I just turned over and went back to sleep."

"You didn't hear anything after that?"

"I heard Angie make a few sounds, but I figured it was none of my business. I know she likes it rough sometimes. I figured they'd be busy for a while, so I just nodded off."

"You recognized this man? You can identify him?"

"Sure I can. It was that Simon Gault fella." Clay heard Chantalle gasp as Charlie continued, "Everybody in Galveston knows him, but there ain't many who know about his late-night visits here."

"You're sure it was Simon Gault?"

"I couldn't miss him. The moon was real bright for a few minutes just about the time he stepped out from behind a tree, and I saw him as clear as if it was daylight. Then they kind of moved a little deeper into the shadows, and I figured I knew the reason why." Charlie paused and then asked, "So what's this all about anyways?"

Clay watched the man's expression as he responded, "Angie was found murdered in the wooded area last night."

"W-what?" Charlie took an involuntary backward step. "I didn't have nothing to do with that!"

Clay did not respond.

"Ask that Gault fella what happened. I saw him, I tell you. His hand was bandaged like he'd been in a fight or something. Check it out with him and you'll see."

"You can rest assured that we will. In the meantime ..." Turning to his sergeant, Clay ordered, "Take this man into custody until we can question him further, and then go to Simon Gault's house and take him into custody for questioning."

"Hey, you can't do this!" Charlie was still protesting as he was dragged away.

When two of Clay's men were dispatched to Gault's house, Chantalle said tightly, "Simon won't stand for being taken into custody, you know."

"I don't think he'll have much choice. Sergeant Walker told me on the way here that an affidavit was delivered to my office this morning charging Gault with numerous crimes committed over a long duration and requesting that my office investigate the matters thoroughly. To be honest, I never did believe Gault's story about his being unaware of Bruce Carlton's *darker side*."

Clay watched as Chantalle took a deep breath. He asked, "Do you have something to add to all this, Chantalle?"

"Not right now."

Clay glanced at Tricia. Her delicate features twitched when he asked, "What about you, ma'am?"

"I have nothing to add, either."

Hesitating only a moment, Clay said, "I won't press either of you for any further information about Gault at this time, but I think you should know that I will be back when I've had a chance to sort out all the charges."

Chantalle responded, "We'll be here."

Clay studied Chantalle and her daughter a moment longer. Tricia's demeanor was tense. She had responded only when addressed directly. A second sense told him there was more to this story than was evident. He suspected that the affidavit accusing Gault of past crimes was crucial to the present case somehow. He did not want to act without reading it first.

With that thought in mind, Clay issued a few clipped orders, nodded respectfully toward the two women, and started toward the street.

One thing was sure. He would be back.

Simon sat stiffly as his carriage traveled through streets beginning to teem with the activities of the day. The sun beamed down relentlessly, raising the heat in the carriage to a suffocating degree, but Simon was unconscious of the discomfort. He had directed his driver to take a circuitous route to his office that would allow him more time to get his emotions under control. He had felt defiled when he'd left Willard's office and returned home, where he had bathed and changed his clothes, hoping he could clear his mind of the panic beginning to overwhelm him.

Simon's mind raced: So, the consortium had received information about an affidavit that had been delivered to the Adjutant General's Office that morning; in it, *in-*

dividuals unnamed by Spunk had charged him with past crimes and had asked that office to investigate the situation.

Those *unnamed individuals* were no doubt clearly named in the affidavit. They must be persons who could provide some proof of their accusations or Willard and his crew would not have turned so completely against him. Yet he could not allow panic to overwhelm him. First he needed to find out how serious the charges were.

Fury flashed as Simon silently ranted. The men of the consortium had treated him shabbily! After all he had done for them, they had not even allowed him to defend himself! He would see that each one of those men paid for his treachery. He would make sure that before he left Galveston, he—

Simon's thoughts came to an abrupt halt as his carriage turned onto the far end of the docks and he saw a military contingent entering his office. He swallowed incredulously. There could be only one reason for the fact that Colonel Madison was not among them. The bastard had obviously ordered his men to arrest him.

All was lost!

Aware that he could not waste a moment, Simon rapped sharply on the carriage wall and called out, "Turn around! I've changed my mind. Take me back home."

Simon's heart pounded as the carriage wheeled obediently and began moving rapidly in the opposite direction. No, he would not suffer the humiliation of being arrested. He had secret sizable accounts in Houston. He would flee before anyone could catch up with him. He would pick up his money, change his name as he had done once before, and relocate to another place. The West was wide. He could make a new life for himself.

Still, Simon seethed. Everything would be all right in the end—he would make sure of that—but the present infuriated him. He knew exactly when everything had started to fall apart for him in Galveston—when everything had started spinning out of control—and he knew the individuals who were responsible.

Their names were Hawk.

The Hawk name haunted him, but he would not allow it to follow him any longer! He needed to shake the dust of the past from his heels forever.

The solution was simple.

He would accomplish it without delay.

Chapter Thirteen

Elizabeth was startled when the train whistle shattered the silence of the compartment. She looked out the window at the fading light of late afternoon. An unexpected delay had made the last few hours interminable, and a vague apprehension had started crawling up her spine.

She glanced back to see Jason's light eyes intent on her. He was frowning, and she knew he was worried about her. In an attempt to reassure him, she said, "We'll be reaching Galveston anytime now. I'm anxious to get back so we can settle the unfinished business we left behind."

Coming to her in a few steps, Jason looked down at her. His expression concerned, he said, "I don't know if we're making the right move coming back here so soon. You've only just started feeling like your old self again."

"Jason, I'm fine. I recuperated from my wound a long time ago."

"If you say so."

"I'm fine," she repeated.

Gathering her closer, Jason whispered, "I almost lost you once, darlin'. The memory of that day is too fresh in my mind to dismiss easily."

"You don't have to worry anymore. Milton Stowe is dead, and Aunt Sylvia …" Unable to finish that statement, Elizabeth continued, "You have business of your own to finish up in Galveston, and maybe—just maybe—I'll be able to discover something about my past, just as Mother Ella and I hoped."

Jason did not reply. Instead he stroked her fair cheek as he said, "It's important for you to remember your childhood, isn't it?"

"It is." Elizabeth whispered ardently, "It's not because I don't love you enough, Jason. I do. I love you more than I ever thought possible, but now—especially since Mother Ella is gone—I need to finish what I started. She wanted me to be able to remember, and I need to know for myself if there might be somebody out there who's looking for me, too."

"And if you find someone?"

Elizabeth clutched the pendant she wore against her skin and whispered, "Then we'll all be a family, Jason. I'll have blood ties to share with you."

"And if you don't?"

Hesitating only briefly, Elizabeth said, "If I don't … I'll know for sure that there's nobody else for me to share with you. I'll mourn that loss, but that won't affect my love for you. It never could."

"Elizabeth ..."

His voice breaking, Jason crushed her close. He was about to speak again when the train whistle screeched, drowning out his attempt. Waiting until the series of long blasts finally ended, he heaved a sigh and said, "I guess that means we'll be in Galveston soon."

Elizabeth swallowed. Responding to the sudden fluttering in her chest, she kissed Jason's mouth lightly.

"I love you, Jason."

Jason's throat choked tight. That was all he'd ever need to know.

The lights of Galveston twinkled as the long day wound down into darkness, and Tricia worked at Polly's side to settle the bordello kitchen for another day. The inhabitants of the house had been sober and occasionally tearful, but the business of Chantalle's establishment had continued unabated. It was a source of amazement to Tricia that the same women who had shaken with fear earlier in the day when Angie's body was discovered, had descended from their rooms as evening approached, ready and willing to greet their customers.

Tricia realized, however, that the same could not be said for Chantalle. Outwardly the same madam of old, extravagantly dressed and with makeup carefully applied, she was nevertheless unable to hide the anxiety in her eyes, and Tricia's heart ached for her.

Glancing up at the clock on the kitchen wall, Tricia sighed. In a few hours the lights of the house would be turned out, ending a day that had started out in tragedy but which had somehow continued on.

Angie's battered body had been taken to the funeral parlor and Chantalle had agreed to pay the cost of burying her. The services had been arranged, but that was as far as anything had been settled. Colonel Madison had sent men to take Simon Gault into custody, but Simon was nowhere to be found. When Colonel Madison returned to talk to Chantalle, Tricia had had as little contact as possible with him, for fear of saying something that might make him turn his attention toward Drew; but Chantalle told her that Colonel Madison had stationed men at Simon's office and at his home, even though he did not expect Simon to return to either place.

Simon's obvious avoidance of being questioned, the affidavit detailing charges against him, and Charlie Frisk's testimony that he had seen Simon with Angie shortly before she was killed, had all but convinced Colonel Madison that Simon was guilty of Angie's murder and of the other crimes he was accused of. Tricia wondered, could Simon also be guilty of Willie's murder and the attempt on Drew's life—just because Whit had dealt Simon's ego a blow?

That didn't make sense.

Her head aching, Tricia raised a delicate hand to her brow. Adding to the weight of those concerns was the fact that she had not heard from Drew throughout the day, and she wasn't sure when she would see or hear from him again because of the Yankee threat hanging over him. She did not know if he had found Whit as he'd intended, if they were together, what they were doing or where they were going, and her ignorance tormented her.

And she ached from wanting to be with Drew.

"Tricia …" Tricia looked up at the sound of Chantalle's voice. She attempted a smile as Chantalle entered the kitchen and said, "We're closing our doors early tonight. Why don't you go upstairs now?"

Tricia smiled. "I need to get some headache powder from Dr. Wesley first."

"After what happened this morning, I don't think going out this time of night is a good idea, Tricia."

"You're worrying unnecessarily, Chantalle." Tricia attempted a smile. "There's no reason to fear for my safety."

"Still …" Chantalle studied the pained frown that marred Tricia's delicate brow and then said, "If you really need that powder, I'll ask Will to go with you. You'll be safe with him."

Aware that it would be senseless to disagree, Tricia nodded. "All right. Thank you. I'll get ready to go right now."

Catching up with her outside the kitchen as the lights of the house began going dark, Chantalle said softly, "I hope you understand, dear. I can't take chances with anyone's safety after what happened, most especially someone as dear to me as you are."

Unable to reply, Tricia hugged Chantalle tightly, and then headed for her room.

Drew unlocked the door to his room at the Chalfonte and waited until Whit followed him inside before pushing it closed behind him. He lit the lamp and then turned to stare at his brother in wordless frustration.

"You don't have to say it." Whit threw his hat onto

the nearby dresser and started unbuckling his gunbelt. "It's been a damned aggravating day."

Drew did not bother to concur. He had come to the Chalfonte to tell Whit about Angie's death earlier that morning and they had gone to Gault's office at the docks. They had drawn back when they saw groups gathered on the dock outside the Gault building and had seen Colonel Madison's men exit the office. It hadn't taken Whit and Drew long to discover that Colonel Madison's men had found a drunk sleeping behind the bordello when they went to investigate the murder, and that the man had seen Gault in the woods with Angie just before her murder. The fact that Gault was nowhere to be found when the military was dispatched to take him in for questioning—although he had been seen safe and sound earlier that morning— proved his guilt in the eyes of bystanders and the military alike.

Whit and he had then spent the remainder of the day canvassing the docks for information that might help them find Gault on their own, or that might help them discover a reason why Gault would have ordered the attempt on Drew's life. The effort had been a waste of precious time.

Drew glanced out the window at the darkness beyond, and his frown deepened.

"What are you thinking about, Drew?" Although separated for years, Whit and he had fallen back into the easy camaraderie of brothers. They had spent the off hours catching up on their lives, and Whit pressed knowingly, "You're thinking about Tricia, aren't you?"

Drew's gaze snapped toward him, and Whit gave a short laugh. "I guess that's my answer."

When Drew did not reply, Whit said, "If you're wondering how I know"—he shrugged—"I guess it's because I was thinking about Jackie and wishing I could be with her right now."

Drew responded, "There's nothing to stop you from going home, Whit."

"Yes, there is." Sobering, Whit said, "There's more to all this than meets the eye, and you know it. Gault has an illogical hatred for the Hawk name. He proved that fact the moment he met me, and things went downhill from there. He hated you from the second he saw you, too—which means, to my mind, that nobody who ever bore the Hawk name is safe. That includes Jenna Leigh and Laura Anne. I deserted them once, Drew. I won't do it again."

Drew nodded. He knew what it was to feel the guilt Whit bore. He shared it.

Whit shrugged. "But that doesn't mean you need to stay here tonight. Just because I'm missing Jackie, that doesn't mean you have to miss Tricia, too."

"I love her, Whit."

Whit went silent. When he spoke again, his voice was hoarse with emotion as he said, "I know what I'd do, then. I wouldn't waste my time here in this shabby room if the woman I loved was only a short ride away."

Drew considered his brother's statement. A small smile touching his lips, he grabbed his hat and left the room without speaking a word.

* * *

Tricia mounted the horse that Will held for her and then waited as Will mounted his horse. Their voices echoed toward Simon as he hid in the same wooded area where he had waited for Angie. He listened intently as Tricia told the stable hand that it shouldn't take her long to get the headache powder from Dr. Wesley, and they'd be back soon.

They rode off, and Simon sneered. Poor Tricia. She had a headache—but she'd have more than a headache before this night ended.

Glancing back at Chantalle's house as the front door opened and the last of her customers exited, Simon raised his brows. So they were closing early—to mourn Angie, no doubt. The bitch didn't deserve the honor, but the timing worked well for him.

Making his way silently toward the rear entrance, Simon glanced around him. It would take Tricia at least three-quarters of an hour to get to Dr. Wesley's office and back. He had time to spare.

Simon waited. He watched the back windows of the house as they went dark one by one. Reasonably satisfied that the private quarter of the upstairs hallway would be empty and the rest of the house would soon be settled down for the night, Simon picked up the container beside him and approached the rear entrance. The stairway was unusually dark as he ascended toward the second floor, but Simon did not falter. He was accustomed to those stairs.

He turned the knob on the back door carefully but was surprised to find it locked.

Of course. He should've expected it.

He searched his pocket for a moment, found his key

ring, and inserted an almost forgotten key into the lock. The lock turned easily. He had Angie to thank for getting him that key—a convenience she had provided in the event that Chantalle's policy of keeping the rear entrance open all night should change.

Simon snickered. He had to rescind what he had previously thought about Angie. Maybe she had been good for something after all.

Simon opened the door to the hallway slowly. Empty, it was only dimly lit. Nothing could suit his purposes more.

Turning toward the private quarter of the house, he slipped down the hallway toward Tricia's bedroom. He turned the doorknob and then froze at the realization that her door was locked. Recalling Angie's incidental comment when she had given him the key to the rear door, he inserted the key into the lock on Tricia's bedroom door. At the sound of a click, he let himself in and locked the door behind him.

Simon paused to allow his eyes to become fully accustomed to darkness relieved only by the muted glow of a small nightstand lamp. He then searched for a comfortable chair and prepared to wait. Tricia would come back soon, and he had no doubt that Drew Hawk would follow at some point during the night. The bastard wouldn't be able to stay away from her. When he had them together, he would take the first step in his careful strategy of retribution.

And before he was done—before he left Galveston for good—his revenge would be complete.

* * *

Grateful to have finally returned home, Tricia climbed the elaborately carved front staircase wearily, and then turned toward her room. Dr. Wesley had been involved in treating an emergency patient in his office when she arrived—a child with a raging fever—and she had been forced to wait longer than she had anticipated to get the powder she had come for. The result was that her head was throbbing. She could not wait to reach the solitude of her bedroom.

Halting when Chantalle opened her door as she passed, Tricia forced a smile and said, "I'm back, and Will was very patient, Chantalle. You can go to sleep now."

Chantalle looked at her assessingly and then said simply, "Call me if you need me."

Leaving her with a swift kiss on the cheek, Tricia walked down the hallway toward her room. She unlocked the door and entered, but her relieved sigh became a gasp when the cold muzzle of a gun was jammed against her ribs and a voice whispered, "I was getting tired of waiting for you."

Hardly able to breathe, Tricia turned toward Simon. She saw his hideous smile clearly in the dim light and she blinked. A tremor shook her as he asked, "You look surprised. You shouldn't be. You should've realized when you saw what happened to Angie last night that my situation in Galveston was at a turning point. And you certainly should've realized that I wouldn't leave this city without making sure that I settled all my debts first."

"Your debts?" Tricia took a breath. "I don't know what you're talking about."

"Of course, you wouldn't. You're just an innocent bystander in this affair. But you're also a key piece in the puzzle because you're so very important to Drew Hawk and Chantalle."

"To Drew and Chantalle?"

"Don't pretend you don't know what I'm talking about!" All semblance of a smile slipping away, Simon continued heatedly, "Chantalle betrayed me! She used my influence to further herself in Galveston, and then turned against me."

"That isn't the way I heard it." Unwilling to allow Simon the comfort of that delusion, Tricia replied, "According to Chantalle, she succeeded here *in spite of you*, although she was unwilling to challenge you at first."

"She's a liar! But even if that were true, it's her alliance against me with the Hawk men that doomed her."

A chill ran down Tricia's spine as she repeated, "The Hawk men ..."

"Whit and Drew." Simon's smile returned. "Dear Drew. He'll be here later, won't he? How could he not come? You've been so generous with your affections. He knows that he can come to you for comfort after the disappointments of the day."

"Disappointments—"

"Do you think I don't know that Whit and Drew have joined forces against me?" Salivating in his anger, Simon continued, "Do you honestly believe that I don't know they've been asking questions about me ... that it was they and Jason Dodd who started the inquiries into my past that resulted in an affidavit against me being delivered to the Adjutant General's Office this morning? But they won't win. They don't even stand a chance, and before this night is over, I will have avenged myself against Drew and Chantalle both."

When Tricia made a soft sound of protest, Simon hissed, "Be quiet! I admit it is regretful that you will become collateral damage along the way. Under other circumstances, we might have had some rather bright times together."

Loathing rippled down Tricia's spine as she snapped, "Never!"

His expression changing into a mask of pure hatred, Simon replied, "No, you'd rather lie in the arms of *Drew Hawk!* And that, my dear harlot, is the reason you have become my enemy."

Incredulous, Tricia managed a single word.

"Why?"

"Why? You're asking why the Hawks are my enemies?" Alerted to a sound in the corridor, Simon said, "Too bad I don't have time to answer you."

He struck out with his gun, and Tricia felt only a sharp burst of pain before darkness overwhelmed her.

Drew glanced down at the flicker of light underneath Tricia's bedroom door. The lamp was turned down, indicating that she had retired for the night. His hunger for her—the thought of slipping into bed beside her and drawing her into his arms—was almost overwhelming as he inserted his key into the door lock.

The house had been unusually dark as he approached and he had entered silently without waking anyone. He was grateful not to have been seen. He did not want to involve anyone in the problems that might follow if he had been seen—most especially Chantalle, who had been more than kind. He had no desire to awaken Tricia, either. He just needed to be near her for a little while, to hold her close so he could reassure himself that in a day filled with frustrations and uncertainty, she was still his.

Drew turned the key and entered the room. He pushed the door closed behind him. The lamp on the nightstand illuminated the bed where Tricia lay.

Drew's breath caught in his throat. Tricia lay atop the coverlet, completely clothed and unmoving. Two steps closer and he saw a bloodied cut on her forehead.

Gasping, calling out her name, he took another step just as a burst of pain exploded in his skull and he crumpled into oblivion.

Drew returned to consciousness slowly. His head ached and his body twitched with discomfort. It was difficult to breathe. He attempted to move his arms and legs, but he could not.

He opened his eyes to the darkness surrounding him—and full consciousness returned abruptly. He was lying on the floor of Tricia's room. He was gagged and bound hand and foot.

He glanced at the bed where Tricia lay to see that she was bound and gagged as well. He turned abruptly toward the darkness beside him, ignoring the pounding pain in his head as he strained to make out the figure standing in the shadows.

Realization twisted tight inside him as Simon stepped

into the lamp's circle of light and said in reply to Drew's incredulous stare, "Yes, it's me, Drew—the last person you expected to find here."

Struggling against his bonds, Drew raised his voice in muffled rage, and Simon whispered warningly, "Don't make any sound. It will be just as easy to leave you unconscious as it would be to leave you conscious and fully aware of what I'm going to do."

Drew glanced at Tricia, who lay unmoving on the bed, her eyes wide with terror. Stifling his laughter, Simon walked closer to her and said, "How do you like your hero now, Tricia Lee Shepherd? He's helpless to protect you as he no doubt promised he would. He's also helpless against *me*."

When Drew and Tricia mumbled heated protests through their gags, Simon snickered. "You're wondering what I have in mind—or are you still wondering what is motivating me?" Simon paused, obviously enjoying himself as he continued softly, "I don't have time to explain my motivation, except to say that eradicating everyone who has ever borne the Hawk name is high on my list."

When Drew tried to protest, Simon hissed, "Be quiet! I'm not going to warn you again!" In the silence that followed, Simon continued coolly, "You're wondering what my plans are. That's simple. I'm going to leave the two of you here just the way you are when I depart. I prefer it that way. It'll be easier for you both to appreciate what's happening if you're conscious. As for what I intend to do next, it's a surprise, but I don't think you'll have any difficulty realizing what it is once I've set things into motion."

Simon walked toward the door. He paused to pick up the container he had left there and then turned back toward Drew to whisper venomously, "I want you to know that *you alone* are responsible for Tricia's death, and that I intend to see to it that every one of your siblings—Whit, Jenna Leigh, and *Laura Anne*—follows you to your reward in quick succession before I leave Galveston. That is my vow."

Taking a moment to draw his emotions under control, Simon whispered, "I'm going to leave now, but I won't hold you in suspense very long. That's a promise, too."

Silent and helpless, Drew watched as Simon walked into the hallway and drew the door closed behind him. He glanced at Tricia. In obvious pain, she looked back at him helplessly, and he started struggling fiercely against his bonds.

His struggles halted at a splashing sound. His eyes widened when the smell of kerosene permeated the room, and then he struggled harder. He had worked his way toward Tricia when he heard an explosion in the hallway outside the door and then smelled the unmistakable scent of smoke.

Fire!

Rubbing his gag free on the side of the bed, Drew struck the nightstand hard with his shoulder. The glass water pitcher crashed onto the floor in jagged pieces, and he said raggedly, "Turn your hands toward me, Tricia. Hurry!"

Smoke began filling the room as he struggled to stand. Coughing, conscious of the flames that flickered underneath the door as sounds of panic on the other side escalated, he began to work a sharp edge of broken glass against the bonds at Tricia's wrists.

Losing his balance, he fell to the floor. Tricia's hands snapped free and she pulled the gag from her mouth as she sat upright and started to untie at the bonds on her feet. Wracked with coughing, she stood up at last, and then fell to her knees beside him to try to untie his bound hands.

The door burst into flames and the smoke in the room thickened. Tears streamed from Tricia's eyes, impeding her progress as she struggled to untie him. She faltered as the heat grew unbearable and Drew gasped, "Cut the rope with the broken glass!"

Tricia was swaying. She was struggling to breathe. Screams echoed from the hallway as the sound of crackling flames grew louder and smoke filled the room.

"Tricia ... concentrate. The broken glass ..."

Tricia found his wrists again at last.

Drew was barely conscious when his hands fell free and Tricia collapsed against him. Maintaining clarity with pure strength of will, Drew cradled Tricia in his arms. The wound on her forehead was bleeding profusely as her eyes flickered open, and he said above the hiss of the leaping flames, "You have to listen to me, Tricia. I'm going to open the window. The air will feed the flames and we'll only have a few moments to get out."

"The second floor ... no way out!"

Drew managed hoarsely, "Are you ready?"

At Tricia's weak response, Drew stood up and dragged her to her feet. He touched the windowpane and winced at the heat the moment before he pushed the window open and said, "Let's go!"

Flames licked at the floor behind them as Drew grasped Tricia around the waist and swung them both out the window. Grasping the vine that had worked its way up the building, Drew clung there unsteadily. He heard the sickening sound of the vine tearing loose from its roots, and they plunged downward.

He was still holding Tricia tightly when they hit the ground with a crack and everything went dark.

Jason stepped out onto the street at the sound of a fire wagon with its bell clanging. Elizabeth and he had just arrived at his quarters when the smell of smoke alerted him to the excitement outside. He glanced up at the unnatural glow that lit the night sky and then shouted to a man racing past, "What happened? What's going on?"

"It's Chantalle's house—the bordello. It's on fire!"

Chantalle …

Turning back toward Elizabeth as she rushed toward him, he said, "I'm going!"

Elizabeth was beside him when he reached the street, and Jason said heatedly, "Stay here!"

"I'm going with you!"

Unwilling to waste time in debate, Jason mounted and pulled Elizabeth up behind him.

A heavy banging on the door of his cottage interrupted Clay's late dinner with Jenna Leigh and brought him to his feet.

Responding in a few swift steps, Clay opened the door to a young corporal who said breathlessly, "Sir,

Madame Chantalle's house is on fire. The whole building is engulfed. People are trapped in there!"

Turning back toward Jenna Leigh as he reached for his hat and weapon, Clay said, "Wait here. I have to go."

Clay rushed toward his mount, which stood still saddled at the hitching rail. He looked back for Jenna Leigh and saw she was already in the yard, running toward the barn where her horse was stabled. He shouted, "I said to wait here, Jenna Leigh!"

But she disappeared inside, and his corporal was waiting.

A sense of urgency awakened Whit from a fitful sleep. At first disoriented, he glanced around the hotel room, and then frowned as the smell of smoke came through the open window. He walked unsteadily toward the open pane, going still at the sight of the blaze that illuminated the sky.

He heard the sound of running footsteps past his door and he jerked it open, shouting, "What's burning?"

"Madame Chantalle's bordello!"

Whit paled. Drew had gone there to see Tricia.

Snapping into motion, Whit turned back to the room, pulled on his clothes, snatched up his gunbelt, and headed toward the street.

Dazed and unmoving after his fall, Drew lay on the ground in the darkness behind Chantalle's house. He looked at Tricia, who lay motionless on the ground near him. She was unconscious, whether from the fall or from her head wound he could not be certain.

His mind cleared when he heard shouts coming from the front of the building. Heat singed his skin, and he glanced up at Chantalle's house, suddenly aware that it was fully ablaze. A brisk night breeze fanned the flames steadily upward. The fire popped sprays of burning sparks into the night sky as he managed to stand, and then snatched up Tricia's limp form and carried her a safe distance from the blaze before sinking to his knees.

His head was throbbing. His lungs were on fire. His eyes were tearing—beside him Tricia lay so still.

"Tricia …"

Soldiers appeared beside him, shouting orders that he did not fully comprehend. He protested when they picked Tricia up and ushered them both toward a waiting ambulance. Secured inside, he fought the darkness threatening to consume him as the horses jerked into motion. He held oblivion at bay as he clutched Tricia's hand in his.

The heat of the fire was intense as flames soared skyward from Chantalle's bordello and smoke followed in billowing spirals. Knowing that he did not dare ride closer, Jason dismounted and lifted Elizabeth to the ground. He tied up his horse and looked back at her, alarmed by her oddly frozen expression as she watched the tongues of fire exploding outward with ever-increasing force through the windows.

"Elizabeth."

No response.

"Elizabeth!"

Elizabeth turned toward him. Her lips were slightly

parted, but no words emerged and he said tightly, "I want you to stay here, do you understand? Don't go any closer. The brick facade could collapse at any minute."

Swallowing tightly, Elizabeth said, "Where are you going?"

"I have to find Chantalle and make sure she's all right."

"But—"

"She's a friend. She helped us both when we needed it. It's time to help her."

Elizabeth nodded.

"Stay here. I'll be back."

Elizabeth nodded again, unable to move as Jason disappeared into the darkness. She stared at the flames as the nightmares that had haunted her came to life before her eyes.

She turned sharply as a horse drew up beside theirs and a young blond woman jumped down to ask, "Did everyone get out?"

Elizabeth swallowed. She said breathlessly, "I don't know."

Beads of perspiration appeared on the young woman's brow and upper lip as she asked, "The soldiers—do you know where they went?"

"They're by the fire truck, fighting the fire."

"Did you see a tall officer—Colonel Madison?"

"No."

"I have to find him and make sure he's all right."

"No!" Elizabeth grasped the young woman's arm. "You can't go near the fire. It's too hot. You can't see ... you can't breathe."

Turning sharply toward her, the young woman attempted to shake off her grip as she said, "That doesn't make any difference to me. I have to—" The young woman halted, and then said, "Did you hear that?"

Elizabeth heard it, a woman's cry for help barely audible over the roar and wheeze of the flames. The woman cried out again, but no one seemed to hear her. Volunteers and men in uniform were running in haphazard fashion around the building, fighting the wall of flame flaring ever higher, but none of them reacted to her cries.

Driven by a suddenly intense need she could not explain, Elizabeth started running toward the sound of the voice. She slipped and fell in the darkness. She drew herself upright as the young woman reached her side and said, "I heard her again. She's going to die in there!"

Elizabeth met the young woman's intense stare. Her eyes were a startling amber in the glow of the fire, striking a chord of memory that Elizabeth could not seem to identify. She turned back toward the fire instinctively as the young woman stood beside her.

The roar of the fire … the chaos surrounding it … flames exploding again and again in fiery sparks that lit the night sky …

She was inside the fiery cauldron. The flames licked at her skin. She could not see. She could not breathe, but she had to save her. She called out, but there was no answer. The fire seared her flesh, but she could not leave her sister behind!

"Get back!"

Elizabeth grasped the young woman's hand as a soldier appeared beside them and ordered again, "Get back! The building is going to collapse!"

"Someone's in there. I can hear her!"

"Sergeant Walker just got her out."

Shuddering, Elizabeth fell back behind the line that the soldiers had established, and then turned toward the young woman beside her. She looked into amber eyes reddened by heat and smoke, and a deep quaking began inside her. A name came to her out of the past. A sob rising, she asked hesitantly in a trembling voice, "Is it … could it be you, Jenna Leigh? Please tell me, is it you?"

Elizabeth waited breathlessly for the young woman's response.

"L-Laura Anne?"

Elizabeth gasped. She tried to swallow past the hard lump that had closed her throat. Unable to reply, she stared at the young woman as full realization dawned with a sob of joy.

Yes, she was Laura Anne—Laura Anne Hawk!

Hardly aware that she had spoken the name aloud, Elizabeth closed her eyes as Jenna Leigh threw her arms around her and hugged her close. She trembled with happiness as she returned her sister's hug with all her strength. She felt Jenna Leigh's tears wet her cheek, unaware that her own tears dampened Jenna Leigh's cheek as well. They were alive—and together again at last!

They were still breathless when Jason appeared beside them and slid his arm around Elizabeth's shoulders. She looked up as he said, "Chantalle is shaken, but she's all right. She managed to get out with the rest of her girls. She—"

Halting when he saw the tears that streaked his wife's face, Jason glanced between her and the young blond woman whose hand she clutched so tightly. He was about to speak when Elizabeth said in a quaking voice, "Jason, darling, I want you to meet ... my sister, Jenna Leigh."

Watching from a distance, Simon saw the rear wall of Chantalle's house collapse. He watched as the volunteers scattered, calling out in distress. He had spread the kerosene widely, and with a single match, the fire had come to immediate life. There was no way that either Drew or Tricia could have gotten out alive.

He had seen Whit running frantically around the fire, looking for his brother, but to no avail. He had also seen the two Hawk women standing side by side.

It wasn't their turn yet.

Turning back to his horse as the frantic scene continued, Simon mounted up.

Smiling, he rode out of sight.

Chapter Fourteen

Drew awakened sharply from a nightmare-ridden sleep. His throat hurt, his eyes burned, and his chest was sore. He looked around him at the dimly lit hospital room. He then glanced out the window, where a smoldering blaze still lit the night sky.

"You're conscious." Drew's attention snapped toward Whit as he emerged from the shadows. He did not reply as Whit continued, "You sure gave me a scare tonight. Hell, when I woke up and found out Chantalle's house was burning, and then learned that you'd been transported here …" His voice breaking, Whit cleared his throat and continued, "Well, I'm glad you're all right."

The fire.

Tricia!

Drew attempted to sit up as he asked hoarsely, "Where's Tricia?"

"Lie back. She's in the room next door. She's fine.

Chantalle and the rest of the women got out all right, too, but there isn't much left of the house."

"I want to see Tricia."

"She's all right, Drew. She's sleeping now. She has a nasty cut on her forehead that's bound to keep her in bed for a day or two. She probably hit it when you both escaped the fire."

"No, it was Gault."

A deep voice from the doorway asked unexpectedly, "Simon Gault?"

The attention of both men turned toward the tall uniformed officer who stood there. His expression stern, Colonel Clay Madison entered the room. He acknowledged Whit with a nod and walked closer to the bed to ask, "Did you say Simon Gault was responsible for Miss Shepherd's head wound?"

When Drew did not immediately respond, Clay continued, "The fire was too hot ... it traveled too swiftly and engulfed the house too completely to have started accidentally. I suspected from the beginning that an accelerant was used, and I have no doubt that it is connected to the recent killings in some way."

Fully alert and aware of the possible danger in his reply, Drew responded, "It was Gault, all right. He was waiting in Tricia's room when I arrived. When I came to, both Tricia and I were tied up. He said he had a grudge against Chantalle, and that he'd get revenge by burning down her house with everyone—including her daughter—in it."

Clay's eyes narrowed. "That's all he said?"

"Tricia and I heard him splashing kerosene in the

hallway. When it burst into flame, I knew we didn't have much time to get out. We barely made it."

"He didn't say anything else—where he was going ... what he intended to do?"

Drew shook his head.

"You're sure that's all you have to tell me, Mr. Collins?"

Whit interrupted opportunely, "Drew has a nasty head wound. I don't think he's thinking clearly enough to answer all your questions yet, Colonel. Chantalle may be able to give you better answers. She and her women were taken here for the night just for safety's sake, but she's well enough to answer your questions."

Clay hesitated, searching both men's expressions briefly before he said, "Of course. I'll come back in the morning."

"I'll go with you." Whit turned briefly toward Drew, his expression speaking volumes as he said, "I think Drew will do better if he's left alone for a while."

Waiting only until both men had left the room, Drew stood up unsteadily. His head hurt and his breathing was still labored, but he needed to get out of there.

Dressed, his gunbelt strapped securely around his hips, Drew moved out into the crowded hospital hallway. The confusion of volunteers, victims, and medical personnel filling the narrow corridors allowed him the anonymity he sought. He looked into the room next to his, and then pulled back sharply when he saw Tricia talking to a uniformed soldier standing there. Relieved that she appeared to be well, he walked a few doors down and glanced into a room where Chantalle sat with several of her women beside her. She was coughing and she looked confused and worn as Whit stood supportively beside her while Colonel Madison questioned her with his back to the door. Drew continued walking. Disoriented and unsteady, he searched for an exit where he could slip away unseen.

Drew stopped abruptly when he came upon a waiting area where Jenna Leigh sat holding another young woman's hand as they conversed. He stared at his sister, his throat choking tight with the realization that he had almost lost the opportunity to talk to her and to know the true joy of being with her again. He'd been wrong to turn against her because she'd married the man she loved, even if he was a Yankee. He would correct that mistake as soon as he could and he would . . .

Drew paused in that thought. A snippet of the conversation between Jenna Leigh and the other young woman caught his ear.

"Jason doesn't like Simon," the young woman was saying, "but I first sensed something was wrong when Simon insisted that Adeline Beaufort's mansion suited me far better than the hotel where I was staying. He explained that Adeline was visiting up North and he was looking after the place for her. He said I would actually be doing him a favor if I stayed there because Adeline had become ill and would be gone indefinitely."

"So?"

"When I arrived, I discovered that the mansion was isolated from the rest of the city, and that, with the exception of an old crone he had hired as my servant but who reported directly to him, I would be totally alone. If it hadn't been for Jason, I don't know what might have happened to me there."

"I didn't know about that place," Jenna Leigh said.

"I expect not. Most people don't." The unidentified young woman went on to describe its location, and Drew's expression grew gradually taut.

The perfect place to hide ...

Drew glanced back into the room where Whit remained at Chantalle's side during Colonel Madison's questioning. He couldn't afford to waste any time.

His decision made, Drew slipped past the waiting room and continued down the hospital corridors until he reached an exit sign. Managing to leave unnoticed, he mounted the nearest saddled horse and nudged him into motion.

Dawn was beginning to make inroads into the night sky when he reined his mount to a halt in the shadows of Adeline Beaufort's palatial estate. The house was dark, and its suitability for any plans Gault might have had for the unidentified young woman was immediately obvious. Drew's stomach tightened at the thought that Gault's perversions were endless. He wondered absentmindedly how far the man was willing to go to sate them, and how long his perversions had gone undetected.

Careful to wind his way to the rear of the building without being seen, Drew paused to survey the premises. The house was large and luxurious, with countless windows to allow light into its expansive interior. There should be at least one of those windows—or possibly a door that had been left unlocked. If there were, he would find it.

Moving cautiously, Drew checked the rear door. It was locked, as he'd suspected it would be. He worked his way around the house, checking each window until a sash at the corner of the house slid upward easily. His heart pounding, Drew slid through the window. He released a relieved breath when his feet touched down on the floor at last.

Darkness and shadows ...

Drew paused to allow his eyes to grow accustomed to the dark interior of the house.

At the sound of a footstep, Drew tensed.

"That's right, Drew, stand there—but raise your hands." When Drew did not respond, the voice demanded, "Do it! No one will hear me if I pull this trigger."

Raising his hands, Drew turned slowly toward the sound of the voice coming from the shadows.

"No, don't face this way!"

Drew went still again.

"Lower your left hand and grip the handle of your gun with your fingertips, then throw your gun on the floor—and remember, I can see you clearly even if you can't see me."

With no recourse, Drew complied. The sound of his gun hitting the floor drew his brows into a frown.

"Kick the gun aside."

Drew followed the order.

"Very good. You're helpless again just like last time—but unlike last time, I won't take anything for granted."

Gault stepped out into a shaft of dawn light coming through the window, and Drew's jaw tightened.

"You don't like this, do you?" Simon laughed in the silence that followed his question. He sobered. "You probably like it even less than I did when I saw you sneaking around to the back of this house and realized that you—and probably dear Tricia, too—had escaped the fate I had planned for you. That was clever of you, however you managed it, but I shouldn't have expected any less from one of Harold Hawk's sons."

Stiffening at the mention of his father's name, Drew demanded harshly, "You knew my father?"

"Of course I knew him, but I did not dream when he purchased my California claim that his intention was to steal my success and take it for his own!"

"I don't know what you're talking about."

"You wouldn't. You and your siblings had been deposited in an orphanage where you waited for your father to fulfill his promise to return and make you richer than you were before he gambled the family into bankruptcy. You had no idea of the lengths to which your father was willing to go to reestablish himself in his former position of influence and power, but I did. I discovered his treachery when he struck gold almost immediately after assuming ownership of my claim, and I realized he had somehow discovered gold only a few feet from the area I had excavated unsuccessfully for endless months."

Drew remained silent and Simon laughed harshly. "Your father was surprised when I confronted him about having struck it rich so quickly. He was so happy and excited about the future he anticipated restoring to his wonderful children—a bright future he would provide for them at my expense—a future that was rightfully mine!"

Seething in retrospect, Simon rasped, "But he didn't

fool me. When his back was turned, I struck him with the same shovel he had used to uncover the strike. I buried his body under enough rubble that it would never be found, and then assumed his identity and sold the claim for the fortune that it was worth. It was only through a trick of fate that I discovered Harold Hawk's journal."

"My father's journal ..."

"You didn't know your father kept a journal, did you? You didn't know that he wrote in it religiously, either, recording every step of his life—his triumphs and defeats, as well as his descent into bankruptcy. He was the reason your family broke up."

Simon took a breath. "I was determined to remain triumphant over the man who had thought to usurp my success. It seemed only fitting that I should change my name and return to the place where Hawk had failed, so that I could prove my worth once and for all by succeeding on the ruins of his failure."

Simon's voice grew colder. "Only one thing stood in my way—the possibility that one of Harold Hawk's precious children would grow up to learn what had happened and attempt to claim my success—that one of them would try to *steal it* from me just as his father had tried. Through a quirk of fate, I found the ranch your aunt and uncle had owned and learned where your uncle had brought you after she died. I then took steps to avoid any problems in the future."

"What do you mean ... *steps?*"

Simon smiled as he said, "No one ever suspected that the fire at the orphanage where you Hawk children lived was *not* an accident."

Drew gasped incredulously. "You set the fire? You're responsible for killing all those children?"

"Those nameless waifs, you mean? Those useless creatures who were slated to grow up worthless and homeless?"

"Bastard!"

Simon's expression stiffened. "I resented being called that name at one time, but I ignore it now. Wealth has its privileges, you know."

Ignoring Drew's heated reaction, Simon continued, "In the confusion after the orphanage fire, no one paid any attention to me when I remained at the scene to make sure the four Hawk children were dead. I was told all the bodies were burned beyond recognition, and I felt safe. The problem was that the orphanage records were destroyed in the fire. I had no way of knowing that both your brother and you had already left the orphanage and only your two sisters remained there."

Simon's expression hardened. "I was shocked when Whit showed up in Galveston. I was incredulous when your sisters arrived, one by one, proving their heritage with the crests that their egotistical father had designed to herald his success. I knew then what I had to do."

His face an evil mask, Simon whispered, "At this point in time, it matters very little to me that the authorities are now aware of the drastic lengths to which I was forced when you all returned. I planned for all eventualities when I established a bank account in Houston and filled it with substantial funds to guarantee my future. It will be easy for me to claim it and reestablish myself under a different name somewhere else, and to live a life of ease from then on."

Simon assured Drew coldly, "You were the last to arrive. It's unfortunate that your friend had to die—but he was in the way. Unfortunately, the attempt on your life failed anyway, but you will still have the honor of being the first Hawk sibling to suffer his father's fate."

Simon added, "But you may rest assured that it will not be long before your brother and both your sisters follow you."

"My sisters? Jenna Leigh is the only—"

"I said, *both* of them." Simon snickered at Drew's startled expression. "Jenna Leigh and Laura Anne— Laura Anne, who is now known as Elizabeth Huntington Dodd because of a lapse of memory caused by the orphanage fire. I watched their joyful reunion tonight at the fire, and I was touched in spite of myself. I allowed them to have that moment of happiness, since it will be so brief."

"You wouldn't dare—"

"Oh, wouldn't I? But I've said enough. Adeline Beaufort doesn't anticipate returning to this house for months, so no one will find your body here until it's too late. By that time I will have systematically eliminated your handsome brother and your two lovely sisters, and there will be nothing you can do about it."

The sudden interjection of a deep voice behind Simon turned him sharply toward the two figures who had stepped into the doorway behind him as Whit said simply, "You're mistaken, Gault."

Simon swung his gun toward them with an evil growl, and Drew dived for the gun he had tossed into the shadows. He joined the burst of gunfire that echoed in the room as Simon's body jerked with the force of the multitude of bullets that struck him, and then fell heavily to the floor.

Standing up, his heart pounding as dawn began brightening the room, Drew looked down at Simon's lifeless body. Feeling nothing but relief, he looked back up as Whit said soberly, "It's finished. Gault is dead and he got what he deserved. I'm damned glad you're all right."

Smiling, Whit gripped Drew's shoulder and squeezed it heartily. Then motioning toward the man standing beside him, he said, "I don't think you've met this man, Drew. I'd like to introduce you to your brother-in-law, Jason Dodd."

Chapter Fifteen

Tricia walked beside Drew at a measured pace as his brothers, sisters, and their spouses accompanied them through the hospital corridor. Three days had passed since the fire. She wore a small bandage on her head where the jagged cut from Simon's gun butt had been carefully stitched, but except for occasional headaches, she was fine.

Tricia stole a glance at Drew. He had recuperated from his trials, and he stood tall, powerfully erect, and handsome. He was the man she loved, but he was unsmiling and his expression was dark. She inched closer to him, feeling his tension in a time of familial sharing that he had never expected—a difficult time for them both.

Knowing she had never loved him more, she slid her hand into Drew's and he closed his broad palm around it. He loved her, too. She had never had any doubt of that throughout the tense moments she had spent wondering what the ending of the Hawk legacy would be.

She had been joyfully tearful at the reunion of the Hawk clan shortly after Simon's demise. She knew she would never forget the moment when the four of them had stood arm in arm, too filled with emotion to speak. The torments of the past had been neutralized at that moment, leaving only wonder and hope.

She remembered when Jenna Leigh had called her husband forward and introduced Colonel Clay Madison of the Yankee Adjutant General's Office to Drew *Hawk*. His expression sober, Clay had produced a memo that—like the first one he had received about Drew—had also taken far too long to reach his office. The second memo canceled the wanted notice for the former Confederate officer, Drew Hawk, who was no longer being sought for the theft of a Union payroll. The memo revealed that the payroll in question was found to have been "appropriated" by a clerk in the Confederate commander's office when the war ended. Drew's resentment of the Yankees went a long way toward being resolved as he accepted the hand Clay extended toward him and shook it firmly.

Tricia looked back and saw the glances that Jenna Leigh and Elizabeth—the former Laura Anne Hawk—exchanged. Elizabeth's memory had fully returned. She was overjoyed that she had been able to realize the dream her dear Mother Ella had kept alive for so many years. With the return of her memory had also come a sense of fulfillment that made her life with Jason complete.

As for Simon Gault—he was gone forever. The problem of the distribution of his assets was formally settled when a key was discovered on his body that unlocked the drawer of the desk where he kept Harold Hawk's journal. In it, written in Simon's own hand as additions to the original entries, was authentication of Simon's theft of Harold Hawk's assets and all the other facts that Simon had related to Drew before his demise. Although saddened by the truth about their father's death, the siblings took heart in the fact that in the end, Harold Hawk proved to be an honorable man who had intended to keep his word to his children, and who had truly loved them.

Whit and Jackie walked beside them. They exchanged a few words, and Whit frowned. It was plain for Tricia to see that the burden of being the eldest weighed heavily on Whit. His sense of responsibility was heavier because of it, and she knew it was harder for him to conceal the feelings this moment raised.

Tricia looked down at the charred metal box she carried, knowing its significance did not lie in its meager physical weight.

Tricia paused at the doorway of Chantalle's room. She took a breath, then walked inside and approached Chantalle's bed, intensely aware of the others filing in behind her. A few of Chantalle's women had suffered burns that kept them in the hospital longer than expected, but Chantalle's problem was different. Her breathing had been temporarily affected by smoke inhalation, and the doctors had insisted that she remain.

Her throat tight, Tricia moved closer to Chantalle's

bed. She looked down at her as the older woman's heavy breathing reverberated in a hospital room that was totally silent despite the number present.

Her face pale in the absence of makeup and her hair liberally streaked with gray, Chantalle retained little resemblance to the flamboyant madam of old as she looked at them and frowned. Breaking the unnatural silence, she asked, "What's going on, Tricia? What's wrong?"

Tears unexpectedly filling her eyes, Tricia responded, "I picked through the remains of your house yesterday, Chantalle. I wanted to see if I could find anything that had survived the fire—something you might want to keep." Lifting the charred metal box into Chantalle's view, she said, "I found this in your desk drawer."

Chantalle gasped. Tears filled her eyes as she glanced at Whit and Jackie; Jenna Leigh and Clay; Elizabeth and Jason; and then at Drew before turning back to see Tricia open the box and lift out a pendant suspended from a delicate chain. The pendant was darkened by heat and smoke, but it clearly bore a crest with the image of a ship in full sail. Underneath it was a banner garlanded with a vine of orchids that was inscribed with the words *Quattuor mundum do*.

His expression strained as he stepped closer to the bed, Whit said softly, "There could be only one reason why you had this pendant in your possession and kept it hidden from all of us when you knew how important a part it had played in our lives. We need to know, Chantalle." Whit hesitated, his voice growing hoarse as he asked, "Are you our mother?"

Tears streamed down Chantalle's pale cheeks. Briefly unable to respond, she replied in a choked voice, "I don't know how to answer that question—how could I possibly lay claim to being your 'mother'? Even now I can't explain what happened to me all those years ago. I only remember the sense of helplessness I felt when I was unable to stop your father from gambling away everything he had worked for. I was defenseless as his problem increased. We were losing everything— our money, our home, the respect of everyone we knew. I watched my marriage and family—my whole life disintegrating around me as the situation continued to worsen. We let our help go. We sold off whatever assets we could. Creditors began banging down our doors. I was panicking, but when I walked to the mansion's pantry and found it empty for the first time, I realized that life as I had known it was changed forever."

Breathing raggedly, Chantalle continued, "There was a man who started paying attention to me sometime around then. Harold was spending all his time gambling. He was never home, and I was still young, beautiful ... and so foolish. When this man told me that he would provide the life for me that Harold seemed unwilling to offer any longer, I believed him. He told me that if I would run away with him and leave my children behind temporarily, he would take advantage of an opportunity that would make both of us rich, and I could then come back for my children and restore them to the life they had always known."

Chantalle paused to catch her breath before continuing, "He was lying, of course, but I didn't discover his deception until it was too late—until he deserted me and left me penniless and alone to make my way in a strange city's slum. I couldn't return to Galveston, and I had no way to support myself. I was hungry and desperate when I finally turned to the only solution I knew. I found a room and shared it with a friend. Her name was Elsa Shepherd. She had been deserted on the streets when she was little more than a child. We lived together, supporting ourselves and her newborn daughter the only way we could until Elsa died of pneumonia."

Chantalle looked up at Tricia as she continued, "I promised myself I would not make the same mistake twice—that I would not desert Tricia the way I had deserted my own children—and that I would raise her to be a lady as her mother had always dreamed."

Chantalle's lined face was sober when she said, "I worked hard at my trade and finally saved up enough money to return to Galveston. By that time my husband and children were no longer there, and I learned that my children had been placed in an orphanage that had burned down—and none of them had survived."

"I cursed my stupidity as I mourned their loss. I could not forgive myself. I left Galveston heartbroken, but I found myself gravitating back years later to the only place where I had ever been truly happy. I knew no one would recognize me by that time. The passage of years and the hardships of the trade had taken care of that. I set up a house, determined to make up for past mistakes by offering the best life possible to the women who worked for me, and by secretly helping as many people in need as I could."

"Then Whit came to Galveston searching for his brother. He showed me his ring and told me his story, and my heart stopped. I was stunned, and I was so proud of the man that Whit had become in spite of me that I could not believe my luck. I was equally stunned and proud when Elizabeth, Jenna Leigh, and finally Drew miraculously came back into my life. Yet I guarded my secret carefully. I didn't want you all to discover I was your mother, because I knew you could never forgive me."

Tears flowing freely, Chantalle whispered, "My only true joy is knowing that you are all alive and that you've been reunited. I dream of receiving your forgiveness, but I don't expect it. I know it is asking too much after all the torment I caused you."

Silence.

Chantalle looked at Whit. His face was white and sober. She looked at Jenna Leigh, Elizabeth, and then almost pleadingly at Drew. Equally pale and silent, they made no response.

Chantalle swallowed, unable to speak again for the thickness that choked her throat.

Equally wordless, Tricia watched as they turned away, one by one—Whit holding Jackie's hand; Jenna Leigh gripping Clay's arm tightly; Elizabeth leaning her head against Jason's shoulder.

Her heart breaking, Tricia watched them turn out of sight. She looked up at Drew. The last to leave, he extended his hand toward her and she hesitated. Tears welled in her throat as she glanced back at the pain on Chantalle's face. She looked again at Drew and saw pain in his eyes, too, and a plea that was bright and clear.

She knew at that moment what she must do.

Unable to do otherwise, Tricia took Drew's hand. She left the room at his side, without saying a word.

Alone in her hospital room, Chantalle turned her face into her pillow and sobbed softly. It was over. Her children had turned against her—but what else had she expected? She had deserted them ... left them for a dream that had fallen flat and empty.

They could never forgive her.

Finding them again, enjoying the beautiful adults they had grown to be, had been a gift ... a treasure that she would cherish through the long, empty years ahead.

Her sobs quieting, Chantalle remembered Whit, with his restrained, gentle respect for her; Jenna Leigh, with her exquisite beauty and unexpected consideration; Elizabeth—Laura Anne—so dear and loving despite all her travails; and Drew ... dear Drew ... so proud and determined to do the right thing and so protective of the daughter she loved as if she were her own—the same daughter in name only who had turned against her for the love of her own son.

She had lost her precious children for the second time, and she feared she would not survive.

"Chantalle ..."

Chantalle looked up at the sound of her name. She held her breath as her grown children filed into her room—the handsome Hawk children that she loved.

Unable to move, unable to speak, she watched as Elizabeth approached her. The others followed as Elizabeth leaned over and clasped her hand. Her light eyes filled with tears, Elizabeth addressed her with a single whispered word of forgiveness.

"Mother."

HAWK'S PASSION

Elaine Barbieri

Jason will do whatever it takes to bring down Simon Gault, the corrupt shipping magnate. The supposedly upright citizen betrayed Galveston during the war, causing untold deaths. But even more disturbing is his twisted desire to seduce innocent Elizabeth Huntington. No matter how determined she is to make her own way in the rowdy, war-ravaged city, Jason swears he will protect the daring young beauty from Gault, help find her missing family and then win her heart.

HAWK'S PLEDGE

Constance O'Banyon

Whit is a gambler by necessity, a loner by choice. Ever since the orphanage had gone up in flames, Whit Hawk has been searching desperately for what remains of his family. Instead he finds Jacqueline Douglas, a rancher in need of a good hand, a woman in need of the right man. Wildly beautiful, she is as untamed as the Texas he loves, and Whit knows that no matter what else life holds in store for him, the fiery redhead must be his.

HAWK'S PURSUIT

Constance O'Banyon

Jena Leigh Hawk has gone by the pseudonym J. L. Rebel ever since she took up newspaper work. To her, writing the truth is more important than anything else, and she hides her femininity behind a man's name, her beauty behind spectacles and drab clothing. But when she goes to Galveston, Texas, to uncover a very personal truth, the origins of her family, her businesslike façade begins to crack. Colonel Clay Madison seems to see right through to her heart, to the yearning, vulnerable woman she is inside. And in his arms, Jena Leigh discovers the pure joy of being female.

TEXAS TR★UMPH
ELAINE BARBIERI

Buck Star was a handsome cad with a love-'em-and-leave-'em attitude that had broken more than one heart. But when he lost his head over a conniving beauty young enough to be his own daughter, he jeopardized all he valued, even the lives of his own children.

Ever since leaving his father's Texas Star ranch, the daring Pinkerton agent and his lovely partner Vida Malone made it their business to ferret out the truth. But the twisted secrets he begins to uncover after a mysterious message calls him home might be more than anyone could untangle. Saving his father will require all his cunning and courage, as well as the aid of the most exasperating and enticing woman ever to go undercover or drive a man to distraction.

HIRED GUN
BOBBI SMITH

Trent Marshall is a hard man. Ever since his older brother was shot down in cold blood, he's pursued justice with only his Colt .45 revolver to back him up. So when he agrees to go after a young girl abducted by Apaches, he knows he has tracking skills, years of experience, and iron determination on his side. What he doesn't anticipate is having the victim's older sister beside him every step of the way. Faith Ryan fires his blood like no other woman. As they penetrate deeper and deeper into the wilderness, Trent knows he cannot resist the primitive urge to make her his own, to take on a much more intimate role than... *Hired Gun.*